Résumé For Murder

Brakes squealed out front, and Officer James P. Smith and another cop built like a bean-bag chair came running in, unpacking their pistols. Caldwell, the doctor, right behind them, impatiently motioned the two officers of the law out of his way.

"You two stay right where you are, out of the way," Big Jim ordered, squinting at us. "Oh, it's you, Wirtz. Stay right where you are, Wirtz."

The back door banged, and someone started clumping up the hall. Smith's partner waddled away to intercept whoever it was. Dr. Caldwell, working silently after his initial grunt of disgust, came back across the hall to call the coroner. "The state police will be able to tell us about any escaped mental patients from across the Ohio line," he said. "There's some maniac on the loose. Darnedest thing I ever saw; after amputating the victim's, ah— organs—he apparently took them away with him. They're nowhere to be found."

CLAIRE McCORMICK

Résumé For Murder

WALKER AND COMPANY · NEW YORK

First published in the United States of America
in 1982 by the Walker Publishing Company, Inc.

This paperback edition first published in 1986.

Published simultaneously in Canada by John Wiley & Sons Canada,
Limited, Rexdale, Ontario.

ISBN: 0-8027-3165-1

Library of Congress Catalog Card Number: 81-71189

Printed in the United States of America

10 9 8 7 6 5 4 3 2 1

CHAPTER I
MONDAY, MARCH 17

IT STARTED SNOWING AS SOON AS I SAW THE LIGHT AT THE END OF the Fort Pitt Tunnel. As I mushed my way toward one of those astigmatic small towns that burrow into the Pennsylvania hills north and west of Pittsburgh, Interstate 79 got progressively wetter and sloppier, while the car radio, crackling with cancellations, periodically keened over this year's St. Patrick's Day parade. Personally, I had no plans to send my Irish friends condolence cards unless they were linebackers; I was mourning my own loss of Monday night martinis at O'Donnell's with a boozy brotherhood similarly addicted to the low-adrenaline snacks vended by the networks to tide us over between Steeler seasons. My name is John Waltz, spelled New Testament style—as I periodically explain to Pat O'Donnell after too many Monday night martinis—the end result of acculturation. Besides laboring under inherited delusions of Anglo-Saxon grandeur, I also serve as recruiting vice president for Pittsburgh Professional Services, recruiter of college seniors for in-service training as executive recruiters. Nevertheless, working for PPS is no crazier than drawing green beer in the middle of a blizzard; my Semitic gift of gab earns me enough to pay the rent on my converted tenement townhouse, my daughter Marcia's tuition at Swarthmore, and the monthly tribute to her mother until she chooses to remarry and lower her standard of living.

And thus it was on this miserable Monday that, prodded by the Protestant ethic, I slogged along toward Witherspoon College in New Arcady, Pa., cursing Pete Simon, Witherspoon's overambitious placement director, with every semi that splattered my windshield. Simon had lured me to his hillside Harvard during a fall workshop in the city after we'd wound up standing side by side at a crowded motel bar, fortifying ourselves for a final two-hour round table on "Business and the Liberal Arts: Stalemate or Symbiosis?"

"You really ought to do some hunting up in our territory, Mr. Waltz," he told me thirty seconds after our ritual pleasantries, fingering his name tag and the noose-tight knot in his cranberry tie. "Witherspoon may not be a big name but, even in this day and age, we still manage to turn out a quality product."

"And you're still in the black?" I asked, hoping my drinking companion might actually have some college seniors for hire who knew how to use a knife and fork in a public restaurant, as well as the family credit cards. "I thought small private colleges were turning into an endangered species."

"We've had football winners at Witherspoon for the last twenty years," Simon said proudly. "And since we're still church-related, a lot of big corporations are interested in keeping us alive. Us and what we stand for up in New Arcady."

"Which is?" I asked, interested despite my distaste for Middle America's current smirks of self-congratulation over its desperate rediscovery of traditional values. And, as another endangered species, Pete Simon—all four-square salesmanship and ingenious boosterism—likewise intrigued me. At the moment he was taking short, nervous sips of bourbon, as if whoever had stuffed him into his dark gray suit was about to loom up behind him and snatch his drink away.

"We don't even have to lock our doors in New Arcady, Mr. Waltz," Simon told me after a last furtive gulp. "I've always said that while we're counting our blessings, we should start including a few of the things we *don't* have up there: crime, violence, racial tensions, pollution. There're probably almost as many horses and buggies as cars on our streets—we're up in Amish country, you know—lucky for us not many people *do* know we've even got any Pennsylvania Dutchmen on this side of the state, or you Pittsburghers might start crowding us out. They don't call it the Eden Valley for nothing! You couldn't find a more perfect place to raise your family. Even if you're like me and never seem to have time to take the kids to the park," he grinned, training his eyes on my suspiciously urban five-o'clock shadow.

"It sounds like a great place to live," I said quickly to forestall Simon's rooting around for his traveling exhibit of family snapshots. "I'll arrange a recruiting date for some time in the spring—after it gets warm enough to play tourist."

"Well, we'll be happy to see you up there, Mr. Waltz," Simon said fervently, delighted that he'd just kicked another field goal for the home team. "You won't be sorry." With a guilty glance at his watch, he threw down a five and hastily signaled the barman. "It's on me, by the way, not on Witherspoon. Our churches keep us pretty dry, so your invitation says BYOB. New Arcady's what you might call a company town."

After cramming some stray printouts into a briefcase big enough to dispense a year's supply of mood elevators to the entire population of Greater Pittsburgh, Simon yanked on his chestnut forelock, straightened his tie, and hurried off to our meeting. "Just give us a chance, Mr. Waltz," he called over his shoulder. "You look like you could use a little fresh air and sunshine."

All admiration for the man's marketing techniques, I ordered a fresh drink—which I needed a hell of a lot more than a lecture on the economic hardships awaiting technological illiterates like my daughter—and saluted Pete Simon's retreating back. Six months later, however, on the gloomiest Monday I'd seen since the end of football season, I had lost even a grudging regard for Simon's proven ability to spot the sucker in every crowd and sell him up the river and into the trees—which it was becoming increasingly difficult to see. And the more I thought about my two-day commitment to Simon's "company town," the less I liked the idea of getting snowed in up in dry-as-a-marble underarm New Arcady. My initial enthusiasm for the place had already been much diminished by the brief history of the borough I had made myself read in the Witherspoon College catalog, full of pictures of the founding fathers, dour old Calvinists with sour Scottish names who'd evidently decided to make things as tough on their neighbors in the green hills of Pennsylvania as God had made it on them back in the land of scrawny sheep and scorched oatmeal.

While in New Arcady, I was to be lodged at a place chastely called "The Inn." Right now this suggested nothing less than cold flannel sheets; and, lacking Pete Simon's air of having vitamin D encapsulated under his toenails, I honestly doubted I'd be able to interest any Christian ice maidens in overnight conversions. Having sworn off Pittsburgh's singles' bars and the zombie-eyed divorcées who haunted them, I had considered turning this trip into a field experiment and finding out whether my Blass-tailored elegance, my silvering Cary Grant hair, and what one extraordinarily perceptive female friend had termed, post-coitus, my "sad Don Juan eyes" ((although in my rearview mirror they more closely resembled a forsaken chihuahua's) might not play better out in the boonies than they had within recent memory on Liberty Avenue. The closer I got to Simon's G-rated Garden of Eden, however, the more I suspected my personal life was doomed to remain a tedious traveling salesman story without a punchline. Nor could I count on much sympathy from Witherspoon's big-hearted placement director, given his devotion to hard work, fresh air, and wholesome family living.

Brooding over my inner weather, I'd stopped reading road signs. Exit after exit had been blearing right by me for the last fifteen minutes. I thought I might even have had the good luck to miss the turnoff for Route 125 and the borough of New Arcady. After only two more dirty green markers, however, I was off the interstate and on a diabolically narrow two-lane highway with potholes yawning like graves every ten feet or so, but no other indications I was anywhere near a human community. Suddenly an oblong black shape loomed up ahead of me, an upended coffin on wheels lit by a single red-eyed reflector. At a slow crawl I followed the bearded Amish sadist keeping his horse and buggy squarely in the middle of my lane up to the top of a steep hill staked out by a large black-lettered sign. "Welcome to New Arcady, Pa.," I read through the swirling snow. "Founded, in God's Name, 1853." Below this forbidding message was stenciled an enormous black cross. Hexed many miles ago, I ignored this further omen of the borough's ill will and crossed the double line. I had no intention of making my entrance into New Arcady behind a horse's ass.

No sooner had I settled back into my lane than I heard a siren. After tailgating me for two miles, the borough cop in the olive-drab Chevy motioned me over to the only wide place in the road. At least six-foot-five and bulkier than his down jacket, he stalked over to my car and stuck his flat custard-pie face in my rolled-down window.

"You didn't happen to notice it's a no-passing zone," he said in a loud monotone after memorizing my driver's license.

"I was late for an appointment," I pleaded.

The cop's near-sighted eyes blinked rapidly, scrutinizing this stranger.

"You think I should let you keep it," he stated, screwing up his eyes to reread my driver's license. "What type of business would you have here in this borough, Mr. Wirtz? Would you be a salesman?"

"Waltz," I insisted, although the cop had at least rechristened me with a good Pennsylvania German name. "No, I'm not a salesman. I'm here to interview some Witherspoon College seniors who think they might like to work for me. As management trainees," I hastily explained, lest the borough policeman think I made periodic raids on the Pennsylvania hills to dragoon a few WASP soldiers into my family of loan sharks and money launderers. "I'll be leaving town Wednesday afternoon," I added encouragingly, handing the cop my glossiest business card.

Monster Mouth promptly shone his huge face in at me.

"Well, Wirtz, I won't write you a ticket right now," he blared into my frozen eardrum. "You're in New Arcady now, and we do like it says in the Bible and act friendly to strange people. You can go on about your business now, Wirtz. You know, though, we'll be watching you."

"Thank you, Officer, uh—" In the spirit of small-town friendliness, I figured I had better call this ungentle giant by his rightful name.

"Officer . . . James . . . P. . . . Smith," he enunciated, weighting each syllable. "And we want to welcome you to New Arcady, Wirtz. In the name of your borough police force."

Officer Smith clanked on back to his car. As I rolled up my window, I heard the tinny tinkle of a carillon that had been playing background music for some time. I recognized the tune; it was "Onward, Christian Soldiers." Welcome to New Arcady.

And onward I went, into the heart of town. The rousing hymn whirred to an end and the clock in the college tower banged out the hour: 9:00 A.M. Miraculously, I chose the right alley to take me from Church Street to College. At the corner of Garden and College, guarded by a squat Victorian chaperone of an administration building, I had to sit and idle while a group of twenty students jogged across, no doubt in observance of some fruitfly-brained fraternity's initiation rites. But instead of the sleek stripes and racing colors generally affected by adolescent athletes, these silent runners wore identical gray sweat suits, hoods up and hiding their faces; I really didn't like this collective lack of style—or the joggers' air of grim self-containment. Hoping they had no plans to honor St. Patrick by driving all human snakes with strange license plates out of the Eden Valley, I stared uneasily after the group and even found myself wishing the hulking borough cop would come thumping up to guarantee their good will.

Reuben Tranter Hall, where Pete Simon's office and my own reserved room were located, turned out to be a long, low, barracks-like building, painted barn red. As per instructions, I pulled into the parking lot at the rear; but, not seeing a back entrance I could sneak through without attracting some police spy's attention, I trudged the length of the building to the front door. Since of course it stuck, I shoved it with my shoulder—into the pelvic bone of a tall blonde hurrying out. I retreated; she advanced. The first real presence I'd felt all morning, and look what I'd done.

I advanced; she retreated. Impasse. A clumsy country dance in a freezing doorway. Copying Officer James P. Smith, I masterfully motioned her inside. "I'm terribly sorry, Miss—? I couldn't get the door unstuck. And I was late for an appointment. Still, no excuse." I smiled ruefully, the picture of penitence.

"I accept your apology. But I'm late for class." She pushed toward the door. "Nor is it 'Miss,' " she instructed me from the doorway. "It's 'Dr.' or 'Ms.,' if you insist on courtesy titles."

Ever resourceful, I immediately switched tactics and bowed low to the ill-tempered Dr. X, simultaneously sweeping an imaginary plumed hat off my head and placing it over my heart. She stopped dead, and I got a glimpse of long sleek legs between the tall boots and the plaid skirt.

"Why not tell me what comes after the courtesy title?" I suggested.

"Christensen. Anne." Then she was out the door.

She looked it, with her Scandinavian snow-queen face, pale and imperious, framed by winter-wheat hair. My internal computer clicked Anne Christensen off a 31.35 years old. Not a Big Ten Homecoming Queen, but the second runner-up.

As I stared speculatively after her, Pete Simon came galloping up the hall behind me. "Hello, Mr. Waltz," he called, without even pausing for a few gulps of the arctic air that seemed to be pouring out of the radiators. "Welcome to Witherspoon. Have any trouble getting up here? Looks like you probably did, but you can relax for a while; your nine o'clock called in and canceled. Said she was sick with the flu, so my secretary rescheduled her for tomorrow."

Before I could even ask him where to hang up my soggy coat, Simon was hustling me down the hall for a whirlwind tour of Reuben Tranter Hall. "Reception room—and coffee pot—right across from me. And here's my secretary, squeezed in between the rest rooms, poor girl. Ask her if you need anything. I had her put us down for lunch tomorrow at 12:15, if that's okay; I've got to make my annual pitch to Kiwanis this noon, so we dig a little deeper in our pockets for the scholarship fund. If you want the White Lion today—that's our gourmet eating establishment —better make a reservation beforehand. Or if you're like me and usually make it a quick sandwich, there's the Golden Grill right up on Main—you can't miss it. Here's your private room—sound-proof so the poor kids won't get so clutched they just sit there and stare at you. And back here's the English Department; we let them share the building with us as long as they mind their manners and stay on their own turf. Isn't that right, Gene?" he called to a large, sweaty young man locking his office door.

Gravely, Gene inclined his gray hood at us.

"Congratulations! Just remember the first fifteen years are the hardest!" Simon beamed up at his athletic friend, who immediately ducked past us into another professor's office. Simon seized my elbow and pointed me back toward his own. "I'll try to stop around sometime later today, Mr. Waltz," he said, frowning down at his large and elaborately functional watch. "But right now I'm just about snowed under."

Shaking his head over his impossibly crowded schedule, my host disappeared into his office and immediately picked up the telephone I had just barely glimpsed on our way down the hall. I went across the corridor in search of coffee. Two fast cups and my first cigarette since I-79 made me my old nerve-gnawed self again. I was further welcomed to Witherspoon by Dr. Eugene Chancellor, the jock from the English Department, who came in for coffee and promptly offered me an apparently anemic cigar in honor of his two-day-old daughter, which cleared up the insignificant mystery of Simon's congratulations.

"My wife and I are, of course, against smoking, in theory as well as in practice," Chancellor announced. "But I told Karen that I somehow still wanted to do the traditional thing."

"Are these gray sweat suits a Witherspoon tradition?" I asked him, since I still had five minutes. "I noticed a whole long gray line as I came onto the campus."

"In my case, it's because I absolutely insist on taking some form of aerobic exercise every morning," Chancellor said pompously. "But you might have seen some of the Covenanters, who are also known, more informally, as the Joggers for Jesus. They believe, as Saint Paul pithily puts it, that the body is the temple of the spirit.

Thus physical conditioning is, in their view, of paramount importance to the true spirit of the early Christian church."

"So these Covenanters are what you might consider a cult?" I suggested, remembering their air of joyless other-directedness.

"I wouldn't consider them a cult at all in the pejorative sense of that term," Chancellor said with a pejorative frown. "About a hundred and fifty students are affiliated with the Covenanters. The group has a faculty advisor—Dr. McKenna—and some faculty support. I personally sympathize, of course, with the Covenanters' desire to take the flab out of religion, so to speak. No, a loose, imprecise term like 'cult' scarcely describes the goals of the Joggers for Jesus."

From the little I knew about academic affairs, I could tell I'd have to be tortured into reading this guy's dissertation. Glancing at my watch, I murmured some polite inanity and walked back down the hall to scrutinize my first prospective employee of the morning.

After three mumbling fraternity men, set apart by their raw new haircuts and strong smell of shoe polish, I headed back to the reception room for more coffee. Simon, his office door open, was wreathing the hall with cigar smoke.

"Do those cigars of Chancellor's taste like anything besides baby powder?" I called.

"Well, if Gene was passing some out, then he passed me over," Simon said, rather crossly. "Can't take a joke, I guess."

I guessed that he'd temporarily misplaced his professional cheerfulness, probably somewhere in the labyrinth of résumés laid out on his desk. And in a town this small, I concluded, the inhabitants must wind up bearing grudges as often as crosses; aside from jogging and churchgoing, what else was there for these pious people to do but develop persecution complexes?

At the moment my own case interested me more than small-town psychoses, since across the hall Anne Christensen was posing beside the drip pot. I fully intended to make her find it in her frozen heart to forgive me, so I decided to be brash. Slow and steady never won any races that I ever heard of, except maybe a couple of local contests for horse-and-buggy hot-rodders. "Would you allow me to take you to lunch?" I suavely asked Dr. Christensen. "In or out of town. For my own pleasure, I mean. The claims-adjusting comes later. Are you black and blue, by the way?"

"I don't eat lunch, and I'm otherwise fine, thank you, Mr.—?"

At least she wanted to know my name. And instead of the Norwegian lobsterman's sweater I would have expected, she had on a turtleneck that told me everything *I* needed to know. "Waltz. John Waltz. To be brief, I'm here interviewing Witherspoon seniors who think they'd like to work for Pittsburgh Professional Services. Are you sure you can't possibly force yourself to gulp down a few gin-soaked olives this noon?" I persisted. "There must be a cocktail lounge buried in the snow somewhere around here."

"I really haven't the time. Or the interest. But thanks anyway," Anne Christensen answered, glancing pointedly at her watch. Swallowing the last of her coffee, she made a quick exit, as if I had been a stinking bore like Gene Chancellor.

Stolid Scandinavian bitch. No doubt she wore thermal underwear and hence had no use for Waltz's warm-water charm. But, as Scarlett O'Hara pithily put it, tomorrow is another day. God damn it, no it wasn't; I was having lunch with Simple Simon, who was probably going to make me order my steak bloody and swallow it whole so he could get back to work.

This noon I wound up as a party of one at the Golden Grill —glowing with grease—and munched room-temperature tuna because a gas leak had forced them to turn off the stove. Since the snow had stopped, I emulated the natives and walked to their dingy café, both to work up some sort of appetite for college-level food and to get a good look at this upright and uptight little town.

All along College Street, I noticed what seemed an abnormally large number of bicyclers and joggers, given the weather. Many appeared well past the student age of unreason. Faculty fitness freaks, I decided, keeping in shape for a lifetime of deferred gratification. At O'Donnell's I had even drunk with a few myself—light-beer men all—and had at last understood that academic males, having chosen a gelded profession, feel compelled to overcompensate by developing ironworkers' muscles. That self-righteous *schmuck* Chancellor was a case in point. Obsessed as he was with his own lung capacity, I also suspected Dr. Chancellor might be the originator of all the "No Smoking Inside This House" signs I saw tacked to front doors—unless the Angel of the Lord had passed over lately.

The houses of New Arcady had a cold tidiness to them. I was watched from behind innumerable narrow windows, their lace curtains drawn although it was noon. Big trees brooded over yards where the snow never melted till May. The Methodist church and the First Presbyterian stood across the street from each other like chessmen; white New England clapboard pitted against blackened sandstone ludicrously edged with petticoat lace. Main Street made a point of reserved parking for Amish buggies, one of which charged me as I stepped off the curb to cross over to the Grill. No doubt its driver had decided to cast out a foreign devil, with the full cooperation of Officer James P. Smith.

I was topping off my sandwich with a plastery piece of pie when a shapely girl wriggled up to me. "Hi, my name is Darla," she breathed. "And I'm here to ask you if you know Jesus."

"Why?" I inquired. "Is he speaking on campus today?" Why in holy hell did this pretty girl have to be hot for my *soul*?

Ignoring my slow-witted sarcasm, Darla smiled at me, showing perfectly straightened teeth. "He can speak to your heart if you'll only listen. He can change your whole life, just like he did mine!"

"Thanks just the same," I told her, "but I'm Jewish. One of the people who made all this possible." I rose to go.

Darla twinkled like a vacant star. "In that case," she persisted, "you can still contribute to our 'Paint the Town Pure' campaign. Since we are struggling to keep printed filth from poisoning the children of New Arcady." She recited her last sentence like a lesson well over her little dandelion head.

"Who am I contributing to?" I asked, suddenly suspicious.

"I'm a member of the Covenanters, a local organization dedicated to the health and cleanliness of body and soul," Darla said brightly. "I'd be pleased to let you have one of our leaflets. And to pray for you."

I thrust a dollar at Darla while she still had her mouth closed and walked out the door and up the street for some survival supplies. Evidently, the purity program hadn't penetrated very far; in Marshall MacGregor's IGA I saw some faculty wives tugging tight pants down over cheeky rears with one hand while yanking their tow-headed brats along with the other.

Since I hadn't found any club soda to float my Scotch down with, I asked the checkout clerk where it was hidden.

Thoughtfully, she cracked her chewing gum. "Well, I guess we haven't stocked any for a while," she finally said. "Not many drinkers here in our town. Can't seem to keep ourselves in root beer and grape soda, though some say they're full of sugar, bad for your health. But nothing like those four packages of cigarettes." She glared at me as she gave me my change. "You might try around the corner, at Whitaker's Store," she grudgingly advised. "They sell all kinds of things down there."

Including Chinese concubines, judging from her tone. Heaven was obviously hounding me; rounding the corner of Main and McAllister, I damn near collided with Big Jim Smith, who raised an admonitory hand. I had to ford a stream of Joggers for Jesus, brandishing leaflets while intoning, "Blessed is the nation whose God is the Lord," to get into Whitaker's Store, a small and shabby Mom and Pop enterprise. Inside I saw—along with cases of club soda and Tom Collins mix—visible evidence of the vintage the Covenanters were attempting to trample out: some soft-core porn beside the stale bread and a few of the gamier girlie magazines. A tall crew-cut blond boy in the regulation baggy gray sweat suit was menacing the small, gaunt proprietor with a thick black Bible. Prepared to club the bullying Covenanter with my non-returnable bottle, I came up beside him just as he lowered his weapon.

"Excuse me, please, I'd like to pay," I muttered into his arm muscles. Did they grow nothing but giants in the Eden Valley? This one was gazing down from Olympus with an air of bemused pity. "Do you realize the nature of the evil that is kept in existence through the money you spend in this store?" he asked softly.

"Whatever it is, I don't think my seventy-nine cents is going to make much difference." I was handing it over to the proprietor, who, unfortunately for confirmed libertarians, had green teeth and a general air of unwholesomeness, like moldy processed cheese.

"Children come to spend their pennies in this store," the Covenanter said sorrowfully. "To buy candy. They choke on the filth clogging these premises."

"Look, I already gave," I explained to him. "At your branch office up the street. And I believe in equal time for impurity."

Having achieved the last word, I made my triumphal exit. I heard the Covenanter's benediction, however, even over the door's jangle. "Thank you," he called loudly. "We shall be praying for your soul."

At that moment I would gladly have sold it to the first street-corner Satan who offered me an easy deal, just to get rid of the damn thing. I wished I had had a hat to pull over my eyes as I slouched toward Reuben Tranter Hall.

As the afternoon wore on, I also wished I had found some Witherspoon College seniors I really wanted to hire. One or two looked worth considering further, but the day was flattening into a stale case of club soda. Even my scrimmage with the lady Viking seemed utterly trivial—hardly even worth dirtying up at O'Donnell's.

At 4:30 I closed up shop and drove the few blocks to the Inn. I had expected a pillared Colonial structure, its decor running to rose-sprigged toilet paper; instead I stood shivering in a draftily turreted castle guarded by an old dragon with dyed red hair and thin blue lips. Scowling at my timid request for ice, she returned from the adjacent White Lion twenty minutes later with a half-pint container of melting cubes. Guiltily, I gulped my drink in my icy room, afraid the landlady would come in any second and drag me off to the stocks, where I'd publicly receive fifty lashes with a whip fashioned from intricately knotted jockstraps contributed by the Joggers for Jesus.

The clock in the bell tower chimed, reminding me to go feed my grease-fired stomach. And so I tripped heavily into the White Lion, a pseudo-British pub minus the ale and conviviality. In what passed for the lounge, my landlady, who evidently ruled both establishments, was welcoming a shrill group of females in fat flower prints and nunlike navy blue. Then, in their midst, I spotted Anne Christensen, a swan in a sleeveless ivory dress. Long ballerina legs shimmered at me; I had caught her with her boots off. Pricked by alcohol and lust, I hurried to Anne's side, ignoring her web-footed friends, who were so startled by my lack of decorum that they moved out of formation to let me pass.

I edged Anne into a convenient corner. "You're beautiful," I murmured, smiling unctuously.

"You're drunk," she whispered back. "I can smell you. Go away before you completely ruin what's left of my reputation."

But I had penetrated to Anne's vain female core. And I also suspected she rather enjoyed shocking her ugly stepsisters, scandal hounds sniffing our trail. "I'd love to," I grinned. "Let me take you away from all this. At least as far as my room at the Inn. Who *are* all these hideous old bitches, anyway?" By now, most of them had brought us into bifocal range.

"Yoo-woo."

"Yoo-woo *who*?" I hissed.

"UWU—University Women United. It's our spring banquet."

"Can I walk you home afterwards? Treat you to a chocolate soda? I hate to sound like such a fast worker," I added, in a belated attempt to convince Anne Christensen I was capable of both earnestness and sobriety, "but I *am* leaving town Wednesday."

"At the moment a soda sounds a lot better to me than a martini, but I promised somebody a ride home. And I still have a class preparation to do. Sorry," said Dr. Christensen. Her tone gave me the impression she actually meant it. Then, with a polite stranger's smile, she turned to rejoin her group.

"Well, I do hope you ladies have a real orgy," I said to her cream-colored back. I could taste it all now. Roast ewe with mint jelly and sheet cake with Emerald City frosting.

The dining room was thick with old-maid odors: talcum powder, lilac toilet water, motheaten sexuality put away in tissue paper. I halfway expected a trail of hairpins leading me into the dining room, dominated by sparse-haired old ladies with canes tilted jauntily against their chairs. New Arcady was a woman's town, then, devoted to mummy manufacturing—virtually a lost folk art, like Bible-quilting. Quaint.

I, of course, was ignored by the student waitress, who was continually being hooked by competing canes. In addition, several diners were immediately taken with coughing fits: the result, quite clearly, of my cigarette smoke, judging from the watering eyes they rolled to heaven. Their plight kept the waitress bunny-hopping back and forth after ice water, so that I finally had to chew my own ashes and wheeze clear across the room to get her attention.

After the few mouthfuls of double-dry Old English roast beef I could manage to swallow when I finally got my dinner, I had to run the gauntlet of walking sticks a second time to go look for the men's room. My landlady—Mrs. Vandervelde by name—staring as if I had a stain on my fly, directed me to her second floor, a maze of parlors where the town's black widows lay in wait. In one of them I heard the UWU'ers calling back and forth, high on dessert and coffee, so I promptly peered in at them, hoping to attract Anne's attention. Instead, I caught the eye of the lady on her left, a grand old dame in a pink pants suit roped with diamonds who, astonishingly, winked at me. She then jabbed at Anne with jeweled fingers until the latter turned her head and acknowledged me with a smooth tea-party smile.

Now, what had *that* all been about? I highly doubted I had found a go-between, all set to smuggle Anne to my room at the stroke of midnight. Or even an ally, since this town had skimmed all human kindness off its blue milk. Mrs. Vandervelde, miserly Dutch burgomistress that she was, wouldn't even light my way to the toilet. Cursing the gloom of her fusty hallway, I stumbled like the drunken bum she thought I was and fell up against a lady leaving the women's john. To our mutual chagrin, I made a soft landing right on her extremely large bosom.

"Pardon me," I stammered, straightening up. "Are you hurt?" I added inanely.

Instinctively, the woman had backed away against the opposite wall. For a moment she merely stood catching her breath and smoothing her dress. Then, even in the indoor twilight, I could see her eyes fill up with what looked like more tears than I could ever succeed in causing Anne Christensen.

This scared me. Perhaps I had actually wounded this woman's size forty D-cuppers as well as her pride. Besides, I wanted no UWU militants springing at me like enraged tigresses.

"Are you all right?" I asked, genuinely alarmed, wishing we both could have laughed about it.

"Yes, I'm all right," the injured lady finally sighed, smiling weakly. "It's good of you to be so concerned, since it seems to happen all the time."

It was about to happen again, as we simultaneously attempted to go our separate ways. Through some after-you-Alphonse maneuvering on my part, we finally succeeded.

Incredibly, I made it to the men's room; in New Arcady, even taking a leak seemed to require broken-field running. As I groped my way back to the stairs, I heard a tinkly piano. Evidently the ladies of the borough were extending their cultural horizons—probably into infinity. But the voice made me pause. It was a rich, passionate mezzo-soprano, as deep and smooth as old brandy. I couldn't imagine which of those blameless and bloodless ladies would even lay claim to such an indecently powerful instrument. Satisfying whatever lingering curiosity I still had about New Arcady could, nonetheless, easily wait until morning. Tonight, I was far too exhausted. Trivia had taken its toll.

At the cash register, Mrs. Vandervelde carefully examined my twenty-dollar bill, but I made it out the door, for once, without further comment from my reluctant hostess. My passage across the icy parking lot, however, was blocked by a small group of truant UWU'ers, call ng in their coloratura voices, "Good night, Sally"; "Good night, Molly"; Good night, Marty," like the high school pep squad. I attempted to skirt them with a sharp left; but, in executing my turn, I slipped on a hidden patch of ice and fell on my ass. For a moment I thought that surely my coccyx had snapped, if not my spine. Then two grinning young women were helping me to my feet.

Rubbing my tailbone, I tried to recover my severely damaged dignity. Fortunately, most of the UWU'ers had gotten into their cars. My strong-handed Samaritans, however, stood regarding me with lively interest.

Automatically, I had already begun appraising them. Like Anne Christensen, they scarcely seemed secular nuns. Both were tall, slender, thirtyish brunettes: one black Irish and the other dark gypsy. Sexy sisters of mercy; but, unlike Anne Christensen, not for me. For each other, maybe. My lone wolf's eyes told me that these two were a couple, very much together, although careful to conceal it from the local witch hunters.

"Hurt much?" asked the taller, with nurselike briskness.

"Actually, I should limp back inside and borrow a cane," I said, trying to square my shoulders into a reasonable semblance of manhood.

"We'd go get you some rubbing alcohol," continued the one who seemed cast in the dominant male role, "but the drugstore closes at six, of course. Along with everything else."

"I could try twelve-year-old Scotch," I suggested helpfully.

"Just don't smoke in bed," said the gypsy one. "The Volunteer Fire Department isn't equipped to handle human torches. Besides, Mrs. Vandervelde would sift through every one of your ashes trying to recover damages."

Much as I applauded them, I wasn't equipped to match wits with this black-comedy team. I was far too tired and too sore and too cold even to ask them up for a drink and unspeakable crimes against nature. Scotch in solitude suited this old recluse. But before I limped off the field, I wanted to tell these delightful dykes to continue the fight. Bore from within, make molehills into mountains, and turn this town over to the twentieth century. Yay, team.

"May I have your names, ladies?" I inquired. "I represent the Miracle-of-the-Month Club. When we find honest-to-God human beings, we notify the Pope. I assume you teach at Witherspoon College?"

"It's a living," shrugged their official spokesperson. "I'm Leslie Fielding, token woman in the Political Science Department; and this is Sally Richardson, who's in music education. Richardson and Fielding, thanks to the literary types on campus."

"Eighteenth-century novelists," Richardson explained. "Richardson is psychological and Fielding is funny."

"Actually, some of my best friends used to be English majors. John Waltz, of Pittsburgh Professional Services. Thanks so much for putting me back on my feet again."

"You're sure you're okay, before we go?" Richardson asked with genuine concern.

"I'll just hobble along up to my room," I assured them. "Good night, ladies."

"Good night. And welcome to New Arcady," they chorused, while I proceeded to pick my way across the alley. It had been a day of pratfalls, mishaps, minor skirmishes; I was taking no more chances. At the half I remained scoreless against New Arcady. And, as for my presumed powers of seduction, so far they had yielded me only a wink from an old woman and a good-will offering from two young ones whose bodies belonged only to each other. Wondering why in hell I'd insisted on being alone with my powerfully negative thoughts so early in the evening, I went up to my silent room, graced only by bottle, Dixie cup, and dollhouse ashtray. Convinced that at the core I was a rotten Jew—given my morbid fears of family gatherings, neighborhood solidarity, and anything else that smacked of ghetto togetherness—I had exclaimed many times over my unrealized Protestant potential for social and spiritual isolation. But now, here in church-centered New Arcady, I found I hadn't the faintest desire to peruse my bedside Gideon Bible or work up a sweat wrestling with my personal demons on the icy floor. Suddenly I understood why so many Scandinavians, locked up in those long, dark winters, did themselves in with such dispatch. I had already named my own poison, however: sufficient Scotch to douse my dreams of thawing out Anne Christensen with my blistering blowtorch. Good night, ladies.

CHAPTER II
TUESDAY, MARCH 18

AT 6:30 I WOKE UP TO EAR-RENDING SHRIEKS I COULDN'T IM-
mediately identify until I looked out my north window and
through a curtain of snow and saw a procession snaking its way
down Main Street: a kilted piper leading a line of hooded
Covenanters swaying like cobras in time to the tune he was tor-
turing out of his instrument. Having mentally launched a personal
vendetta against those goddamn Sunday-school grafters, I opened
the window. I could hear the Joggers for Jesus howling out a
refrain as they dipped their way down the street, their leader strut-
ting in approved regimental style. "Are you washed in the blood
of the Lamb?" they asked mournfully, over and over and over.
Then the piper changed his tune and New Arcady's native-born
Red Guard took their Great Leap Forward, jogging through the
snow until they faded from view like gray ghosts.

What a way to start the day. Washing myself in Mrs. Vandervelde's rusty water, I noted that my bruised butt strikingly resembled a baboon's, although I had no reason at all to wish it white
and smooth. Cautiously, I drove to breakfast at the Golden Grill,
hoping to avoid town cops and stray cultists until I reached the
sanctuary of Reuben Tranter Hall.

"Get a good night's rest over at the inn, Mr. Waltz?" Pete
Simon called from behind his snow pile of morning mail as I came
up the hall for the key to my room.

"Not in *this* nice quiet town," I said, walking into the office of
its one-man chamber of commerce.

"Sorry about the bagpipes." Simon grinned. "Wish I could

24

miss the next meeting of the borough council. But I look at it this way: by the time my daughters are old enough to join, the group'll be long gone, just like bobbysocks and the hula hoop."

He smiled indulgently, paternally, while I looked at the large framed photograph dominating the wall behind his desk, centered among a collection of citations and certificates. Mom and Dad beamed down at four blonde daughters, including two well-rounded teenagers. Their mother, a smug little partridge, was dwarfed by a leaning tower of lacquered hair.

"And you do have a fine family," I said, to get it over with.

"Well, they cost a bundle, but I guess they're a good investment," Simon said proudly. "Provided they all market themselves into marrying millionaires."

"Thought you'd sworn off the state lottery, Pete," Leslie Fielding—her arms full of thick, plastic-backed notebooks—said from the doorway. "Don't tell me you finally got lucky! I checked out your entire civil service jobs file," she explained. "My poli sci majors all seem a little worried about their futures. Hi, John Waltz, how are you? You holding up your end okay?"

With a grin and a wink, Fielding straightened her pile of government pamphlets and ducked back out into the hallway. Simon hastily went out to hold the front door open for her, but when he came back, he was making a face I would have expected to see only on my landlady sniffing my water glass.

"Nice gal," I observed.

"Yeah, if you go in for bull dykes," said Simon. "I was kind of surprised to see Leslie in here all by herself. She and her —friend—try pretty hard for a low profile, but I don't think either one of them's going to last very long around here. You can't fool all of the people all of the time, if you know what I mean. And I guess I'm pretty old-fashioned, but I don't especially want that type teaching my daughters. Kids that age really do need some kind of role model. And a lot of their parents just can't be bothered. Which is why I teach Sunday school, I guess. Senior high boys. My substitute sons." Simon grinned.

Before I could clear my throat to award him a verbal merit badge, he was flipping through his desk calendar. "I've blocked us out enough time for lunch out at Nino's. Italian place on Route 34 East. Has a liquor license." He turned to glance out the window behind him. "Weather permitting, of course. We may have to stick to the White Lion. Anyway, I'll see you up here at 12:15."

Here Simon took a look at his big fancy watch to signal the end of our three minutes of small talk and then glanced out his half-open door, which Anne Christensen was just passing on her way down the hall. "Hi, Anne, how's the job hunt coming?" he called.

"Nothing yet, I'm afraid. Hello, Mr. Waltz, how are you?" Anne asked with clipped courtesy. Ignoring my challenging stare, she tapped on down the hallway.

Too bewildered to want to catch up with her, I showed myself out of Simon's office and went across the hall to warm up with coffee before my first appointment of the morning. Running the length of Reuben Tranter Hall was beginning to make me feel like a zealous convert to Convenanterism, although I doubted I could survive an induction ceremony; hurrying to my temporary office, I put my foot into a surgeon's tray of lug wrenches and damn near broke my big toe. The man in blue denim disemboweling the sputtering radiator outside my door hastily got up and held out a powerful arm to steady me as I reeled back against the wall.

"Yes, yes, I'm all right," I said impatiently, before this member of the maintenance staff I intended to sue had a chance to ask.

"Goddamn college's fault if you ain't," he said sourly. "Radiators all ought to be sold for scrap. If it was me, I would have had this whole damn rathole razed ten years ago. Cheap bastards. Crooks, too. Every goddamn one of 'em," the maintenance man growled, waving his wrench in the general direction of the placement offices up the hall. With a grunt and a shrug, he stooped again to his hopeless task.

A dog ready to chew to pieces the hand that reluctantly fed him his horsemeat. As he began savagely banging away on the pieces of metal spread out in front of him, I paused at my office door to give this glowering fellow a second look. Most women would have, I supposed. The man operating on my radiator was short, compactly muscled, dark as a matinee pirate, with sideburns and mustache to match: the Turkish Terror, chained to Christian galleys. He looked completely incapable of being submerged into this community.

The future Jaycees I saw that morning, by contrast, all had pleasant, instant-pudding faces. None exactly lived up to Pete Simon's advance billing, although one fraternity man did look like suitable desk dressing for PPS's Monroeville Mall office. My patience with these Protestant mainliners was finally rewarded at 10:30, when a Ms. Melissa Parsons arrived for her duly scheduled appointment. She had Slavic cheekbones, High Renaissance eyes, auburn hair, and a dual major in business and modern languages. I knew immediately that PPS had to engage in affirmative action and hire Ms. Parsons as a management trainee. Curiously enough, however, she lacked the poise that should have accompanied her beauty and presumed intelligence; she kept shredding tissues while she answered my questions.

"Cigarette?" I asked, hoping I had made the correct diagnosis.

"No, thank you," she said, shuddering slightly. But all these kids had been warned, probably by Pete Simon, that smoking in a recruiter's presence would impel him to rip the buttons right off their blazers. The writers of interview tip sheets had obviously never met John Waltz, who had once lit up his own toothbrush.

"What's going to keep you happy with yourself and your work, say five years from now?" I asked, in my most sincere talk-show-host voice. "What about your own performance standards?"

Ms. Parsons looked panicky. "Only the Lord can decide how I can give my life to him in order to meet *his* standards for me," she said in a dull monotone.

"Ms. Parsons," I said urgently, "I'm trying to suggest to you that PPS would be very interested in making you an offer, if you're still interested in working for us. As I naturally assumed you were." *This is the real, evil world, kid,* I wanted to add, *so make room for Mammon.*

"I was, a month ago," Ms. Parsons said, braiding her strips of tissue. "But—"

"Something happened?" I prompted her.

But the girl just sat there littering the rug. "Now—well, I just don't know, Mr. Waltz," she finally answered. Her burnt-almond eyes begged my pardon. Then Ms. Parsons's face closed, and her voice came out like a doped-up pop singer's: "God has his own plan for my life," she said.

Her God sure as hell sounded like a selfish old bastard, always yelling, "I'm Number One." And since PPS couldn't stand the competition, I'd have to give up on Melissa Parsons, whose brains had been bleached out in the blood of the Lamb. "Give me a call between now and the end of the semester if you decide you might like a second interview with us," I said, rising, knowing Ms. Parsons had chosen not to hear me. Still, hell-bent on saving her for herself, I made one last attempt at interpersonal communication. "And you can always reach us through Mr. Simon," I said encouragingly.

The girl's head jerked violently, her face desperate as a drowning woman's. In the instant before her eyes filmed over again and she marched herself out of my office, Melissa Parsons gave me a look of sheer terror. Picking up pieces of tissue, I stared after her in mingled alarm and relief as she sleepwalked her way down the hall. Next patient, please.

Although Ms. Parsons had left early, my 11:00 appointment, a gangling senior given to repeating both himself and me, stayed late. And I still had to squeeze in yesterday's cancelee, one Susan Snickelburger. So I trotted back up the hall to let Simon know I might be a few minutes late for our luncheon date. The sky still had the gray opacity of a Covenanter's sweat shirt, but the snow had stopped, placing a one-martini lunch at least within the realm of possibility, unless my host ruled, as he very well might, that my five minutes' tardiness dictated Mrs. Vandervelde's sepia-toned tap water instead. Hoping to convince him the state health inspector was hot on my landlady's trail, I paused outside his door, which was only slightly ajar, to announce my presence with a few well-bred taps, in case he had gotten stuck with some student almost as crazy as the gorgeous Ms. Parsons. Then I realized Witherspoon's placement director was talking on the phone, with somebody who was giving him a far harder time than even the flakiest undergraduate could have aspired to. Giving up on good manners, I stood there and listened.

"Oh, come on, you know I'd help you out if I could," Simon was telling his caller in a low, nervous voice. "Loan you *fifty* thou if I had it. But you have to realize I'm a little strapped right now. You know, plywood doesn't come cheap these days," Simon added, his patience clearly as strained as his humor.

The person at the other end of the line apparently had no intention of allowing him to change the tone, or the topic, of their conversation because, after a long pause, Simon sighed, "Okay, Thursday night, then. Say around 8:30. I'll see if I can't work something out for you. Yeah, we had some good fun on the old couch over there," he agreed unenthusiastically. "Yeah, sure. See you then."

Stunned, for at least thirty seconds, I stood in the hallway with my mouth hanging open like the village idiot's, gaping at one of the bulletin boards. I felt almost outraged that Peter Simon, my vanishing small-town American had, between his Sunday school classes and borough council meetings, somehow managed to squeeze in secret bouts of adultery. Simon's rather strenuous double life was, of course, most emphatically his own business, but I did hate being forced to find out that as a judge of character, John Waltz ought to be immediately and permanently removed from the bench.

Shaking my head over my own naiveté, I moved stealthily up the hall to Simon's secretary's vacant office and dropped a note on her desk saying I'd meet him at 12:30. Idly, I wondered just which faculty wife had Simon hustling up some money for their meeting Thursday night at 8:30; while his secrets were certainly safe with *me*, he hadn't sounded at all sure they were safe in the greedy little paws of his ex-girlfriend. I felt briefly sorry for Pete Simon, who'd picked such a poor sport to play with on his office couch, but if the lady wouldn't give up gracefully, that was his worry, not mine. At the moment I had other things to think about besides any complications arising from Simon's sex life or his own glaring errors in judgment; as I turned to start my fifty-yard dash down the hall, the front door of the building banged, and a large furry female came running up to ask me where room 18 was. So I ended up escorting Ms. Snickelburger to our rendezvous father-of-the-bride fashion. With pop eyes fixed on my increasingly glassy ones, she pleaded for a position with PPS while I tried to murmur polite ambiguities. Forced, after fifteen minutes or so of not getting my point across, to indicate our lack of interest in Ms. Snickelburger's way with embroidered pillowslips more clearly, I realized that, even with all her padding, she wasn't built to absorb the shock of rejection. Quivering with hurt feelings, my interviewee started to cry. Unlike Ms. Parsons, however, this blubbering baby whale carried no tissues, so I presented her with my own large white pocket handkerchief and waited patiently while she swaddled herself in her coat. Several minutes later, she at last heaved herself out of her chair and left the room, leaving me even later for lunch than I had predicted.

By the time I had locked up and brushed Ms. Snickelburger's fake fur from my own coat, the clock in the silent corridor said 12:29. I set a new record reaching the other end of the building, but where in hell was Pete Simon? *Now* he had had to close his damn door, which I stood idiotically hammering on like the town constable until I remembered Simon's pride in his own punctuality; I could almost picture him neatly printing "Pay-off: 8:30" on his appointment calendar for Thursday, March 20. Which meant he'd sent *me* a message nobody had remembered to give me and was waiting for me out in the parking lot.

My feet felt suddenly sticky; I'd obviously stepped into the spilled dregs of somebody's sugared coffee. I trudged slowly back down the hall and out the back door. Nothing in the parking lot, however, but crystalliferous cars and a few sad, rusty bicycles. Then I realized that Simon's car had to be standing out in *front* of the building, with its owner impatiently waiting inside it, foot trembling over the accelerator. I slopped wearily through the sooty snow to the front entrance of Tranter Hall, where there was no car either idling or cruising. As I turned to go back inside the building, an orange Camaro—Daddy's advance on graduation with honors—whipped fearlessly around an Amish buggy and splattered me with melting slush. Swearing like a Christian soldier, I shoved through the heavy door and searched for a note on the outside of Simon's. Nothing. I knocked perfunctorily, then turned the knob. The door was locked. Patches of the same sticky reddish-brown substance that I had stepped into on my trip to the parking lot had dried around the latch. Above it I traced what looked like a crude triangle daubed on in the stuff. It flaked on my numb fingers. Dumbass Waltz had blood on his hands. Real blood. I reared back toward the main door of the building, right into Anne Christensen, who was coming through it.

"Oh no, not again," she groaned. Then she saw the look on my face and took two frightened steps backwards.

I pulled her over against the wall. My stained fingers froze to her wrist. "Anne," I said. Period.

"My *God*, what's the matter, John?" she gasped. "And you've got a death-grip on me. *Please*!"

Somehow my hand relaxed and I achieved coherent speech, although I heard myself mumbling like an old man missing most of his teeth. "Simon's door's locked. There's blood on it. Blood underneath it," I managed to tell the marble-pale woman beside me. "We've got to break it down. The door. I mean, I've got to. Unless—can we get a key from somewhere?"

"I've got a master," Anne answered, carefully enunciating. "It will open the coffee room. The receptionist in there has a key to Pete's door in her desk. If she left it unlocked."

Without any female fumbling in her purse, she presented me with the key as quickly as she had grasped the situation. A twitching spastic, I fumbled open the door across from Simon's.

Anne pulled out the right desk drawer, produced the receptionist's key ring, and extracted Simon's.

To coin a cliché, we were in this together. Whatever it turned out to be. At the moment I didn't fancy our conducting a joint investigation, but Anne obviously intended otherwise. "You stay over here," I ordered her. "*Please*," I pleaded urgently.

Hearing the fear in my voice, Anne nodded and stood gripping the cold metal edge of Simon's receptionist's desk while I force-marched myself back across the hall. The lock clicked, but I had to wrestle Simon's stuck door open. Surprise! The lights were on—and the place was festooned with streamers of blood. Pete Simon lay slung in his chair like a bloody bag of laundry. He was all torso; someone had hammered his head into hamburger so that it sagged into his neck. At least I was spared a look at his face. The dead man's chair was pushed far enough back from his desk, however, for me to see that Simon's spread legs, sheathed in the rags of his trousers, seemed glued to a stiff sheet of blood, because his penis and his testicles had been cut out from between them.

I began to try to read the papers piled on top of the desk through their bloody punctuation marks. Then I focused on the wall and stared at the spatter-painting of blood on the Simon family's studio portrait. I also started making a mental checklist. In case of death, call a doctor, call an ambulance, call the police. Notify the next of kin. The next of kin.

I started to gag. Anne Christensen stood blocking the doorway behind me, but I pushed past her, hurled myself out the front door, and vomited into the dirty snow. Immediately I felt a little better.

Anne had had the sense not to follow me out. When I returned, she was on the phone in the reception room, dialing the state police.

"I've already called the locals," she said quietly. "And I caught the doctor having lunch at home. It's 12:40; I hope they get here before people start coming back from lunch and classes. With that door open over there. We can't even close it. Fingerprints."

I had averted my eyes from the gaping doorway, and I was trying hard to blank out the TV screen in my brain. Or at least change the channel. "Well, so much for my strong, silent routine," I said with a sad clown's smile. "But you're marvelous. Wonder Woman."

"My stiff upper lip is all that's holding my face together," Anne said faintly. Then her crossed leg began swinging violently back and forth. "John—how did—it—get out? What if *it's* still in the building—hiding in somebody's office?"

I had ignored this possibility. During my absurd chasing around after a dead man, Tranter Hall had appeared completely deserted. But I had been, after all, interviewing in a soundproof room while Pete Simon's carcass was being so bloodily carved up—the obvious suddenly punched me in the stomach—and the killer would have had ample opportunity before Ms. Snickelburger's departure and my own circuit of the building either to find a nice dark place for himself right here in Tranter Hall or else run along home. Besides making better sense, the latter alternative appealed to me strongly.

Hoping I sounded reassuring, I suggested it to Anne. "Whoever it was would want to get the hell out of here without leaving any more bloody traces than absolutely necessary. Why trap himself in the building? Why be surprised by Dr. Christensen towing a student into her office? How could he get into your office, or anyone else's, in the first place?" My voice was faltering along with my forensic skill. "Unless he had a key," I admitted.

"Yes—*unless he had a key*," Anne said fiercely. "He had a key to Pete Simon's office, remember? He locked Pete's door behind him."

"And put his coat on, and walked out the front door. Or the back door," I insisted.

"He wouldn't have to!" Anne cried. "It's one of *us*! It could even be you. Or me. Somebody who works in the building. And who's maybe in here right now!"

I could have slapped her. "Oh, come *on*, Anne," I said angrily.

"The *last* thing we need is you trying to scare us both to death! For God's sake, there's nobody in here but us. Nobody else in the whole damn building!"

Then, mercifully, before we had any more opportunities to try second-guessing the killer, we heard sirens screeching down College Street. Brakes squealed out front, and Officer James P. Smith and another cop built like a bean-bag chair came running in, unpacking their pistols. Caldwell, the doctor, right behind them, impatiently motioned the two officers of the law out of his way.

"You two stay right were you are, out of the way," Big Jim ordered, squinting at us. "Oh, it's you, Wirtz. Stay right where you are, Wirtz."

The back door banged, and someone started clumping up the hall. Smith's partner waddled away to intercept whoever it was. Dr. Caldwell, working silently after his initial grunt of disgust, came back across the hall to call the coroner. "The state police will be able to tell us about any escaped mental patients from across the Ohio line," he said. "There's some maniac on the loose. Darnedest thing I ever saw; after amputating the victim's, ah—organs—he apparently took them away with him. They're nowhere to be found."

I got a grotesque image of somebody shuffling around with Simon's bloody member in his pocket and struggled to suppress my own insane cackle. "You two holding up all right?" Caldwell asked gruffly. "Don't see any signs of shock; you'll do fine." He doled us out some Valium. "Five milligrams now; five at bedtime. And no refills, Anne," he admonished her.

The doctor sat down beside us to fill out his forms for the coroner. "First closed-casket funeral for this town ever, as far as I know," he said suddenly, shifting in his chair.

Sirens again. The state police. Immediately, the men in khaki began winnowing the building. Two of them went next-door for the master keys in possession of the maintenance supervisor, who came storming over to Tranter Hall to expostulate with Detective Lieutenant Hershey for several precious minutes before he finally surrendered his key-ring like a miser dredging Krugerrands up from his mattress. After handing over our own keys, Anne and I were warned to stay put until the lieutenant, a male-model type, could find a quiet place to question us. For the moment he was satisfied with our formal identification of the body, cheerfully corroboratéd by Dr. Caldwell, and with having one of his subordinates obtain our fingerprints.

His function usurped by the state trooper now posted at the rear door, the fat local cop came huffing and puffing back up the hall. Lieutenant Hershey, thank God, told both Fat Freddy Mays and Big Jim Smith to go get some fresh air and make some attempt to control the crowd beginning to ring Tranter Hall.

Members of the English Department were muttering to each other outside the windows, while both the placement office receptionist and Simon's secretary had begun to protest being barred from their own doors. In the soothing tone of a suicide hotline, one of Hershey's men kept telling them repeatedly, "A police investigation is underway. No one is permitted to enter or leave the building."

Tragedy was rapidly turning into farce. Up and down the corridor, telephones were jangling with maddening persistence. Through the front window we could see Big Jim trying to crowd the coroner back into his car. The state squad seemed to be unbolting the urinals in the men's room as well as measuring, photographing, and scraping off blood samples.

"Subject of present homicide investigation apparently left the death location by means of the men's room window, north wall of building," the detective lieutenant was saying for the benefit of his tape recorder. "Splashes of what appears to be dried blood found on upper portion of left-hand lavatory. Streaks of what appears to be dried blood found on six linoleum squares of men's room floor. Disarrangement of shrubbery and appearance of surface snow at ground level, thirty inches below window, further indicate suspect's method of egress. Faint configuration of tire marks, approximately seven-eighths of an inch in width, apparent in driveway adjacent to north side of building, suggest subject's employment of two-wheeled racing bicycle to leave the neighborhood.''

I glanced at Anne to read her reaction. Bizarre as the bicycle business sounded, at least it proved my point; no mad doctors of philosophy had been crouching in any of Tranter Hall's dark corners. Across the hall the coroner was placing plastic bags on the victim's hands and feet. I wondered if he had brought along any sandwich-size, in case he came across the dead man's missing pieces. At last he signaled the ambulance attendants, who removed the present remains of Pete Simon. The crowd outside was keeping up a low, steady growl.

I needed a stiff drink before I snapped my leash and bolted clear back to Pittsburgh. ''You need a stiff drink,'' I told Anne, whose pallor rather alarmed me, especially since the Valium Dr. Caldwell had so grudgingly given her didn't seem to be doing anything to control her intermittent shivering fits.

''The end is not in sight,'' she reminded me. ''We still have to be grilled by Lieutenant Hershey.''

Right on cue, Detective Lieutenant Miles Hershey, who had round, chocolate eyes and fair, curly hair—a combination that would have had my own daughter begging for a strip search —came back in to summon us to my own former office for our individual interrogations. ''First I have a personal question for Miss Christensen,'' he said soberly. ''Are you at all friendly with the victim's wife, Mrs. Mary Sue Simon?''

Anne's crossed leg began to jiggle again. ''Am I supposed to be? No, I wouldn't say so. I've spoken to her two or three times at ladies' luncheons.''

''We haven't been able to locate her yet—no one's home—but I thought when she gets the news, she ought to have another woman with her. And we hope she doesn't hear it on the radio. I might as well caution you two right now about giving any information out. Even if that seems sort of obvious,'' the lieutenant added with a smile of apology.

Definitely a nice young man. Every father's favorite son-in-law.

Once settled in my own recruiter's chair—which reminded me

that I'd probably missed meeting the one student who could have made PPS into a multinational giant—Hershey glanced at the preliminary reports one of his men had made out of whatever personal data Anne and I had remembered.

"Looks like you're stuck in New Arcady for the duration, Mr. Waltz," he said. "Or until further notice—whenever we tell you you can leave town. In view of your discovery of the body. To start off, would you describe in detail your own activities between 12:00 noon and 12:39 P.M. today, when our dispatcher in Coal City recorded Miss Christensen's telephone call?"

All at once I found myself prepared to champion Dr. Caldwell's escaped-mental-patient theory, since I had just realized that Ms. Snickelburger and I had to provide each other with alibis. Hershey duly noted her existence. As I told him of my perambulations through and around Reuben Tranter Hall, climaxed by my second crash into Anne Christensen, I myself sounded like a candidate for permanent custodial care.

"What was Miss Christensen's manner when you met her at the main door of the building?" Hershey asked.

"I seem to be missing something, Lieutenant," I said, genuinely bewildered.

"Had she been hurrying? Did she seem agitated? Noticeably upset?"

Although I knew Hershey was merely doing his job, and would have to question Anne Christensen just as closely about any possible deviations on my part from the behavioral norm for finders of mutilated bodies, I decided to set him straight about Anne at once, before he wasted any more of his own valuable time. "Considering that I practically knocked Miss Christensen down and that I was barely this side of sanity at that particular moment, she seemed in a perfectly normal state for a gray Tuesday noon," I assured him. "And no hysterics. She behaved like a—you should pardon the expression—trooper through the whole thing."

"Are you personally acquainted with Miss Christensen at all?" Hershey inquired gravely.

"Not as well as I'd like to be. I mean, I met her for the first time yesterday morning," I hastily explained.

The lieutenant acknowledged Anne's charms with a non-committal nod. "Did she make any comments to you concerning the possible identity of the killer?" he went on, briskly returning us to the business at hand.

I could tell the lieutenant had no intention of being soft on beautiful blondes. "Did Miss Christensen mention her reason for returning to the building during the noon hour?" he persisted. "We'll have to round up everybody who works in Tranter Hall, but apparently nobody else happened to."

"I don't think she eats lunch, but we hardly had a chance to get down to trivia. Lieutenant, as you're well aware, I'm becoming an extremely hostile witness."

"Be useful in spite of yourself, Mr. Waltz," Hershey grinned, suddenly all melting marshmallow. "What about the extent of your own contact with the victim?" he continued with his usual briskness. "Any knowledge of his personal life, conduct, moral character?"

His eyes brightening at once, the lieutenant leaned forward expectantly; my face had obviously given me away. Honest John Waltz, perennial flop at playing himself. *And* at zeroing in on the essentials; I should have brought up Simon's telephone call ten minutes ago, before Hershey had even started stewing over the circumstantial evidence. "Three hours ago I would have thought the U.S. Bureau of Standards ought to issue Pete Simon some kind of certificate but, as it turns out, he was a phony," I told my interrogator, who impatiently signaled me to get on with it in plain English. "Simon liked to play dedicated workaholic and devoted family man," I explained, "but, judging from the telephone conversation I almost walked in on about an hour before I found the bloody mess somebody made out of him, he'd had an affair with some woman who'd decided to ask him for a little remembrance. Money. So—"

"So?" Hershey echoed, obviously waiting for some facts he could actually use.

"Simon didn't sound too happy about it, but he told her he might be able to work something out for her. She was supposed to meeting him Thursday night at 8:30 in his office—at the scene of the crime, so to speak; I guess he never blew his cover taking her to a motel. Maybe she didn't trust him to come up with her dough and decided to drop by a little early. Or maybe Mrs. Simon found out what her husband was actually doing all those evenings he bolted his dinner so he could rush back to Tranter Hall. Or," I went on, plunging ahead while I still had the lieutenant's semi-respectful attention, "maybe some other civic-minded soul found out Pete Simon was getting a little action and thought he'd help the Lord punish the poor bastard. Sure as hell looks like *somebody* here in the borough got furious over Simon's sex life."

Hershey, obviously not a local boy, looked at me quizzically, so I made an effort to enlighten him. "Lieutenant," I said earnestly, "in New Arcady, murder is probably more forgivable than adultery. This town sees its earthly goal as the extinction of smoking, drinking, and sex for recreational purposes. There's even a clean-up-the-smut campaign going on at the moment, sponsored by a local cult called the Covenanters."

Hershey was extremely interested in my eyewitness account of the group's morning devotions. "Know who any of their leaders are?" he asked me after I had numbered my own grudges against the group.

"Possibly the tall astronaut type who wanted to throw the Good Book at me in Whitaker's Store. But I've been assured, even by Pete Simon, that the Joggers for Jesus are only out to get souls."

One of Hershey's men knocked on the door, and he excused himself for a hasty conference in the corridor. "I do have a statement for you to sign, Waltz," the lieutenant said when he came back. "And I still have to talk to Miss Christensen, although the president of the college wants to see me immediately. Says he wants to shut the whole damn place down. Send all the students home. Which we can't let him do, of course," Hershey sighed, a muscular Atlas with a crick in his neck. Then he squared his shoulders and raised his head. "Waltz, I'm unofficially deputizing you," he informed me, suddenly inspired. "Since you have to stay here anyway—until we tell you it's okay to leave—why don't you try and see what else you can find out that might be of interest to us? The way things are, I'll be tied up with paperwork in Coal City part of the time, so I might have to miss some of the fun up here. Who knows, Waltz?" he added jocularly. "You might even end up with proof positive that Miss Christensen didn't do it."

My daughter Marcia would have loved the lieutenant's lame-brained irony, which I was momentarily content to ignore, since I suddenly felt like an overgrown Hardy Boy, ready to rush into the Golden Grill and demand all the dirty napkins so I could put them under my mail-order microscope.

"Under the circumstances, I think you're entitled to hear the results of the coroner's preliminary investigation," Hershey was saying, even solicitous. "Here goes: 'The white male identified as Peter Simon was the victim of a homicide occurring between approximately 11:30 A.M. and the alleged discovery of his body at approximately 12:35 P.M.,'" he read. "We'll have to change that outer limit to about 11:40 or a couple minutes after, when you told me you heard Simon talking on the phone—looks like you were also the last one to see the victim alive, Waltz—or at least you heard him moving around in there?"

I nodded, rather grimly, since I supposed that despite Ms. Snickelburger and his own decision to feed me privileged information, Lieutenant Hershey would probably be keeping an eye on me, as Officer Smith of the borough police had assured me he intended to do when I came over the drawbridge yesterday.

"Well, anyway, there's no evidence of anything fancy, like a tape the murderer left playing in Simon's office." Hershey continued: "'Immediate cause of death, apparent subdural hemorrhage of the brain due to extensive crescent-shaped lacerations, apparently created by blows made with the head of a claw hammer. Presence of what appears to be an occipital fracture indicates assailant initially rendered victim unconscious. Presence of several incised wounds on various portions of the body, resulting in further severe blood loss, indicates additional use of a knife blade, double-edged, approximately seven inches in length. No weapons available for examination and identification.' ''

The same trooper was standing at the door with another piece of paper. ''Mary Sue Simon is being driven home from her bridge club,'' said Hershey after glancing at it. ''Waltz, what about going along with Sergeant Hendricks? You might be able to make it less awkward.''

Incredulous, I nodded and obediently followed Sergeant Hendricks, who was now silently handing me a message as well out to the parking lot. What in all hell was I going to say to Mrs. Simon? ''Sorry some psycho did a fancy amputation on your schmuck of a husband? Remember what a good provider he was, even if it turns out he was screwing every skirt in town?'' Why me, with all the local ministers on call?

Anne's scribbled note, which I examined in the car, simply said, ''Come for a drink. After five. More later,'' and gave me directions. It was now 3:30, and what I really wanted was less, not more. And maybe about ten hours' sleep. Still, I was curious to see if I could do a better job of summing up Mary Sue Simon than I had her late husband.

Simon's house on Somerset Street had a brick neo-colonial exterior that included a doorless garage half-paneled with sheets of the plywood I'd heard the dead man bemoan the price of only four hours ago. Mary Sue, dyed to match the tangerine throw pillows strewn over her living room, came steadily enough to the door and graciously seated us near her enormous fieldstone fireplace, which I judged hadn't come cheap either.

After assuring Simon's widow she'd be spared questioning at present, Sergeant Hendricks gave her a carefully condensed version of the murder story. White-faced but dry-eyed, Mary Sue stood silently plucking invisible threads out of the arm of the orange plush recliner next to the fireplace while Hendricks stammered on. ''Mr. Waltz here found your husband's body,'' the sergeant suddenly announced, obviously eager to wind things down.

''I'm so terribly sorry, Mrs. Simon,'' I said in a dutiful monotone. "I didn't know your husband very well, of course, but he was certainly a fine man."

Mary Sue, however, seemed to have hung out a "Do Not Disturb" sign; she scarcely even nodded her head to acknowledge my painful effort. Then, after a long moment of silence, Simon's widow straightened up and looked me right in the eye. "We'll lose the house, you know," she told me in a thin, flat voice. "We'll never pay for it now. That would have been his den out there in the garage—with built-in shelves for all his trophies and things. That was what he'd always wanted. And he always got whatever he wanted. So there's no money for anything now. Nothing at all for me or the girls," Mary Sue said with a tight little laugh.

Hendricks vigorously cleared his throat.

"Thank you very much for coming by," murmured Mary Sue, extending her hand first to Hendricks and then to me. "I'll answer questions for your lieutenant whenever he thinks it's absolutely necessary," she told Hershey's sergeant. Then she pointedly stepped aside to give us a clear path to the front door.

After listening to that lifestyle-conscious lament, I suddenly felt a lot sorrier for the late Pete Simon than I could manage to get for his widow—grief-crazed or not. I was also ready to scratch a prime suspect off Hershey's master list, since I couldn't see Mary Sue caring enough about her husband's method of easing his tensions—which she'd certainly helped to create—to kill him. Any castrating this woman chose to do would be neat and bloodless, so as not to ruin her velvet-pile shag. No wonder Simon had warmed himself at a friendlier fireside.

"We'll still have to check out her alibi, but so far as we know, she was playing bridge with about twenty other people from 11:00 A.M. on, until we finally got ahold of her about an hour ago," Hendricks said on our way back to Tranter Hall, thoughtfully answering my unspoken question.

The sergeant's well-marked car was tying up all forms of traffic. Despite the cold weather, everybody in town seemed to be standing around staring at us and each other, all set to start jabbering and finger-waggling any second. At the corner of Church and Main, there was even a small huddle of Amish women: black crows flapping around in the snow.

I retrieved my own crusted car and drove back to the inn, unaware that my own fame had spread until I saw a well-tailored six-o'clock-news type violating Mrs. Vandervelde's "No Loitering" ordinance at the foot of the stairs. "Lousy day, isn't it? No further comment," I mumbled, and bounded up the steps to my room, eager to escape into sleep, Scotch, and shower. Then I remembered that I had to call PPS and tell them I was stuck up here in the middle of a murder. Mrs. Vandervelde was obviously listening in, which took care of telling her I was extending my stay. I thought of calling Marcia at college, to let her know where she'd have to wire for any emergency funds; but since she was rooming with the daughter (or possibly the son; I had never been quite sure which) of some bigshot at NBC and I valued my own privacy, if not quaint little New Arcady's, I immediately decided she could eat cornflakes for the duration.

The nap I'd also decided on was no good; my subconscious chose to remind me at ten-second intervals that a Grade AA maniac was probably stocking up on grape soda at MacGregor's IGA right this minute. I kept seeing a tall, slender blonde with her head smashed like a golden-haired doll's. *Somewhere in the back of her watch-spring mind, Anne might even know who it is*, I thought. And there were a couple of other questions—besides where I could take her for dinner—I really wanted to ask Anne Christensen.

I found her apartment, on the top floor of a shabby white frame house sloping up McCorkle Street, easily enough. As I got out of the car, I began waving wildly at every neighboring window. It suddenly occurred to me, however, that given the day's events, I just might be mustering up a lynch mob, so I hastily clamped my arms to my sides.

"Aren't you worried about your reputation?" I inquired of

Anne when she came out to guide me up her steep steps. "Besides, I may collapse on these things. Put myself in a compromising position."

"Watch that loose board so you don't," Anne said. "The maintenance crew's never got around to fixing it; I'll have to get the Greek over here again."

"You mean the guy I saw working over at Tranter Hall this morning—the one who thinks the whole damn college ought to be torn down?" I looked around Anne's living room. She'd trellised her place with plants, but the plaster needed patching, and the woodwork needed painting. What she really should have had the Greek do was tack a "Condemned" sign up over the doorframe.

"Tony does do a lot of griping, but he also spends a lot of his off-duty time doing repair jobs for helpless females like me," Anne said, motioning me into her one comfortable chair. "I really shouldn't even use his nickname; Tony's not too bright, but he's a Christian gentleman. Unlike his employers. And mine," she added bitterly. "But don't get me started on the subject of Witherspoon College; I had enough of it all afternoon. What can I get you to drink?"

"How did it go with Hershey?" I asked when she came back with a styrofoam pitcher of martinis.

"He's . . . insidious," Anne said. "You don't notice because he's so busy being a boy scout."

"And . . . ?" I prompted her.

"Well, I guess I have what you'd call an alibi. After my 11:15 class—which, today of all days, I let out half an hour early—I did stand there in the classroom quite a while. Trying to talk a student out of having a nervous breakdown before spring vacation."

"To our mutual health, and the preservation of our sanity," I said, raising my glass.

Anne nodded soberly. "Apparently, the educational process will be ongoing," she informed me. "Without interruption. In Dr. Horton's estimation, given his emergency hotline to heaven. At least this was what Witherspoon's twelfth president told us at his all-college convocation. At great length. Dr. McKenna, who led the rest of us in prayer, reminded us that only the Divine Physician can cast out devils. In other words, we shouldn't try a do-it-yourself approach. You're right," she said, staring darkly into her own glass, "people do want a scapegoat. So there aren't any cracks in that damn cheap shiny varnish they stain the pews with. I swear, John, living here is like spending your life in a church basement! You get a few scraps tossed to you from out of the missionary barrel, every once in a while. And then you're expected to keep proving how grateful you are for them—as if you might go back to being some kind of ignorant savage any second. Quite a few New Arcadians have been known to sit with their curtains closed and drink themselves into boiled cabbages because they couldn't take this town anymore."

Awkwardly, Anne jerked herself up to pass me a plate of crackers and cheese. "Relax," I said. "Sit down and gulp your own drink."

"I'm sorry," Anne said in a strained voice that aroused both my concern and my curiosity. "Talk about Tony Antonides! At the moment my own resentments against this place are coming out of the crumbling woodwork. Somehow this horrible thing set me off. How did you like consoling the widow, by the way?" she demanded before I could invite her to number her grudges against the fundamentalist slumlords who probably underpaid her so she'd have to rent from them.

"Mary Sue seems to be grieving, all right," I told Anne. "But I'm not sure it's for Pete Simon."

"Yes, I can imagine," Anne said acidly. "She'll find out damn soon what it's like to be without a husband here in this town. I saw you staring at my wall-to-wall library. But you have to realize that what's charitably known as the 'inner life' is the only kind an unmarried woman in New Arcady is even supposed to have—"

"Unless she opts for a little deep analysis on Dr. Simon's handy office couch?" I asked quickly, before I completely lost my nerve.

Anne took a long swallow of her martini and began scraping away at the rim of her hard plastic glass with her fingernail. "I guess I can't accuse you of insensitivity, can I?" she sighed. "You seem to be picking up all the right vibrations. I thought maybe you had even earlier this morning—that's why I practically ran down the hall when I saw you with Pete, there in his office. What did it? The way I reacted when Lieutenant Hershey wanted me to rush right over and throw my arms around Mary Sue?''

I nodded and, carefully examining what looked like an incipient crack in my own plastic glass, waited for Anne to either tell me the story or put me out in the cold.

''That's why it happened,'' Anne went on after a moment, earnestly if not coherently. ''Last winter, for a couple of months. Because I needed someone to put his arms around me. I was lonely; Pete was sympathetic. He always was, when he had the time. And we were fond of each other. But I honestly didn't like creeping around to his office after-hours, and there wasn't really any time for *me*; I started feeling Pete was putting me into the same category as he would a coffee break. So it was over very fast.''

''But I wasn't the first, John,'' she continued, after a very loud pause in which we could hear each other trying to scrape all the electricity back into the rug. ''I get the impression Pete might have been trying to act out every fantasy he ever had when he was seventeen before he hit the Big Four-O at the end of this year.''

''Well, if you weren't the first, Anne, as it turns out, you sure as hell weren't the last!'' I told her. ''Somebody a little more recent decided it was time to cash in. I heard Simon on the phone with her maybe ten minutes before his killer walked in. I guess the lovely lady who called him up at the office to ask him for money wanted to call it a 'loan,' but he sounded pretty damn scared.''

''Actually, I'd been wondering about the possibility of somebody trying to blackmail him myself,'' Anne said, rising to think things through by pacing the length of her bookcases. ''There were these notes Pete wrote me. When he was too tired to sleep, he said. He'd get up and go downstairs and write down all his thoughts and feelings about me. All the things he'd always wanted to do—oh, don't make me explain, damn it. You know. Sex things. So if this—person—saved anything Pete had put in writing—''

"Did *you*?" Save any of his letters?" I asked, trying to sound as though my curiosity was detached from the rest of me. "I'd like to see one."

Resigned, Anne rummaged through a desk drawer and produced a thickly penciled sheet of yellow legal paper from underneath what looked like a pile of old bills. "I have this awful habit of saving absolutely everything so I won't accidentally-on-purpose throw out anything from Witherspoon College or the IRS," she said, thrusting Simon's letter at me. "What you have to understand," she added, almost apologetically, "although I guess only another woman really would, is that Pete had this very definite appeal. *Elan vital*, I suppose. At least, unlike my own colleagues, who all turned institutional beige at around twenty-five, he wasn't *dead* yet."

She got up abruptly and went into the kitchen while I read Simon's midnight message to her. Evidently, he'd seen seduction as a black-negligeé art; his fantasies ran mainly to Frederick's of Hollywood. Most of his stuff was so disappointingly stale it would have yellowed on the shelves at Whitaker's Store.

Anne, meanwhile, had come back with another pitcher of free-flowing martinis, which she immediately set down beside her chair after she'd filled her glass to the brim. "I think it's finally time for tonight's triple-bogey question," I announced, moving the pitcher to my end of the coffee table. "Who's the would-be black-mailer? Which one of the lucky gals Simon wanted to rig out in flame-colored garter belts wanted *him* to either pay up or get fired? For moral turpitude."

"If anybody had actually tried that," Anne said slowly, "before they got rid of Pete, they'd probably have paraded *her* down Main Street with her head shaved and then stuck her out in Mac-Dougall's Woods by the county dump. What you do have to understand, John, is that Pete Simon and his beautiful family and his PR work for Witherspoon and his Sunday school class and his seat on the borough council were exactly what New Arcady wanted to see when it said, 'Mirror, mirror.' So the whole town would be totally furious with anybody who tried putting the whammy on us by smashing our looking glass. And around here, John, it's *always* the woman who pays. Me, for instance," Anne added in a tense, angry voice, her eyes fixed on a pile of student papers beside my chair.

"You mean you got fired?" I stammered. No wonder all the junk had come crashing out of the closet. "Those dumb *putzes* actually put a pink slip in with your last paycheck?"

"It was politely suggested, right after the New Year, that I resign," Anne said, and squeezed her emptied glass hard enough to send chips of plastic flying into the cheese spread. Two years ago, she continued, she had gone through a knock-down, drag-out divorce from a husband who, while a part-time lecturer in the History Department, had unsuccessfully attempted to sponsor a student rebellion against single-sex dormitories and had successfully organized a pot party that sent him soaring above Main Street. Anne, whose own career had been considerably more flourishing, hadn't been able to live him down—nor his allegations in suing for separate maintenance.

"So I did the only decent thing and resigned," Anne said savagely. "And I don't have a job lined up for next year yet."

"Uhm—to get more or less back on the case," I said, hastily blundering on, since my sessions this morning with the Misses Parsons and Snickelburger had already indicated I was a proven flop at winding down overwrought females, "what about the woman Simon was on the phone with this morning? Who *were* the other women in his life?"

"Well," Anne finally said after several more swallows of gin, "I'll certainly tell you as much as I know. I really can't figure out who might have acutally asked Pete for money. I'm not positive," she went on, getting up to retrieve her pitcher from my end of the table, "but I think for a while last year—right after me—Pete was seeing Karen Chancellor. She used to be Dr. Horton's secretary. Her husband Gene's in the English Department."

I nodded. The big, scarlet-pimpled jock who'd given me a cigar and a pain in the inner ear.

"She just had a baby," Anne went on. "I've heard just a few

arch little hints to the effect that it might not be Gene's. But I can't see why Karen would have tried to get money from Pete. Or want to threaten him with a paternity suit, thereby ruining her own neat little life.''

''Any blackmailer-turned-murderer would be pretty much past the point of caring about doing damage to herself,'' I objected. ''Especially if she got into a rage at Simon because she knew she'd be expected to pay the house for *his* fun and games as well as her own.''

Anne gave me a sharp look but continued with her catalog. ''And there was Ellen Leach, who's the wife of the chairman of the History Department. But that was over a long time ago—way before I ever got involved with Pete. And somebody else quite recently. A student this time, a senior girl. Apparently, it was fairly serious on her part—and obviously fairly dangerous for Pete. All I know is what I wasn't supposed to hear while I was having my morning coffee over at the union one day last week.

''Pete was always very careful to behave in public like a model citizen,'' Anne added meditatively, tracing some kind of pattern in the dust on the arm of the ancient rocker beside her. ''He practically put his coat down in every mud puddle on Main Street for all the old cats in the Christian Women's Club. But he did seem to have been getting a little careless. Or maybe by now there'd just been too many of us. For safety's sake.''

''Then what about some real nut finding out about Simon and this young girl? I think we might be looking for somebody else besides the blackmailer,'' I went on, rising to pace off the living room in my own turn and reactivate my remaining brain cells. ''Especially since the blackmailer would have had to dash right over to Tranter Hall the minute Simon hung up the phone so she could beat him bloody. Which, as long as we don't know what was in her slimy little mind, doesn't entirely make sense under the circumstances—unless, of course, we find out she instantly went berserk when Simon tried to stall her just a little. So what about somebody else going berserk over Pete Simon's sex life? Suppose some closet psychopath finally gave in to his—or her—irresistible urge to carve up New Arcady's number one hypocrite. Any ideas on who around here might fit into that particular category, Doctor?''

· ''I keep expecting to turn into a psychopath myself any day now,'' Anne said, with a sudden dry-martini giggle. She put a hand to her own flushed face, feverish from nervous tension and gin.

''I think we'd best adjourn for dinner while I can still drive,'' I said quickly, and offered my arm. ''Shall I take you to Nino's?''

So I ended my second day in New Arcady by patronizing that dusty, red-velvet Italian place after all, drinking corky Chianti and inhaling Parmesan cheese crumbs, making sure Anne blotted up the booze with garlic bread. It wasn't a festive, first-date evening for either one of us; Anne had opened up a pretty wormy can of resentments for herself along with her jar of gin-soaked olives. And, to be perfectly honest with myself, I had to admit I was developing enough of an interest in Anne to violently, if irrationally, dislike the idea she'd ever wanted anything from the late Peter Simon except a little help with her résumé. All in all, after the events of the day, we both needed numbness.

On the way home, we tentatively agreed to get together the next night to see if we couldn't pool our insights and come up with the New Arcadian most likely to have murdered Pete Simon. During dinner I had told Anne of Hershey's interest in the Covenanters, so she suggested I attend their Wednesday morning pep rally —which she, of course, had to miss because of her class schedule. Since she declined to let me see her up to her door, on the grounds that she was too tired to manage the requisite pleasantries, I watched Anne Christensen scale her purgatorial stairs and returned to my cold room at the inn.

CHAPTER III
WEDNESDAY, MARCH 19

I WOKE UP FEELING I HAD BEEN TRAPPED IN A TIGHT TIN BOX BY some sadistic three-hundred-pounder doing a Cossack dance on the lid. I crawled out of bed to detoxify myself in icy water, but the ringing wasn't all in my ears. I had slept late; it was 8:00 A.M., time for the morning show, with the Witherspoon carillon creaking out its combination of sacred and profane melodies. I was even getting so I could Name That Hymn Tune; in this instance, "Nearer, My God, to Thee." New Arcady liked to laugh at its own bad jokes. Still, like the doomed Titanic, its passengers singing their way to the bottom of the sea, this town had indeed struck the tip of an iceberg. During my solitary breakfast at the Golden Grill, I tried to make my mind cut through the morning-after mist and develop a sharp set of mug shots. Instead, I got a sudden picture of Pete Simon glad-handing his own murderer into his office. I remembered Anne saying, *It's one of us*, and I hunched over my coffee and scowled at two Witherspoon students and a fork-bearded Amish farmer seated at the counter.

Seeking to separate the sheep from the goats, I dwelt on the wronged woman possibility, last night's most logical assumption. There'd been so damn much messy blood spilled all over Simon's office that it was hard for me to consider his murder a woman's sort of crime. My latent male chauvinism stubbornly insisted on seeing women as dedicated household drudges, perpetual scrapers of pots and scrubbers of toilets—which, come to think of it, would hardly rule out a woman who'd mentally walked off a cliff.

And, perhaps, ridden away on a bicycle—not that picturing Pete Simon's killer furiously pedaling down College Street was going to help me follow his, or her, twisted tracks. This town was full of damned fools who loved to get that healthy glow at five below. One of "us" . . . Somebody habitually in and around Reuben Tranter Hall. Somebody in the English Department? As usual, I had overlooked the obvious: Gene Chancellor, big, strong, fanatically fit, and possessed of a wife who had apparently offered the supreme insult to his self-conscious masculinity. I suddenly recalled that the proud father had both tried to ignore Pete Simon's expression of congratulations Monday morning and deliberately neglected to offer him a cigar. Lieutenant Hershey, whatever his opinion of my more subtle psychological probings, would want to know this particular fact of the case at least. And I wanted to know what results hard police science had yielded since yesterday.

However, I had other matters to attend to; it was almost 9:30, when the Covenanters were scheduled to rally round the old rugged cross. Scouting a parking place, I noticed a number of townspeople hurrying into MacTavish Memorial Chapel. Whatever brand of snake oil the local cultists were selling, New Arcady was all ready to rub it in. As I sought an obscure corner, I attracted some glances of frankly hostile curiosity, the kind generally given the Yellow Peril in ancient Saturday afternoon serials. How nice it would be for New Arcady if the stranger among them could be marked as the murderer, fingered for them by a huge celestial hand.

But suppose it actually was one of *them*—not a blackmailing mistress or a cuckolded husband, but some stalwart member of the ruling clan, conspicuously clothed in self-righteousness, eternally raising money for starving South Yemenites and praying for New Yorkers' souls. Somebody, say, like the old bellwether beginning to orate up front.

I spotted Hershey's curly halo in the back row and went to crouch beside him, tripping over somebody's size 13D Converse sneakers in the painful process of making room for myself. The Covenanters all seemed to be sporting purple armbands; I hastily pantomimed my ignorance of their possible import to the handsome lieutenant, whose profile was making several of the female faithful squirm with unrequited lust. He merely shrugged. I saw Darla, the girl who had tried to steal my soul away in the Golden Grill, smirking hard at Hershey; catching my baleful eye instead, she quickly sent herself into transports over the sermonizer up front. Melissa Parsons, lost to my own cause, was listening intently, her Renaissance profile tilted toward the speaker. Hoping to stir up the muck of my subconscious, I tuned my own ears to his high, clear tenor.

"Deliver me from bloodguiltiness, O God," the wispy old minister was begging.

"Wash me, and I shall be whiter than snow," his congregation chanted.

"The sacrifices of God are a broken spirit," their leader told them tearfully. "A broken and a contrite heart." Clutching the lectern like a life preserver, he swayed so that wings of white hair swooped over his forehead. "Let us pray," he sobbed, his own voice breaking.

I was afraid the old goof was having a heart attack, but he straightened up briskly and motioned a tall Convenanter to the altar. It was the Bible-wielder of Whitaker's Store.

"For those of you who do not know these young people, sprinting with the Spirit," the speaker said solemnly, "I present Jack Campbell, pre-ministerial student at Witherspoon College and Convener of the Covenanters." Then he left the lectern, literally taking a backseat to the younger man.

"May I ask all Covenanters to acknowledge Dr. McKenna's divinely inspired presence and to pray for the eternal light he lends to our cause," Campbell said in the tone of a Central Committee member preparing to offer an hour-long toast to the memory of Chairman Mao. He fixed his eyes on his assembled listeners. "Blood has been shed here in New Arcady. And we of the Covenanters also mourn the dead." He lifted his left arm. "But this band of mourning is purple in color to remind us, in this Lenten season, of the guilt we share in shedding blood that should be far more precious to us."

The cult leader exhibited to the crowd the inside of his wrist, where a red cross had been carved. In the dramatic pause he had carefully created, I could hear gasps of awe and admiration. "Thus we mortify our flesh to break our spirits," he stage-whispered. "I ask you all to kneel in supplication and submission."

Submission to *whom*, I wondered. As the Joggers for Jesus dropped silently to the cold stone floor, I judged them about as harmless as a Pennsylvania copperhead waking up from its winter nap. I looked at Hershey, who nodded; in our hard-soled shoes, we went noisily out.

"I'd be most interested to know how both McKenna and Campbell were occupying themselves yesterday during the noon hour," the lieutenant said on our way to his unofficial headquarters in Tranter Hall. "And I think I'll have Hendricks start checking on them right now, while I *do* know where they are. Waltz, how did you make out?"

I gave Hershey an innocent bystander's version of my conversation with Anne and the information she'd given me on Pete Simon's intimate friends. I also mentioned my reasons for thinking he should check on Gene Chancellor as well as the frenetic father-and-son team performing their psychological miracles in the chapel.

Hershey was pleased with the Chancellor connection. "The more we can narrow it down to somebody with a motive that makes sense," he told me, "the quicker we can solve this case and get the town settled down. Before they start crying for *our* blood." He unlocked his soundproof cell, turning to greet the chairman of the English Department, a small, worried-looking man creating seismographic disturbances by not wanting to make waves. I saw no sign of Anne among the faculty members collecting their belongings.

"Dr. Horton is complaining he's got the trustees as well as the parents breathing down his neck," Hershey continued, tearing up several telephone messages scattered on his desk. "The borough council is complaining about the effects of adverse publicity on a place where nobody locks their doors. The Pittsburgh papers have picked the story up. Everybody's spooked; they need a few facts as a pacifier, but so far we haven't got many to give them. Not much real evidence at all."

I gave the lieutenant an inquiring glance. "You're talking about something tangible? After our morning devotions, I don't know what 'real' means anymore."

"To try and pacify *you*, Waltz, the murderer was—unfortunately for us—nice and neat. No blood types other than the victim's; no clear fingerprints other than yours, Miss Christensen's, and Simon's. The murderer locked Simon's office door with Simon's own key and took it along. The maintenance people on the south side of the building work staggered shifts, so some of them go to lunch at 11:30 and the rest an hour later. I finally got their supervisor to sit down long enough to tell me he let one of his second-shift men off at 12:00. Haven't had a chance to chase down this guy yet—if it turns out to be worth the trouble. And the homeowner on the north side of Tranter Hall, across the driveway from Simon's office, had some kind of seizure last night—delayed hysterics, most likely—and was too sick to be questioned. We'll have to try to get with her later today, too. And naturally the murder weapons are still missing." The lieutenant sighed. "Nobody in town has as yet seen or heard anything suspicious. Or at least volunteered any information indicating same."

Sometimes Hershey sounded like a directive issued in triplicate. Too many midnight memos. But I got the message: New Arcady had already determined to "See No Evil," as Anne had said the town judiciously chose to do on occasion. "What about the bicycle tire marks?" I asked.

"That sure looks like the way the killer took off, but those tracks aren't taking *us* very far." Hershey frowned. "A professor in the Religion Department, a Dr. DeVore, reported her bicycle stolen on Sunday to the borough police. She told Hendricks she thought it was probably some fraternity prank and assured him they'd undoubtedly bring it back. There were also two racing bikes stolen from Witherspoon students in the past two weeks. They haven't turned up either. Doesn't prove much, one way or the other."

"Yes, it does," I said. "It proves that not only should these trusting souls start locking their doors, but they also ought to padlock their bicycles."

I don't think Hershey exactly relished my sense of humor. While he opened one of his many manila folders, I lit another cigarette, trying to comprehend somebody's cutting himself with a knife for theatrical effect. "Blood on the door!" I exclaimed.

Hershey looked at me as if I had just come down with an acute case of glossolalia. "Would you mind explaining that for me?" he asked, struggling not to sound as exhausted as his patience.

"I remember touching a big smear of blood on the outside of Simon's door, just above the knob, while I was still standing there stupidly trying to figure out why the hell he'd locked himself in his office. I think it even had a definite shape to it—something like a triangle—and I seem to remember there was another big patch of blood smeared on above *that* one. What were they doing there if the killer tried so hard to tidy up?"

Hershey frowned once more. "*I* remember making a note of them, Waltz, but I really don't see your point, so let me look through what I have from the lab again. Here it is: 'Two areas of virtually coagulated blood, roughly triangular in shape'—looks like you were right about that, Waltz—'each approximately four-and-one-half inches high and vertically juxtaposed'—that means one on top of the other, Waltz, so your memory's okay, anyway—'upper triangular area inverted over lower.' "

"You see what I mean?" I prompted the lieutenant. "The murderer put them there on purpose. Spread his bloody triangles on like a couple of paint samples."

"But *why*, Waltz?" Hershey asked impatiently. "Are you supposed to be telling me I ought to be out looking for some kind of a geometry freak?"

"Hershey," I smiled sadly, "with this entire community practically taking sitz baths in buckets of blood, you really expect me to read the murderer's Rorschach test for you? What I mean, Lieutenant," I added, by way of apology, since Hershey looked ready to throw his regulation loose-leaf binder straight at the bridge of my nose, "is that since there seems to be no shortfall of fruitcakes here in New Arcady, how do we find out which one of them—whether it's one of Simon's old mistresses or one of their husbands or some Jogger for Jesus who should have shipped out for Guyana—has exactly the right kind of craziness? I mean, to take the time to draw a couple of triangles in his victim's blood on said victim's office door before he took off with the guy's private parts? Believe me, under these particular circumstances, I wish I were as smart as you seem to think I am."

"Okay, Waltz—if you're finished—" Hershey said, trying to rub the dust out of his eyes, "let's assume for the moment that drawing bloody triangles on Simon's door fits that clown Campbell's style, for example. Where does that get us? What kind of stupid graffiti was he scrawling on his way to the men's room?"

I ground my teeth in irritation at my inability to answer my own questions as well as Hershey's. I'd have to consult Anne, who had doubtless read all the right books. "We ought to ask some of these academic types," I suggested.

And here was one of them now, sullenly following Sergeant Hendricks down the hall. Our boy Gene Chancellor, who'd die someday in mid-sentence with his mortarboard on. Although Hendricks had collared him as courteously as possible, Chancellor immediately began threatening Hershey with a telegram to the Pittsburgh chapter of the American Civil Liberties Union.

By guaranteeing his loutish suspect a whole bill of rights, Hershey finally got him calmed down enough to talk sense and even persuaded him to let me remain in the room, as long as I kept my prejudices to myself. The lieutenant's line of questioning, however, quickly turned Dr. Gene Chancellor into an enraged turkey gobbler. He had been home Tuesday noon, he said, babysitting from 11:30 A.M. until 2:00 P.M. while his wife kept a hair appointment and picked up a book he'd ordered six weeks ago. He'd had to turn down a student who'd requested a conference just as he was leaving Tranter Hall; moreover, he'd asked a neighbor if the mail had arrived when he came out of his house to walk back to work. But why, in God's name, he wondered aloud,

57

were we committing the crowning indignity of demanding an alibi from Gene Chancellor?

"My good name is of the utmost value to me," he protested. "How could you possibly impute a motive in a gruesome murder to *me*?"

"Your relations with the victim were friendly, then?" Hershey probed.

"Why would they be otherwise? Why must you ask?" Chancellor sputtered, his face a study in apoplectic scarlet.

"And your wife's relations with the victim? Were they also friendly?" Hershey persisted.

"We did not see the Simons socially, but certainly they were," Chancellor said huffily. "Lieutenant, I am outraged. I simply will not be badgered like this." He started to get up, then abruptly sat down again.

Prick Gene Chancellor's festering ego, and you'd find a hell of a lot of pus, I concluded. He really should have hoped his daughter had, in fact, inherited somebody else's DNA.

Hershey's face remained blank. "Were you aware that your wife was engaged in a sexual liaison with the victim?" he asked Chancellor.

"Of course I wasn't aware!" the English instructor shouted. "How could I be aware of something that did not exist? There was nothing between them. I could not have tolerated anything between them." This time he rose, to his full lumpy height. "Lieutenant," he proclaimed, "I intend to sue you for defamation of character. Forthwith."

"We request your cooperation in signing this statement, Dr. Chancellor," Hershey said in a monotone, and produced a typewritten form he'd obviously had run off solely for intimidational purposes. "Afterwards, you are free to go. We may wish to ask you additional questions at some future date. The lieutenant looked utterly bored.

Chancellor's Hearty Burgundy face ballooned alarmingly. Then it collapsed, and he started to cry, in great, gut-rending sobs. "I wanted to kill him. And her too. Karen. She's the guilty one," he whined. "Lying to me! Humiliating me! Making people *laugh* at me!"

I should have felt sorry for the poor bastard, but instead I was wishing one of us out of town before sunset. Hershey, however, as a man of practical action, had solved the more immediate problem of getting Chancellor out of the room by handing him over to Hendricks like an oversized puppy who'd just crapped on a clean floor. But even after his forcible ejection, I could hear my prime suspect whimpering his way down the hall.

"Well, so much for working hypotheses," I said to Hershey.

"He's not out of the running. Hypothetically," Hershey replied, flashing his teeth like a badge. "One thing I'm getting more and more convinced of by the minute: we're going to have to work on this case from the psychological angle. That's the only way we even have a prayer of solving it. Maybe we can even find some Covenanter with enough of a grudge against McKenna and Campbell to do a little spying for us."

I could picture Hershey patiently running countless rats through his mazes. As for me, I wanted to get to the source of all my own psychological problems: call up Anne Christensen, waylay her after class, sprawl on a strategic sofa in the faculty lounge, get her mind off her problems and onto my own.

Hershey, meanwhile, was taking an exceedingly short stroll through New Arcady's Yellow Pages. "With all these churches in town to keep everybody here on the straight and narrow," he explained, "the logical thing is to ask one of their own ministers who else besides Simon might have been getting set to jump right out into the fast lane. Or have enough money problems of their own to be heading straight for a crack-up. I'd expect most of the preachers here to have a pretty good idea who the bankrupts are. Not to mention the alcoholics who pour it out of their grandmother's teapot, and anybody who might be planning to use a .30-.30 on themselves before the next deer season. There's a Reverend Von Ruden listed here; that sounds pretty venerable to me, so we'll give him a try."

"He says he'll be glad to give me forty-five minutes or so

around three o'clock," Hershey announced after a few respectful murmurs into the telephone. "You can come along if you want, Waltz—so you can further your education." The lieutenant paused to squint at me like Big Jim Smith before glancing down at his neatly hand-lettered schedule. "Hopefully, Mrs. Hammill next-door has recovered enough for questioning."

So I trotted along like the lieutenant's faithful husky. Mrs. Hammill, a small, frail, elderly widow, peered at us from behind her fenced-in face with the indoor paranoia that was probably New Arcady's number one killer. She said she had been resting in her living room "at the time this terrible Judgment fell on us" and had glanced out her front window only once, when she'd heard buggy wheels, because she'd been thinking about placing an order with Samuel Mueller, the Amish butter-and-egg man. It might have been Mueller passing, she added; he did deliver on Tuesdays. It was most likely a very few minutes after twelve when she'd seen the buggy go by because the noon news had just come on. No, she couldn't be of any more help, Mrs. Hamill said, and bolted the door behind us.

I was equally as glad to be out of the old lady's gloomy mohair-shirt parlor as she had been to see us go, although Mrs. Hammill had certainly fingered the pulse of the community for us self-styled, out-of-town specialists. When I asked Hershey, however, just how many New Arcadians he estimated might be similarly inclined to interpret Pete Simon's murder as some kind of divinely ordained community punishment, he referred me to Reverend Von Ruden's higher wisdom. He also suggested I occupy the hours until our appointment with the old minister by playing spy at MacDougall Memorial Union to see if I might possibly be able to pick up any gossip about Simon's as yet unidentified student mistress. Although I suspected the lieutenant was trying to get rid of me so he could munch on a little manila in peace, I immediately agreed, since staking out the student union would also give me the opportunity to observe the reactions of various members of the college community—female English professors, for example.

At 12:45, the union's basement cafeteria was operating at full production capacity, assembling and gluing enough cheeseburgers for an NFL banquet. In between corrected bites, students seemed to be conducting their mysterious business as usual. A tableful of Covenanters in one corner solemnly feasted on fish specials and sucked up strawberry milkshakes. So much for the Joggers' low-cal approach to life. Several students were asking each other, "What were you doing during the murder?" but, self-preoccupied, none saw fit to indicate they'd ever bothered their precision-cut heads about their former placement director's private life—if they even knew anything about his involvement with one of their own, which on the whole I was forced to doubt. For an hour I sat and sipped sedimental coffee, pretending to scribble profundities in my pocket notebook while watching for Anne. She finally came in, flanked by that formidable pair, Richardson and Fielding. Smiling broadly, they motioned me to a larger table. Safety in numbers. But at least I could now sound these two out while dazzling all three women with my logic-defying cognitive leaps.

"What information can you leak to us?" Fielding asked once we were seated. "While protecting your unidentified sources, naturally." She looked mockingly at her lover.

"I'm trying to give Les a little reality therapy," said Richardson. "She's secretly convinced she works for the *Daily Planet*."

Fielding elaborately flourished her own pocket notebook. "But seriously, folks, we're about to start charging a consulting fee," she said. "Every single faculty member has his own favorite solution, which, especially for our benefit, he has turned into an introductory lecture."

"I was hoping you'd expound on your own theories," I told them. "Good help is hard to find these days." Actually, I was trying to read Anne's mind on more personal matters. Our table was an ark arranging us two by two: boy, girl; boy—I guessed —girl. But my heterosexual friend, who sat brooding over bitter coffee, had apparently gone off somewhere by herself.

"Well, if you want the results of a little nonlinear thinking," Fielding said slowly, "somebody finally took Pete Simon almost as seriously as he took himself. Impossible as that might sound," she added, glancing from Richardson to me to Anne, who had evidently found at least two souls of discretion here in New Arcady.

Anne looked up, frowned thoughtfully, and stared back into her coffee as if she could divine the dregs. Richardson was also frowning. "My gut-level reaction is that the Covenanters couldn't possibly have done it," she said. "That there really is a woman in the case. Maybe not a rejected lover, even. But somebody in a mad rage finally striking back. Or would you give me an 'I' for incoherence on that one, Anne? Anne?"

"Are you sure you wouldn't like to share the results of your research with the rest of us, Doctor?" I asked, but succeeded only in sounding full of pique instead of the friendly interest I had intended to convey.

"Like everything else around here, my brain isn't working too well today. Sorry, gang," she said with a slight smile.

"What about cooking me dinner before you and I get down to business this evening?" I asked boldly, hoping to make Anne's conversation take a somewhat more intimate turn.

"Oh, gosh, John, I was so rattled last night I totally forgot about the Sacred Cow covered-dish supper tonight," Anne sighed. "I mean the Christian Women's Club's having a good-riddance gathering just for me; and the dean's wife will be there, or I'd gladly opt out."

"Great time for a party," I drawled. "Or is it a wake, maybe?" I'd already choked on the stale cake crumbs of New Arcady's barbaric female festivities.

"It was of course suggested we cancel, but many of us are lonely old maids," Anne said wryly. "We're supposed to be 'sharing, in solidarity, our sorrow.' At least according to Lillian McKenna."

"Well, spread a few unfounded rumors for us," Fielding said, rising.

The departure of the two lovers left a silence lumping around us like gravy. "I can certainly watch and listen for you this evening," Anne said at last. "I really *am* sorry, John. And as far as getting together afterwards goes, I kind of got put on the spot the other day and told somebody I'd come over for a drink after our dinner. Dr. Blackstone," she went on conversationally. "You'd like her; she used to be a somewhat prominent psychiatrist, and now she seems to have turned herself into a seventy-five-year-old swinger."

"Too bad Dr. Blackstone gave up her practice," I said dolefully. "She might be able to tell me why I keep having this ridiculous delusion I might be attractive to women." Voicing my equally absurd jealousy of an old lady, however, had reminded me I'd meant to ask Anne about any possible ritual aspects of Pete Simon's murder, specifically the bloody triangles daubed on the victim's door; and so I switched to that topic—certainly one of more mutual interest than my wounded vanity.

"I can't help you on this," Anne pondered, caught up in the problem. "But Becky DeVore might be able to—she teaches comparative religion—and she's stopping by a little after five for a ride to the CWC dinner. So why don't you come by around then and ask her about it yourself?" Dr. Christensen suggested, reaching for her coat and her enormous black briefcase. "I do have a class now, John."

"And I have an engagement," I said, wishing I did, preferably with a beautiful and antisocial coed. It was actually time for me to hit the road again as Hershey's idiot sidekick, the hero's ill-favored friend who always winds up without the girl.

Driving to Reverend Von Ruden's, Hershey told me he'd had brief conversations with both Campbell and McKenna, who'd promised to pray for the success of the investigation. They'd shared the same alibi; the older man had said he'd had Campbell at his own house yesterday noon for a humble yet nourishing meal prepared and served by his good wife, rightly concerned about that saintly young man's careless eating habits. Campbell himself, instead of answering Hershey's questions, had praised God for filling the overinflated old windbag full of the Holy Spirit. "And all three of them would lie for each other, as their Christian duty," Hershey observed. "Ask your girlfriend to see if she can get Mrs. McKenna to say something she shouldn't," he suggested when I mentioned the Sacred Cow supper. Whatever form of surveillance I thought I ought to be keeping Anne under, I gathered the lieutenant had pretty much taken her out of any "Suspects, Active" file folder he'd started—as he apparently had me as well—although I'd never accuse Hershey of not knowing how to manipulate people.

The Reverend Von Ruden I disliked on sight, mainly because he looked like a sterner and more authoritarian incarnation of McKenna, *his* wavy white hair held by Final Judgment net. Nor were my instant prejudices overcome when the old minister opened his mouth. "Gentlemen, how can I help you on this dark day for us all? How can I be of service to you?" he inquired, ushering us into his musty tan study with a good deal more bowing and scraping than I thought strictly necessary. However many sermons he'd given down at the First Presbyterian, there were still enough murky undertones to Von Ruden's vowels to make me think he ought to be humming the overture to *The Flying Dutchman* instead of whatever hymn the Witherspoon carillon was currently saluting the hour with. Thus I deliberately seated myself on the sidelines, on a high-backed wooden bench in the corner behind the old preacher's huge rosewood desk, so I wouldn't be tempted to make any nasty remarks about the good old days back in the Reichland.

"Reverend Von Ruden, I understand you've been living here in this borough for almost forty-five years," Hershey—no doubt trying to sound like the kind of anachronistic young man who doggedly respects all his elders—began in a suppliant's tone. "You must know more about what goes on in New Arcady than just about anyone else in town."

"Ah," said Reverend Von Ruden, holding up a large hairy hand to forestall any more idle chatter. "On almost every occasion I find that I must first always ask myself, 'What is the situation?' And today the situation is this: One of our own—our brother, our son—has been taken from us: a man in the prime of his life, giving service to us all—as husband and father, as a leader in his church and in his community, as the shaper of the best of our young people, just as he was the best of us. This man has been ripped from our side, so cruelly and so savagely that some of us think God must have found all of us wanting; and for all of us a cloud has been put over the sun, completely hiding his purpose from us. That is the situation.''

"And, in this situation," Hershey, losing his prudence, rashly broke in, "which my men and I are trying to clear up as fast as we can so we can all start sleeping at night again—believe me—we really need as much help from all of you here in New Arcady as you can possibly give us."

"Ah," said Von Ruden again in the low rumble I assumed was his warm-up voice, "having once made a situation clear to myself, I must then find out what is required of me in that particular instance. So now I must ask, 'What does Lieutenant Hershey want?' And what Lieutenant Hershey wants," said Von Ruden, favoring that grossly overworked public servant with a *basso profundo* chuckle, "is for Pastor Von Ruden, who has ministered to these people so long and knows them so well, to make for him an accurate judgment of who it is that has done this terrible thing and to give this individual to him, Lieutenant Hershey. And so what must Pastor Von Ruden say to Lieutenant Hershey?"

Here Von Ruden, placing his hands palms-up in the one dustless rectangle of his desk directly in front of him, demonstrated his mastery of the dramatic pause for so many seconds that I almost called out from my corner, "Okay, we give up!"

"What Pastor Von Ruden must say," the old man finally went on, while Hershey picked at the faded claret brocade on the arm of his chair, "is that here in New Arcady, saved or lost, we are all sinners, surely. We borrow money from those who trust us, and do not pay it back when our obligation is due; we refuse to obey our husbands or to cherish our wives; we show no respect to our teachers and parents; we show envy and bitterness to our neighbors and friends. Mostly, we are like those good housewives who keep telling their husbands they need an increase in the household allowance so there will be a little money left over to hoard up in the cookie jar. Some few of us, true, are—how should I say it?—misfits here, malcontents who nevertheless will not try out the hospitality of some other town. But most of us here in New Arcady are what I must call cookie-jar sinners, Lieutenant.''

Again Von Ruden paused to let us digest his message while I entertained myself by planning to stay around New Arcady long enough to whomp up a big batch of Alice B. Toklas brownies (a recipe Marcia had carefully copied out for her Cordon Bleu father) as my own charitable donation to the next UWU bake sale.

''Reverend Von Ruden,'' said Hershey, foolhardy enough to start all over, ''can you think of anything at all—any firsthand information, any rumors going around about anybody's unusual behavior, any consultations you might have had where somebody said he or she was really worried about their old friend so-and-so—anything at all you could tell us that might help us find out who murdered Pete Simon?''

''What I have been saying to you, Lieutenant,'' Von Ruden chided him, mournfully shaking his head, ''is that while I very much wish I could help you, there is nothing I can tell you. Nothing of any use to you. Pastor Von Ruden cannot find out this wolf in our fold. But, Lieutenant Hershey,'' said the old schizo, raising his voice in order to glue Hershey's arms back to his antimacassars, ''God moves in mysterious ways. And God will find him out. *God will find him out!* God has somehow marked this man for us. As he did the first murderer.''

Reverend Von Ruden rose to his feet and lifted his arms in obvious benediction. ''Gentlemen,'' he announced, ''I believe our time is up. I am now semi-retired, but I have a sermon to prepare for tomorrow.''

''Do you think Von Ruden was telling the honest-to-God truth about not having the remotest idea who might have a knife with a double-edged blade tucked away in the cookie jar?'' I asked Hershey as we slid our way down Somerset Street—the old minister lived just up the hill from the Simons, so they had been almost neighbors—to the lieutenant's parked car.

''That's actually a good question, Waltz,'' Hershey said, frowning down at a patch of snow dyed dog-piss yellow. ''I think the old bastard believes what he says he believes; and I don't think he'd deliberately lie to us. But he just might know something he doesn't know he knows, or doesn't want to. Something that he doesn't want to think might be relevant to Simon's murder because it might tend to incriminate some nice respectable New Arcadian. Say, one of his old friends or parishioners. One of these so-called pillars of the community.''

"Pete Simon was one of these so-called pillars of the community," I reminded him. "I may skip the funeral tomorrow. I'm not sure I can take another eulogy from Von Ruden. As it is, I'm counting on the Second Coming any day now."

My witticism was wasted on Hershey, who had at last lost his temper. "I really am getting damn sick of all these good people covering up for each other, intentionally or not," he said. "I hope to hell I get something out of Simon's lady friends. And find Mrs. Hammill's Amish farmer. Even if the egg man's the one we want, there're probably six Samuel Muellers out in the sticks. And the hell of it is, they *do* all look alike."

Personally, however, I would have preferred setting speed traps for Amish buggies to corralling Anne's sacred cow friends. And at five o'clock, toiling up Anne's stairs, I almost became New Arcady's second most dramatic statistic of the week. One of my shoelaces wound itself around the bent nail protruding from the loose board on the third step from the top, and I wobbled like a falling Wallenda until Anne, hearing hideous animal noises, rushed out to steady me.

"Lady, one of these days you're gonna get sued," I said angrily, once safely inside. "Not to mention charged with manslaughter."

"I *asked* Tony if he'd come over and fix that damn step before the end of the week," Anne said tearfully. "*I'm* the one who's likely to land in the hospital. But he said somebody took his good hammer right out of his toolbox—"

She had broken off because, for the second time in thirty-six hours, I had gotten too good a grip on her. "Somebody stole this Antonides's *hammer?*" I demanded, my hand wringing her slender white wrist. "When? Did he report it to the police?"

Once more, Anne got my message; it was our personal signals

that somehow stayed scrambled. "I think Tony said over the weekend. I don't know if he told the borough cops; he doesn't have much use for them."

Suddenly I had a long-overdue inspiration. "Was Antonides doing any work on Pete Simon's remodeling project? That he maybe didn't get paid for? He was muttering something yesterday morning about the 'crooks' who run Witherspoon College, but it naturally didn't occur to me I ought to take him literally."

"Oh, gosh, I should have thought of that myself," Anne said excitedly. "Because he started bending *my* ear about it the other day in Tranter Hall. From what Tony told me, Pete had hired him, along with a couple of helpers, to take care of the whole thing. The deal was that Tony would get half the money for the job—including what he'd spent for supplies at the hardware store and the lumberyard out of his own pocket—at the beginning of this month when he had the job half-finished. But, according to Tony, Mary Sue didn't like the way he was doing the paneling and told him she wasn't going to pay him for *anything* until he did it over. And Pete, I guess, backed her up. And then Mr. Fitzmeier at the hardware store promptly told Tony his credit wasn't good there anymore. Tony was practically foaming at the mouth while he was telling me all this—I guess I must look like a sympathetic listener—and so I really was afraid he was going to march down the hall and take a swing at Pete then and there. Luckily, the maintenance supervisor came over to yell at him about something before he could do any more than cuss the Simons out."

"I'll have to try to track down Hershey," I said when Anne had finished, letting her go at last. "Where does Antonides live?"

"Just down the street; in fact, his rooms are downstairs from Becky DeVore's."

At precisely that instant, Anne's buzzer rang. Dr. DeVore was climbing the steps, and Anne ran out to warn her about the booby trap near the top.

Poor Dr. DeVore would have had an even harder time keeping her balance than I had, since she was the top-heavy lady who had inadvertently taken me to her bosom in the White Lion. For a moment both of us pretended to be perfect strangers. Then Dr. DeVore extended her large white hand. "I'm sorry we couldn't have met again under happier circumstances, Mr. Waltz," she said, earnestly smiling up at me—no mean feat since, with her high-heeled pumps on, she must have been at least five-eleven. "Anne tells me you've more or less put yourself on our murder case, and that I might be able to give you some help. I can't imagine what kind, but I'll be more than willing to try. Like all the rest of us—although most of us wouldn't dare admit it, even to each other—I *am* rather fascinated by this grisly thing. Horrible as it is," she added with a shiver. "My heart just aches for those four little girls of Pete Simon's. And I keep thinking about how much he did for all of us. He actually got sixteen-year-old boys showing up for church school Sunday mornings at nine o'clock. I used to think they almost worshipped him; I could hear his boys talking in the hall sometimes while I was letting out my own class. To be a little briefer about it, Mr. Waltz," Becky DeVore said with another hundred-watt smile, "what can I do to help?"

"I was hoping you might have some time to talk to me tonight after your dinner party," I told her, as courteously as possible, although I knew I'd never match Dr. DeVore for skilled diplomacy.

"Well, since it certainly sounds more interesting than my students' homework assignments—I don't know why the college has to pretend it's conducting business as usual—I'd be glad to, Mr. Waltz. Can you pick me up at the Methodist church about 9:30? I suppose we'd better be off, Anne," she added, turning to her less radiant companion. "I set my three-bean salad down on the porch, and it's probably turning into vinegar popsicles."

Since I had gotten into the habit of carefully inspecting all New Arcadians not genetically engineered into xenophobia, while Anne went to get her coat, I took a good look at Becky DeVore, who had indeed sounded almost girlishly excited about doing her bit for John Waltz and his misunderstood genius. Although she was probably closer to fifty than forty, this middle-aged spinster had the smooth rosy skin of a pre-teenager, which made me remember my mother's Aunt Tilly, who'd gone to her grave believing I'd someday amount to something and—probably because of her indomitable optimism—had had that same air of arrested girlhood until she was well into her sixties. Our Lady of Perpetual Adolescence. But, whatever the extent of her spiritual serenity, Dr. DeVore's boobs, I could tell, were—even in this age of silicone implants—a queen-size source of embarrassment to this woman, who was otherwise firm and well-fleshed rather than fat. The general effect was much like a mustache of thick black pencil scrawled on the Mona Lisa.

"Anne told you I had some kind of hunch about the blood smeared on Pete Simon's office door?" I asked this smiling expert on organized cruelty, since she was looking at me expectantly.

"Well, I hope some kind of inspiration strikes me pretty soon because right now I haven't got any vibrations about it at all," Dr. DeVore sighed, her clear blue eyes clouding. "But if I can't come up with something for you tonight, I promise to do some library research for you. After tomorrow, when I'll have a little more time."

"Becky's been asked to sing at the funeral," Anne explained as she came back into the living room to hold out her coat so I could forget all her previous fuss about female emancipation. "As on all other occasions. We none of us leave her in peace."

Of course, with that rib cage. I had been misled by the silver-bell tinkle of her speaking voice. Becky DeVore was the owner of the powerful contralto I had marveled at Monday night. "Do you give classical concerts?" I asked, with real interest, having been brought up to share my mother's faith in high culture, if little else.

"I was trained as a concert singer," Dr. DeVore admitted with a self-deprecating smile. "But with my schedule, I don't get much chance to sing anything besides sacred music."

"Somebody ought to insist the MCP's at the First Presbyterian immediately break with tradition and make Becky a deacon," Anne put in, her eyes flashing with sisterly indignation. "I think they only put her on the church building committee because they knew she'd do all their work for them."

"You mean, with your voice, you make time for everything except Verdi and Wagner?" I asked Dr. DeVore, indignant in my own turn. Anne, however, was again holding out her coat to me, so I gave up and bundled her into it. "And so the Valkyries ride again," I murmured dramatically. Determined to get this motley show on the road, Anne promptly snatched my own coat off the footstool in the hallway and tossed it at me as if it contained hardy winter cockroaches; but I had finally remembered my supposedly urgent business with Lieutenant Hershey. "Ah—do you mind if I stay here a minute and use your phone?" I stammered, although Anne had yanked open the street door and plainly expected me to precede the ladies downstairs. "Do you happen to know if Tony Antonides is home right now, Dr. DeVore?"

"Oh my goodness, do the police want *him* for something?" his upstairs neighbor asked breathlessly.

"There are more thieves among us. Tony had his hammer taken right out of the toolbox he keeps in the cellar," Anne explained, resignedly shutting the street door.

"Oh dear," Dr. DeVore sighed, unbuttoning her large shapeless coat. "I hate to complain—Mr. Antonides tries so hard to be helpful—but he seems to be getting more and more careless. I've never understood why he doesn't have anything except a padlock on his door to the basement, especially as it's the outside entrance. I guess I'll have to talk to him about having all the locks changed, whenever he gets home this evening. His truck's not in the garage, Mr. Waltz, so I don't think he's around right now; but he gets awfully hard to keep track of."

Pledged as she was to loving her neighbor, I didn't think Dr. DeVore liked the one downstairs much—not that I could say that I blamed her—and for all I knew, Antonides might have gotten himself stinking drunk enough to stumble upstairs and make a grab at those boobs. "Was your bicycle also stolen out of the cellar?" I asked, righteously angry at all the sots and oafs who'd ever distressed Becky DeVore. "I take it nobody's brought it back yet."

"No, they haven't, Mr. Waltz," Dr. DeVore said, clasping her gloved hands as if to pray for a quick restoration of her trust in humanity's fundamental harmlessness. "But it's really my fault it got taken at all—I had it up on the porch. Like most of the rest of us in New Arcady, I'm apt to believe it can't happen here. So, like all of us, I'm almost as outraged by our petty crime wave as by Mr. Simon's murder. Which probably sounds to you as though we're all stark raving mad up here, with the way things are in the city."

"Actually, Dr. DeVore, I've always believed that if I ever did discover an island of sanity, a coconut would immediately fall off the nearest tree and onto my head and I'd forget where I was. So—"

"So," Anne interrupted with a horrible grimace, "we'd better go rescue your three-bean salad, Becky, and not be late for the invocation. You can telephone from here if you want, John, but please don't forget to lock up when you leave."

"I'll see you at 9:30 then, Mr. Waltz," Becky DeVore promised, verbally stepping between us while Anne scowled from the doorway. "I'll wait right in the vestibule for you so you won't have to come down to the social hall and feel you're at our mercy."

"Fine," I said heartily, wishing Anne were half so concerned for my sensibilities. "Have a good evening, ladies."

The ladies hot-dogged on down the steps to their covered-dish supper, and I tried to reach Hershey who, of course, wasn't to be found either at the state police barracks out on Route 34 or at his apartment in Coal City. Leaving instructions with the dispatcher for him to call me at the inn, I went to Frank Fitzmeier's Friendly Hardware Store to buy some basic tools.

The minute I walked through her narrow front door, Mrs. Vandervelde held out the desk phone to me. "It's the police, for you," she said, ready to trumpet to the town my imminent incarceration.

"I'll take it in my room, thanks," I said pointedly, for the ungenerous portion of privacy my overemphasis might buy me.

When I gave Hershey my news, even though he was quick to assure me he'd been trying to catch up with Antonides all day, I could tell from his tone that I'd at last given him reason to feel like a police officer examining traces of tangible evidence rather than another set of wildly oscillating brain waves. Since I had nothing to do for the next two hours except stand in front of Mrs. Vandervelde's wavy mirror practicing gargoylish faces that I'd probably never have the nerve to try out, I asked the lieutenant's permission to meet him and Sergeant Hendricks back at Antonides's apartment and was granted it with the stipulation I stick to my role as passive observer.

The two officers had even broken out an unmarked car, I saw, when I pulled into Antonides's snaking gravel drive. In a few minutes a Galliano-gold pickup pulled in, and the Greek got out, bearing groceries and beer. Hershey and Hendricks fell into formation on either side of him and marched him into the house.

"I ain't done nothin'," Tony told them belligerently, "and somebody better not be sayin' otherwise."

"You're right; there's something you didn't do," Hershey said crisply. "Report the presumed theft of a hammer out of your tool chest to either us or the borough police. The law states that in the event of a homicide investigation, all persons who knowingly withhold pertinent information have themselves committed a felony."

"Did *she* say somethin' about my damn hammer to you?" Tony asked sharply. He raised his hooded hawk's eyes to the ceiling.

Hershey, correctly gauging Antonides as the garrulous sort, settled himself into the latter's sprung couch.

"Old Becky upstairs," Antonides added, after Hershey had also stared studiously at the ceiling for several long seconds, "she's got it in for me. She don't like me livin' down here, bein' a goddamn janitor and all, drinkin' my beer and bringin' my girlfriends over

73

here every once in a while. And I done more jobs for that woman! It was probably one of them damn kids she has comin' upstairs all the time for her tea and her cookies who done it. *I* ain't supposed to do any bitchin', not to *her*; and besides takin' off with my hammer, one of them little bastards of hers is scrapin' his toenails with my German commando knife!

"That my uncle got off one of them sonavabitchin' Krautheads he shot over there in the war," he complained to Hershey in the high-voltage silence. "Put it down-cellar so I could varnish up the handle." The Greek banged his fist on his own end table. "Think I'm gonna get another one of *those* from Frank Fitzmeier down at the goddamn hardware store?"

"In other words, Antonides," Hershey said slowly, his eyes fixed on the Greek's, "somebody not only broke into your cellar and put you to some inconvenience by taking a hammer out of your toolbox, but also stole a keepsake from you that you put a pretty high personal value on. But you decided not to report these thefts to the borough police."

"Them two? Them two can't even tie their damn shoelaces!" Antonides snorted. "Think them dumb bastards'd do anything about it anyway? For the likes of *me*? And who told you the cellar was broke into?" he asked truculently. "Old Becky, tryin' to cover things up? Hell, one of her little Christians swiped my spare keys, right out of the ashtray on the hall table!"

Hendricks immediately got up to go have a look at the basement. Hershey calmly asked Antonides to account for his activities yesterday during the Witherspoon maintenance crew's two lunch periods, from 11:30 until 1:30.

"Went to lunch at 12:30, same as always," Antonides answered promptly. "But yesterday was different than usual. Had to take the whole afternoon off, so I missed all the goin's-on up here. Got a goddamn bad toothache over the weekend, so I had to go see my dentist, clear down on the other end of Coal City."

"And what time was your dental appointment, Antonides?"

"Supposed to be one o'clock. But they kept me sittin' there in the goddamn waitin' room till about quarter of two," the maintenance man grumbled.

"Hope you weren't trying to set any speed records on your way down there, Antonides," the lieutenant said blandly.. "In this kind of weather, it usually takes Hendricks and me at least forty-five minutes to get to the south side of Coal City from up here. What time did you say you actually left the maintenance building?"

"It must of been about 12:35 before I signed out," Antonides said, shifting his glance from the window behind Hershey's chair to the one beside me. "Old Wilson was standin' there jawin' at me—didn't want to give me the whole afternoon, but I told him I was hurtin' so bad the dentist'd probably have to operate on my whole goddamn mouth right then and there. Forgot I didn't have my appointment till 1:30, Lieutenant," he added with a shrug, but without turning to look at Hershey. "Last one I had must of been at one o'clock. Yeah, I remember now, because that was the time old Wilson told me he was gonna dock me for half a day an—"

Hershey cut the Greek off before he could bring any more grievances against the *ad hoc* committee he'd somehow appointed. "I saw your supervisor's time sheets, Antonides," the lieutenant said evenly, "and yesterday you signed out exactly half an hour before your scheduled lunch break. So you left the maintenance building at twelve o'clock."

"I never did!" Tony snarled. "Old Wilson must of doctored up them time sheets just to make things look bad! Because I ain't lyin'!" Shifting around in his low-slung chair, he began to try to stare Hershey down, his stupidest mistake so far.

"Who's your dentist, Antonides?" the lieutenant asked brusquely. "And where's your telephone book? If he has a listed number, we're going to call him at home in about twenty seconds. If not, I'll get it out of his answering service Got his card on you?"

"Okay, so I didn't have no dentist's appointment," Tony

agreed desperately. "Went down to the Eagles' to try to talk this good-lookin' new barmaid they got workin' afternoon turn in there into spendin' an evenin' or two with me. Took off at noon because old Wilson owes *me* some time! *That* ain't no crime, is it?" Antonides said with a sudden ill-advised smirk that nevertheless showed us teeth as unimpeachably white as Hershey's own.

"And I understand somebody else owed you some money, Antonides," Hershey said conversationally, ignoring the Greek's rhetorical question. "Pete Simon."

"I ain't done nothin'," Tony protested, shrinking back in his chair. "I don't bother nobody." Then he slowly followed Lieutenant Hershey's gaze, and mine, to the living room doorway; Hendricks had silently returned from the basement and stood holding a gleaming, curved claw hammer, its oiled leather handle protectively sheathed in the sergeant's handkerchief.

"This yours, Antonides?" the lieutenant asked his cowering suspect. Both Hershey and Hendricks remained absolutely motionless, waiting for the maintenance man to finish the job of self-incrimination.

"It's them Covenanters who done it!" cried Antonides, a black rat slowly drowning in bilge. "That's why I told you I took off work when I did! Think I want them maniacs findin' out about how I practically seen 'em do it? An' now they're tryin' to pin it on me just because one of 'em found out Pete Simon'd pulled a goddamn grifter's trick on me! So they snuck back down in my cellar and planted my hammer they took on me!

"Looky here, Lieutenant," Tony went on in a less frantic tone, once he'd made sure Hershey's hands were still at his sides. "Yesterday noon, when I was crossin' the parkin' lot out in back of Tranter Hall—walkin' home after my truck, so I could go down to Coal City and all—I seen one of them Covenanters, with a hood on and everythin', goin' down the drive. Ridin' on a bicycle. And that's the God's truth!" Earnestly shaking his head, the Greek focused his desperado's eyes directly on me, as if seeing in another dark alien a potential ally.

"And what time was this, Antonides?" Hershey demanded.

"At exactly what time did you actually leave the maintenance building?"

"Guess it must of been a couple minutes after twelve, maybe about five after, 'cause I got talkin' to George Maxwell about the start of trout season and all, right before I walked out the door. You can ask him," Tony added in an injured tone.

"Did you see anything else? Anyone else?" Hershey prodded him, pressing his advantage.

"No—yeah—wait a minute," Antonides said wildly. "I think I seen a Dutch buggy comin' down College Street. Out of the corner of my eye, like. He was goin' pretty damn fast."

Hershey signaled Hendricks, still standing in the doorway holding Tony's hammer, to come over and flank his subject's chair. "Antonides, you're under arrest. On suspicion of homicide," the lieutenant announced briskly.

As Hershey cleared his throat to recite his prisoner's rights, the Greek straightened up and looked squarely at his arresting officer. "I ain't never killed nobody, Lieutenant," Tony said levelly, as if he'd just rediscovered some lost code of Mediterranean manhood, "except about a dozen gooks in Korea, like I was supposed to."

Hershey studied Antonides in silence. "I might of wanted to bust Pete Simon one for causin' me all the trouble he did, but I ain't no killer," Tony said again. "Hell, them Covenanters is more 'n likely ready to come chasin' after *me* any day now with my own goddamn knife! Let them freaky little bastards hear how I saw one of 'em around Tranter Hall right after he used it on Pete Simon—and how I figured out about them puttin' my hammer back down-cellar to make me out a damn liar—and I'm next in line. But why the hell should I care?" he added sardonically, getting to his feet at last. "The whole damn town'll probably vote to give McKenna and every last one of his little freaks a thousand dollars' cash money for gettin' the place rid of me!"

Antonides kept up his bitter laughter even while getting his coat to accompany the two tall, blond police officers shepherding him to the county jail, where legally constituted authority waited to strengthen the harsh case against him. After Hershey and

Hendricks had led him outside, the Greek paused for a moment beside their suddenly conspicuous car. "You got what you wanted, you cocksuckers!" he shouted up the street. "Enjoy the funeral!"

"And they all of them will," Tony muttered, hunching himself into the car. "That's the God's truth, too."

I sat in my own car for a few minutes, trying to piece together all these parchment scraps of what purported to be God's truth, since God, according to the Reverend Von Ruden's barbed-wire logic if not mine and the law's, had just fingered New Arcady's murderer. Cettainly Lieutenant Hershey had just arrested the borough's knee-jerk misfit—grumbling against the holy order of things, exhaling resentments with every beery breath; on the job, muttering against his superiors; off the job, gambling at the Eagles' Club in Coal City, where he picked up the brazen-haired waitresses he brought home to fumble around with in his dark bedroom underneath Becky DeVore's. No doubt that poor lady, gagging on the odors of stale sex and Seagram's Seven, mingled pailsful of Lysol with her Saturday morning devotions. Stavros Antonides, moreover, was also irreparably non-middle class and irredeemably non-Protestant. And so, after all of this was over, the borough of New Arcady could enshroud itself in the hills again while its good citizens sighed, "Thank God it wasn't one of *us*."

Nevertheless, I didn't like the pattern so neatly pinked out by the ladies' sewing circle; I could not in the least convince myself that Stavros Antonides had killed Peter Simon. In my own judgment, the ability to carry out an efficient and silent vengeance was simply not among the Greek's marketable skills; nor was decorating his victim's door with bloody triangles within Tony's imaginative range. I also felt forced to rule out the possibility that Simon might have stolen Tony's woman as well as welshed on their verbal contract; Hershey and I would have heard about *that* particular theft from Antonides himself, who—if my own instincts weren't totally skewed again—would have been literally caught red-handed making Pete Simon pay for it. Nor could I conceive of Hershey's having stopped all further developments in the case along with Antonides, and shredding his stack of folders without even collecting any more scraps of information to put in his nearly empty file on Simon's mysterious telephone caller. At any rate, until Hershey chose to tell me our case was officially closed, I saw no reason not to proceed with my self-assigned task and have Tony's upstairs neighbor interpret the marks the killer had made on Pete Simon's office door.

When I pulled up, a few minutes late, at the doors of the Methodist church, Becky DeVore and another woman were standing outside, anxiously peering into the darkness for me. "Mr. Waltz, we almost thought you'd decided to stand us up!" Dr. DeVore exclaimed when I pulled up beside them. "Lillian's ride had to get home to her sick grandson, so I told her if she wanted to stay a little longer, you'd be more than happy to take her home. Lillian, this is Mr. Waltz, our visitor from Pittsburgh. Mr. Waltz, this is Mrs. McKenna. You'll probably have the good fortune to hear her husband speak to us tomorrow, if you haven't already."

"Yes, I have, today in the chapel," I told the ladies as I hopped smartly over the ice to escort them into the car. "Your husband seems to have quite a following, Mrs. McKenna," I said heartily, hoping she'd turn suitably and unguardedly boastful enough all the way home to tell me her husband spent so much time spiritually conditioning his hamstrung brats he never made it home for lunch.

Mrs. McKenna, a wizened-faced little lady with a classically center-parted bun bleached Easter-chick yellow—no doubt to prove to her husband's understandably skeptical charges that she still thought young—gave me, however, only a nod and a look that hinted she thought Pittsburgh was somewhere in Sinkiang Province. After I had settled the two women into the car and blamed my tardiness on Lieutenant Hershey (without mentioning his current prisoner, since prudence had just dictated that the ladies hear about Tony's arrest over their lukewarm Sanka at the White Lion instead of from me), I tried again.

"With so many young people turning their backs on any kind

of religion these days, Dr. McKenna's had an amazing success with the Covenanters," I said, beaming into the rearview mirror—for I was up front by myself like the commandant's chauffeur.

"That's exactly why we should have one, Rebecca," Mrs. McKenna said in an urgent voice to her companion. "We need to make things a little livelier for our young people. You'll see—if we have it at Easter, we'll have fifty new members in two weeks. Be fruitful and multiply!"

"But, Lillian, a book-burning on a college campus?" Dr. DeVore protested. "And do you really think Easter's the most suitable time—"

"Of course it is!" said Mrs. McKenna, breathing fire at the back of my neck. "What better time to show the Lord we mean to set a match to two thousand years of wickedness, just as he will one day put this earth to the torch? Burning and purifying. Purifying by burning! All kinds of books, and magazines, and long-playing records, and tape recordings, and whatever else they squirrel away back in the dormitories. With you faculty people egging them on. I've seen some of the smut you people hand out as their homework. That even their Sunday school teachers give them to read, Rebecca. Peter Simon was letting his boys' class paw over something he was trying to tell me was sex education—with some pictures to look at that not even a married couple should see! I told Will he ought to make sure the Session never let Peter Simon have another Sunday school class at the First Presbyterian!"

In her agitation Mrs. McKenna began thumping the back of the driver's seat with the huge crocodile purse I'd noticed her carrying—quite big enough to cart babies from heaven to the doorsteps of local innocents gamely joined together in wedlock. "And *you've* never supported our programs at all, Rebecca!" she proclaimed when she'd finished jabbing away at my spine. "Will has said to me more than once, 'Lillian, Rebecca means well, but she's much too much of a liberal.' And I'm beginning to think he's right. But you'll see; we'll have our bonfire, and we'll put New Arcady right on the map."

Before I could tactlessly remind the Covenanters' PR director that Pete Simon's murderer had, presumably, beat her group to it, Becky DeVore was signaling me to stop the car in front of an ugly firebrick cottage at the corner of McAllister and Garden—a good three blocks away, I was relieved to see, from Whitaker's Store.

"Well, Mr. Waltz, now you've had a chance to hear some of our infighting," Dr. DeVore sighed after we'd watched Mrs. Mc-Kenna disappear behind her living room draperies. "I'm sure Lillian really *does* mean well, but. . . ."

"But no one could accuse her of anything half so rational as liberalism," I finished for my passenger, since making negative judgments seemed to cause Dr. DeVore acute cardiovascular stress. "I think I'd better check under the backseat when I get home and make sure your friend didn't leave me a few oily rags. Did she sic herself on somebody else long enough this evening for you to do any more thinking about our problem? The triangles of blood on Pete Simon's office door?"

"I did, but it's rather involved," Dr. DeVore answered. "And under the circumstances, it just doesn't make much sense, so I won't even try to explain it until we're safely upstairs. You can park right here in our drive; just don't block Mr. Antonides. But I guess he must have come back and then gone out for a walk or something. He does seem to stay out so late; I wonder sometimes how he ever gets to work in the morning."

I was sorely tempted to give in to my nobler impulses and tell this much-maligned lady that tonight she wouldn't have to leave the porch light burning for her downstairs neighbor; but, figuring my first loyalty still lay with Lieutenant Hershey and his more oblique approach to the problem of Tony Antonides, once upstairs I started exclaiming over Becky DeVore's modest collection of family heirlooms, most of them piled to the breaking point with books and sheet music.

"Actually, it was your mentioning the Valkyries this afternoon that set me off," said my hostess, embarrassing me further by offering me both tea and the chocolate grahams she kept for her student visitors. "Because when the Valkyries ride into battle, they choose those who are to die in it. That's what the name means: 'the choosers of the slain.' So I must confess that, while Anne's tribute book was being passed around tonight, I started thinking about religious rites in pre-Columbian cultures that might involve making some kind of mark on the dwelling places of victims selected for ritual slaughter. But that didn't get me very far, and all at once—right in the middle of dessert—it struck me that the closest parallel was in the Old Testament."

Then Dr. DeVore, carefully spooning out her teabag for future use, did exactly what I had been afraid she might do (since I didn't think my noble Roman nose had fooled her a hell of a lot) and recited something, very fast, in what sounded like flawless Hebrew. " 'Hear O Israel, the Lord thy God the Lord is One'?'' I ventured, as Becky DeVore, sitting there smiling encouragement, obviously expected me to, even though it meant becoming an ungrateful pre-adolescent again, the boy who got caught trying to develop his throwing arm out behind the consolidated high school when he was supposed to be sitting at the rabbi's feet catching the old man's intolerably accented mumblings. "I'll have to give up on the rest, Dr. DeVore," I said before she could throw me any more spitballs. "I don't even know enough to give you a compliment. I was one of those young people who tried very hard to turn his back on religion, and the only reason I went to Hebrew school at all was because my great-uncle Solomon insisted, and my father thought he was probably as rich as the original. Not that it turned out that way, of course."

"Well, of course we all hate anything we're forced to learn as a child," Dr. DeVore said, offering me amnesty as well as more hot water. "I learned some Hebrew because I thought anybody who teaches the Judaeo-Christian tradition ought to be able to recognize at least a few words of the original Scriptures. Not that you'd need Hebrew or really any kind of special knowledge at all to be familiar with the ritual I had in mind. All it is is your own Passover—when the Israelites, you remember, smeared the lintels of their houses with blood so that God's angel would spare their firstborn sons but kill the Egyptians'. But, as you see, that's just the opposite of what it should be to make any sense in our murder case; the victims' doors are the ones *not* marked. So I'm probably being more of a hindrance than any kind of help to you, Mr. Waltz. But after tomorrow I'll be glad to check into some more informed sources than myself for you. Right now I really do have to ungraciously ask you to go home so I can get to bed. I'm such a terrible insomniac I never seem to get enough sleep, and it really does literally put me right out of tune.''

"Actually, we might both be smarter than we think," I told Dr. DeVore as she led me down to the street door; *her* steep stairs were at least indoors. "Maybe the murderer's counting on us to think he's copying something more esoteric than the Old Testament. Maybe he did it backwards on purpose."

"I guess I always tend to think most things are just what they seem. But then I usually seem to be wrong," Dr. DeVore sighed, wrinkling her large white forehead. "Good night, Mr. Waltz. Sleep well," she called from the door of her shabby old house.

Driving back to Mrs. Vandervelde's, I heard a couple of girlish shrieks as I hit the stop sign at the corner of McAllister and Garden and devoutly hoped I had run over a strayed Sacred Cow, preferably some iron-bosomed buddy of Lillian McKenna's. Late as it was, a dozen or so Covenanters were out patrolling Main Street like a Phisohexed militia. "Yah, keep your bowels open and your minds closed," I yelled, rolling down my window. Since they didn't seem to have heard me, I gave these storm troopers in tennis shoes a good-night curse as I pulled into the inn's unplowed parking lot. That night I dreamed that some enterprising funeral director had finally smartened up enough to offer special group rates.

CHAPTER IV
THURSDAY, MARCH 20

WAKING UP COLD AND STIFF AS A DAY-OLD CORPSE, I UNWOUND enough of myself from the sheets to get a call through to Hershey at Tranter Hall and—while Mrs. Vandervelde breathed obscenely over the line—arrange a short breakfast meeting at the Golden Grill between the lieutenant's projected search of his prisoner's apartment and Pete Simon's funeral. Not only did I badly need a debriefing, but my mind had been methodically unreeling a TV movie dismembered by too many sponsors. Somebody had also snipped several key scenes out of the film, so I was hoping that Hershey—the type who had always read the book first—could restore them for me.

This morning New Arcady was being blessed by Christmas-card snow, tastefully etching every tree branch in town, covering up the piles of horse manure in the buggy lot behind the IGA, and washing the walls of the First Presbyterian Church a chaste bridal white. Hershey, I saw, as he came loping into the Grill, had opted in favor of a sober blue suit for the morning's solemnities; together, we resembled either a couple of loan officers forced to announce that interest rates had soared to the heavens or the last two mourners hired to insure that Pete Simon's soul did the same.

"I wish I could tell you locking up Antonides solved all our problems for us, Waltz," Hershey said by way of greeting, as we slid into a notably inconspicuous back booth, "but everything's still pretty much up in the air. We called up his lady friend who works at the Eagles', and she told us Antonides didn't even show up there Tuesday until pretty near two o'clock. *Then* Antonides finally told us what he should have about fifteen hours ago: that he stopped a couple of other places first, to get his courage up—'You know how it is, Lieutenant, when you're worryin' over a woman!'—Wish I had time to!'' Hershey grunted, and went back to chipping the breading off his menu.

"What about the hammer Antonides says somebody's using to frame him—whether or not somebody actually used it to brain Pete Simon?" I inquired.

"Well, *somebody* cleaned it all up for us," Hershey said glumly, once a pimply seven-footer had come ambling out of the kitchen to take our order. "No blood, no prints—and no W. W. Two German dagger on the premises either. Not that we have enough from the lab yet to target anything that specific as one of the murder weapons. And as far as Antonides's story about some kind of a frame-up goes, I did get with your friend Miss DeVore for a few minutes this morning. Wasn't really much of a conversation—I think the good lady had a hangover from some kind of sleeping pill—but she did tell me she'd been keeping more of an eye out lately because of her bicycle being taken, and she hadn't noticed anybody hanging around the house or the neighborhood who looked like they might be trying to sneak into her basement. Just like Antonides told us, there weren't any signs anybody'd tried to break in," Hershey said with a long sigh. "Miss DeVore did agree to let us go over the whole damn house inch by inch, as long as we show a little respect for the dead and wait until tomorrow. Since that's a hell of a lot easier than getting a warrant to do it today, I said okay."

"What about this hooded character on a bicycle Antonides says he saw riding away from Tranter Hall Tuesday noon?" I asked the overburdened lieutenant, now listlessly probing sodden clumps of the Cream of Wheat he'd just had shoved in front of him. "If he or she turns out to exist, and also turns out to be an actual Jogger for Jesus—armed with Antonides's keys to the basement—it's for damn sure not because Becky DeVore holds any tea parties upstairs for the Covenanters. I would say she tries to ignore that particular group as much as she's allowed to. In other words, Lieutenant, Antonides has been lumping his upstairs neighbor in with the

Covenanters just because he likes to keep things simple: put his favorite targets for abuse all in a row and start blasting away. So in this case—if we assume for the moment Antonides might be telling the truth about this person on the bicycle he says he saw Tuesday noon—*could* this hypothetical individual have just dashed into the house, grabbed Tony's spare keys so he could let himself in and out of the cellar, and dashed back out again? Would he *have* to be somebody either Tony or Dr. DeVore invited in?"

"Well, operating on your particular assumption, Waltz, probably not," Hershey nodded. "Antonides did let it slip that he's not too careful about keeping his outer door locked, especially if he just runs over to Whitaker's or he's busy down-cellar. And you wouldn't believe the collection of junk in that ashtray he kept his duplicate keys in. So somebody probably could have fished them out of there, maybe even quite a while ago, without Antonides even noticing there wasn't anything in his ashtray but rusty nails."

"But who knew to look underneath the rusty nails?" I pressed the lieutenant, who had gone back to turning over clots of cereal. "Yeah, I know," I admitted grudgingly, "the half of New Arcady Antonides happened to mention where he kept his keys to and the half of New Arcady *they* happened to mention it to. I take it you wouldn't advise laying any odds that you've got your man. But you're still keeping him in custody?"

"Until somebody gives me a better idea," Hershey said sternly, "or tries to sue me for false arrest. And I'm also going to have his arrest announced at Peter Simon's funeral. Right from the pulpit. So everybody can start to relax and go on about their business. Like Antonides's bicyclist, if it turns out there was one, and maybe even this blackmailer or whatever she was that I can't seem to find enough time to chase after. One thing doing your job and taking a prisoner seems to do is to keep you away from your work."

"What about this Amishman you were looking for?" I asked cautiously, not wishing to raise the lieutenant's anxiety level any further.

"Well, I did manage to get Hendricks off his duff and out

beating the back roads for this guy. Told him to hop into bed with as many farmers' daughters as he had to," Hershey added with a grin, making every effort to raise our gravediggers' spirits. "Hurry up with that half cup of coffee, Waltz, or whatever it is in there. I intend to be right on time for *this* funeral. Out of respect for the dead, I mean." Out of his own sense of delicacy, Hershey covered the remains of his breakfast with a napkin and reached for the check, which stuck to his hand.

As we joined the mourners slip-sliding toward the First Presbyterian Church, I told the lieutenant I'd had a personal encounter with Mrs. McKenna; and, that since she didn't believe in two-way conversations, among other things, we'd have better luck wearing down her obviously hag-ridden husband. I also summarized my own conversation with Dr. DeVore and added that she'd promised to keep on researching bloody religious rituals for us. It struck me that in the event Antonides turned out to be as innocent as he so vehemently proclaimed, before long Lieutenant Hershey and I would be deputizing our murderer as well as most of his or her nodding acquaintances and faculty colleagues.

"Give the killer enough margin for error, and he'll make one," Hershey said. "Maybe even in church."

As long as we crossed Antonides and all of the Covenanters except their elderly guru off the suspect list, Hershey, I realized, had to be right; our murderer—along with every other New Arcadian who'd ever wished Pete Simon any harm—was dashing through the snow to be on time for his victim's funeral. The church itself was massed with friends, enemies, and flowers. My eyes started to sting as I struggled to the back of the sanctuary. After I had compressed myself into a coffinlike space between a faculty wife and a huge heap of her worldly goods, I kept frantically trying to dam up my nose before the service began. A furry ball began to form in my stomach. Then I recognized that hot, sticky odor up front at the altar. Orange blossoms. The day I was married in Passaic, New Jersey's poshest hotel, I had discovered my hideous allergy to them. Madeleine's mother had had a triumphal canopy of these traditional wedding flowers all rigged up, ready to fall right on the groom, who had wheezed and sneezed his way through every minute of the chanted orthodoxy. As a perhaps not entirely unforseen consequence, my new mother-in-law had managed to more or less emasculate me for the first day or so of my Ocean City honeymoon. Now, Simon's funeral stank of orange blossoms; poisonous petals were carpeting the entire front of the church, spilling all over the shiny black casket.

"Is this some village idiot's idea of a joke?" I whispered to my companion, who was nudging her belongings toward her.

"It's the florist's fault. They never should have given the business to Bullfinch's," she whispered back, inching herself away from me.

Screwing up my runny eyes, I looked for familiar faces, Anne's especially. Then, on the other side of the church, I saw the four or five rows of women forming a wailing wall across the back. Given all the learned old men displaying their patriarchal profiles up front, I thought I'd blundered into a Bohemian-style synagogue, with the women unashamedly partitioned off. Lillian McKenna peered out malevolently from underneath a picture hat that appeared poised for flight, and I finally spotted Anne sitting next to the same old babe who'd winked at me during the UMU dinner Monday night, presumably Dr. Blackstone, New Arcady's dowager empress. Since, once again, I couldn't catch her companion's eye with my own rheumy ones, I scrunched back into my seat, hoping, with each snuffling breath, for full-volume sobs in my corner of the church. I did get a glimpse of the widow gathering her four golden-haired girls to her: a masterly metal sculpture, with Mary Sue straining to hold a Jackie Kennedy pose.

After alternating attempts by the home and the visiting ministers to match Reverend Von Ruden's capacity for overstatement, the old German himself got ponderously to his feet and for nearly fifteen minutes thundered out an account of cruel and unusual punishments meted out against Old Testament trash like Jezebel, who'd had her blood lapped up by packs of police dogs. From there Von Ruden went on to the story of Esther, deliverer of the Jewish people from bondage—and various other sordid and kinky practices, as far as I could gather from his deep abdominal groans. Thus far, however, the clerical consensus was that New Arcady really needed a Messiah, or at least a tall stranger brandishing a police special. I wondered how Hershey's sense of timing was operating, at what sob-split second he'd choose to stop the show. But just as Von Ruden rumbled out his last indigestible amen, Dr. DeVore, in an opera diva's flowing dark dress, came out to take center stage.

I wanted to hear only her miraculous voice, capable of transcending even the most turgid pieties, but Becky DeVore's perfect diction forced me to listen to the tallowy lyrics as well. These pathological Presbyterians should have been plunged into communal vats of sheep dip; here they were again, bleating out the same old gory refrain:

> Just as I am—and waiting not
> To rid my soul of one dark blot,
> To thee, whose blood can cleanse each spot,
> *O Lamb of God, I Come!*—I come.

Dr. DeVore disappeared into the darkness on the left side of the sanctuary, and Holy Willie McKenna walked slowly to the lectern, his aging angel's face beaming like a beatified bit player's. "Our prayers for deliverance have been answered," he proclaimed. "Detective Lieutenant Hershey of the state police, who is here sharing with us our grief over the loss of our good friend Peter Simon, announced to me just prior to the service today that Stavros Antonides has been arrested on a charge of murder. Let us now pray for the salvation of this poor lost child of God, that God in his infinite mercy may offer him forgiveness, as his victim, and I'm sure his victim's family"—here McKenna paused dramatically, leaning over the lectern, poised either for flight or a long leap right into Mary Sue Simon's lap—"would wish us to do."

The congregation had barely collected themselves enough to start making self-satisfied noises when Reverend Von Ruden got up and stomped over to the lectern in order to raise his hand and cut off McKenna with one swoop of his big black sleeve. "If you have your Scriptures by heart, Mr. McKenna," he admonished his quaking rival, "you must begin by quoting for us the fourth chapter of the book of Genesis. On the curse our God placed on the first man to kill his brother. God has turned his face away from Stavros Antonides, Mr. McKenna! It is the will of God that damns Stavros Antonides, Mr. McKenna! For—all—*eternity*!"

Von Ruden stood hiding McKenna from view and glaring sheet lightning at his captive audience until the church's regular minister, a virtual adolescent, hastily signaled for a recession. Then he marched stiff-legged off the platform.

Frightened out of their communal complacency, the assembled mourners began to crowd each other out of the church. "They ought to save that guy for the senior citizens. He really knows how to ruin Witherspoon's image," a hollow-eyed admissions-office type lamented, guiding his group around three old ladies wearing identical black straw hats waggling with eye-gouging glass cherries.

"It's also most unfortunate that Antonides was employed by the college, in whatever capacity," noted another member of the same tribe of administrators.

"Who's this foreign fellow who went crazy with drink?" an old man asked petulantly, plucking indiscriminately at coat sleeves.

"They say he went around with loose women. Right out in the open," a matron with cast-iron curls suddenly announced to me, as I fought my way toward fresh air.

"Just who do you mean, lady? Which one of them?" I breathed into the woman's chin-buttressed face. She recoiled back against the cherry-crowned threesome.

Wolfing down crisp country air and cigarette smoke, I took up a past near the parking lot, intending to cut Anne out of the herd of charging Cows. But Dr. Blackstone was clinging to her arm like an all-day antiperspirant. "And how do you find New Arcady, Mr. Waltz?" asked the borough's archduchess, giving me a carefully inscrutable glance.

I was just about to tell her that only massive radiation therapy—resulting, say, from a thermonuclear explosion—could cure the town's ills when Hershey hurried up, beating off his many admirers as well as several reporters and the entire Witherspoon power structure. Some frenzied fan had actually ripped a button from the lieutenant's coat. "If you feel like coming along on a wild goose chase, Waltz, you can meet me at the usual place. In about an hour and a half," he said hastily. Then he squeezed through a narrow gap in the crowd and shoved toward his car.

"Now, there's a truly handsome young man," Dr. Blackstone said with satisfaction. "Tall, fair, well built. Very good body, even with his clothes on. Sexy. Don't you agree, Anne?" she asked slyly, her eyes sparkling behind her smoke-tinted trifocals.

"I think she likes them short, dark, and illiterate," I said, looking Anne straight in the eye. I was tired of having my leg pulled at the expense of my other vital and increasingly insistent organs. "Ol' Black John done bought hisself some brand new tools," I told her, grinning and rolling my authentically bloodshot eyes. "Whut time y'all want him to bring hisself over and fix yo' broken step, Missy?"

"Why don't you take her out to dinner instead, Mr. Waltz?" Dr. Blackstone urged. "I know a *real* restaurant, no farther away from here than Nino's. Fresh oysters, in season. I promise to draw Anne an extremely detailed map, provided you come to lunch tomorrow, since it appears that you'll still be here in town in connection with this most intriguing murder case." She smiled with an irritatingly ironic smugness; I was sure the old woman was perfectly aware that, in arresting Antonides, Hershey had furnished New Arcady with a toothpick instead of its prepaid piece of the True Cross. For this very reason, I was also sure that Dr. Blackstone would contribute to our own cause and give us the psychological judgments Reverend Von Ruden had washed his hands of.

"I'm beginning to have this horrible feeling I belong here," I told the old woman. Then, emulating Hershey —a two-ton grizzly disguised as a koala bear—I gave her the smile I usually saved for Marcia's most mature female friends. "I'd be delighted to come to lunch," I said, making sure she heard my meaningful pause, "provided you draw me that map."

"I'll do my best, Mr. Waltz," Dr. Blackstone said emphatically, her tone telling me that it had paid to advertise subliminally. "No, Anne, you're not invited. I want him all to myself."

"Was I invited out by someone somewhere this evening?" Anne asked in exasperation. "Something's been left out of this conversation. Me."

"I offered to do all your dirty work," I reminded her. "But I'll settle for the privilege of picking you up at six o'clock, barring acts of God or his gang of Good Humor girls. I think we could both use a good dinner. And a night off from New Arcady," I added in a lower tone. Actually, I was beginning to worry about both of us, me especially since, despite all the help I'd been getting from the generally paralyzed hand of fate, I was still doing a lousy job of promoting the kind of beautifully uncomplicated relationship that, under Anne's and my present circumstances, should have been at least twenty-five percent established as of 10:00 A.M. this morning.

Anne, determined to misunderstand even my least questionable motives, gave me a look that told me the only frontier I could expect to cross, at least this evening, was the line of credit on my Master Charge. "Come along, Anne, I'm freezing," Dr. Blackstone ordered her, getting a firm grip on the younger woman's arm. "I'll tell you how to get where I want you two to go over a cup of rum tea. And do ask Jimmy Caldwell for some Drixoral for that allergy, Mr. Waltz. Have the pharmacist at Alden's tell him I sent you. That *is* an allergic reaction you're having, isn't it? I *am* a doctor as well as an outrageous old woman."

I could have sworn the old dame winked again, over her shoulder, as the two women moved toward Anne's car. I walked back to the Golden Grill to get my own car, and some more coffee, since I'd decided against serving as UN observer at Simon's interment. Through Alden's gritty plate glass, I glimpsed Jack Campbell paying for a purchase at the cash register and promptly went in to spy on him as well as ask for my antihistamine. Thus I came up behind the Covenanter just as the clerk was emptying her entire stock of sugarless mints into the small paper bag he held out to her. Fumbling with mittened fingers, Campbell dropped the sack on the tile floor, and a poison-green bomb burst: Absorbine, Jr. Rivulets of wormwood flowed over my feet; the Convener of the Covenanters had baptized me at last.

"Hope it wasn't for shin splints," I said as pleasantly as possible, determined not to blow up at Campbell and give him an excuse to go into one of his Jesus routines and start lapping the stuff off the floor.

"I'm so terribly sorry," the Covenanter murmured, stooping to pick up the shards of glass nearest my toes. "If I've ruined your shoes, my organization will be *very* happy to buy you a new pair. Out of the funds we've been collecting for our campaign against printed filth."

"No thanks," I said, stepping around Campbell to the rear of the drugstore before I gave in to my temptation to plant my aromatic foot squarely on his skinny gray ass. "Getting out into the fresh air ought to kill the smell."

Watching Campbell, still on his knees, try to scrub Alden's linoleum with his muffler, I thought about the dangerous—even potentially criminal—effect this stiff-necked humility might have on his followers. As long as Hershey was chasing phantom Covenanters on bicycles, I decided I should tell him to concentrate on any Campbell or McKenna groupies we might see wilting into the arms of their leaders, since somebody straining to prove her love to Jack Campbell was actually a more likely killer than the Convener himself, whom at the moment I could scarcely see jeopardizing his promising career as the Bruce Jenner of evangelism by committing an imprudent murder.

However, all the way out to Samuel Mueller's farm (at the extreme end of a rutted cowpath that touched all four corners of Schimmerhorn County), Lieutenant Hershey proved much more interested in his own sins of omission than any dubious insights into Campbell and his group that I thought I might have to offer.

"You ought to congratulate me, Waltz," he said with forbidding sarcasm. "I finally got some of the unfinished business cleared off my desk this morning, and it didn't do me a damn bit of good."

"In other words, we still don't know who the woman I heard Simon talking to on the telephone Tuesday morning is?" I asked disappointedly.

"All I found out is who it isn't," Hershey complained, trying to keep his eyes focused on the slush-covered ice he was plowing through in low gear. "Ellen Leach—one of those three Miss Christensen thought we should check on. So I did. After the funeral, which Mrs. Leach decided not to attend. She was home with a head cold, which she said she must have caught at the Campus Wives' Club meeting. At 11:40 Tuesday morning, while you were listening to Simon trying to stall his caller, Mrs. Leach was bidding three spades against Mary Sue. Made her contract, I guess."

"Just another one of life's little ironies," I said consolingly.

"Quiet, Waltz. If you'll let me finish, once I'd let her know she was pretty much off the hook, Mrs. Leach got very chummy—even offered me a cup of peppermint tea. So I hinted around a little about the idea of somebody blackmailing Simon to see if she might have any clues as to who and—although she said she was really sorry she didn't, since Pete Simon had been a very nice guy who didn't deserve that or any other kind of trouble—she hinted back she might be willing to keep her ears open and see if she couldn't work the conversations she has with her girlfriends on to any rumors that might be floating around about how the late Peter Simon might not have been all he made himself out to be. Mrs. Leach said she thought trying to churn up some gossip was really the least she could do—couldn't hurt *her* much at this point, she told me. We were getting so cozy over our peppermint tea by then, Waltz, that Mrs. Leach came right out and told me she and Simon had been lovers for quite a while almost two years ago, but that she'd had to break it off because her husband was up for some kind of chairmanship, and she thought she'd better make her own profile pretty low for a while. I guess Professor Leach got his promotion, because Mrs. Leach went on to tell me she's about ready to climb the walls with him and his departmental budget. She even started hinting around to the effect that she had been pretty much getting set to try to start things up with Simon again. I guess the lady needed somebody to tell all her problems to who wasn't going to blab 'em all over her bridge club.''

"Since Mrs. Leach sounds like such a champion hinter," I said slowly, just as law enforcement's Ann Landers concentrated on bringing us out of a skid, "maybe the professor neglected his balance sheets long enough to figure out that, in addition to her dreadful cold, his wife was coming down with another bad case of the hots for somebody else's husband. Just like the one she'd gotten two years ago. So where was *Mr.* Leach Tuesday noon?" I demanded, hoping I'd for once grasped a subtlety that had escaped the lieutenant.

"Out of town, Waltz. At a conference. Won't be back until tomorrow. Everybody in the whole damn town—when they haven't got their big fat butts in a pew—seems to spend their life in some kind of a meeting. If you were smart enough to wonder why the murderer picked a Tuesday, Waltz, it's because our friend knew that's when all the secretaries at Witherspoon have official permission to knock off for lunch at 11:30 so they can have their weekly hen session at some dump in Pine Village Shopping Center. So he or she figured they weren't going to have to worry about running into Simon's secretary or his front office girl on a Tuesday noon.''

"Anyway, Waltz," Hershey went on—after I'd dutifully admitted my lesser intelligence—"it made a hell of a lot more sense to check on Miss DeVore's bicycle than it did on Professor Leach. Hendricks's team finally found it during the funeral. In an old storage shed—open to the weather, of course—on the alley that runs behind the Alpha Phi Beta fraternity house on MacKendree Street. Four or five doors down from them. It had had too much snow dumped on it—and we don't know how many days ago somebody stuck it there—for paint samples or metal scrapings to tell us anything. And Hendricks was too damn dumb to cover it with plastic in the first place," the lieutenant said plaintively, "so

I gave him the job of interviewing every active member of Alpha Phi Beta. Spoke to their pledge president myself; he seemed to think stealing bicycles was a little slow for his group, that most of them might be more interested in spending their spare time wiring blue boxes or something. So it looks like we'll have to waste a hell of a lot *more* time looking for the right bicycle thief. Or the right bicycle. If there *is* one," Hershey finished, sounding exhausted enough to settle us cozily into a snowdrift as he slumped down in his seat.

"And you didn't pick up any vibrations from the funeral service?" I asked, holding onto the dashboard as we slithered around on S-curve. "Or tune into anybody's evil thought waves?" I myself had seen the mourners' eyes measuring their neighbors, plotting criminality curves, calculating to six decimal places each other's potential for bloody murder.

"I didn't exactly expect some joker to come charging up to the altar yelling, 'I confess! I confess!' " Hershey said disspiritedly, "but our old buddy Von Ruden sure as hell stole whatever show anyone else was planning to put on. People were either egging him on—eye for an eye, tooth for a tooth, all that bloodthirsty business borrowed from *your* people, Waltz—or placing side bets on the old bastard's senility."

"Hershey, you sound positively anti-Semitic. Which is a right I reserve exclusively for myself. However," I admitted, "you're right about that old-time religion. If God wanted to locate his lost heirs, he'd find the real children of Israel right here in New Arcady, Pennsylvania. What about these Amish, by the way?" I asked, through lips as blue as Mrs. Vandervelde's. "Would they extend their charity enough to give us a cup of coffee?" It was getting progressively colder and darker on this freeze-dried road designed for wooden wheels. It struck me that I hadn't seen the sun shine even for a millisecond during my seventy-eight hours in New Arcady, not from the moment I got stuck in my snow-covered rut.

Hershey reached cautiously under the seat and handed me a thermos. "Courtesy of the cook at the Alpha Phi Beta house. She was even all set to have one of her boys fork over his fur-lined gloves for me. We're stuck in a rut with this case," he said meditatively. Obviously the lieutenant and I had been spending too much time together.

"Even if Ellen Leach and the bicycle thief are a lost cause, what about the Chancellors?" I reminded Hershey, in an attempt to console him with the prospect of two good solid candidates for suspicion. "If Mrs. Leach is climbing the walls, Gene Chancellor seems about ready to jump right off the top brick. And we don't know that Karen didn't have blackmail on her mind the other day. I assume you haven't had time yet to ask her to share her most cherished moments with the deceased, the way we were all urged to do at the funeral?"

"We'll try to catch her on our way back from Mueller's—if we can find his damn farm in the first place. Don't these people even believe in marking their own lanes with mailboxes?" Hershey asked, peering ahead as if he had suddenly acquired middle-aged eyes. "I'm having Colton find out how long it actually took Karen Chancellor to get her hair done Tuesday. I'm no expert, but even if she had to run an errand on her way home, two and a half hours sounds like a hell of a long time to spend getting yourself blow-dried."

"Hershey," I said, "you haven't lost your youthful innocence yet. My ex-wife used to spend *three* hours being beautified every Friday. Even so, when I picked her up after all that investment of labor and capital, I used to think that the productivity of the American worker had declined another half percent."

"Waltz, stop babbling and watch where we're going. Wherever the hell it is," Hershey said in annoyance, flipping his lights from dim to bright and back again, in some secret code of his own.

"Smoke up ahead on the right. Looks like there might be a lane coming up in a quarter of a mile," I said, trying to make out an actual building. I had the feeling that somebody had just struck the set.

Soon, however, I could see the entrance to the crooked mile-long lane, marked by a rusty mailbox. We had to leave the car beside it and hike to the house, a toy cottage with a bright blue door, dwarfed by the big, solid barn—visible proof of Mueller's prosperity—and a Mies van der Rohe chicken coop, a rural triumph of modern functionalism. Mrs. Mueller, a stringy stewing hen of a woman plumped out by a big black dress, inspected us for a moment before motioning us inside. "He's back by the fire, doing his sums," she informed us. "Can't do much real work today."

I had a vision of Abraham Lincoln sprawled on the hearth, scrawling his calculations on a shovel. But the Muellers' small, hand-scoured house was unromantically lit by kerosene lamps rather than candles; and Mueller himself, frowning over his accounts in a ladder-backed kitchen chair pulled up to the fireplace, merely seemed a tired businessman with a sprung attaché case—until I smelled his socks, which in the heat of the fire were releasing a bouquet of bran mash and horse manure.

"Lizzie, go get some chairs so's the English gentlemen can sit," said our host, pointing at one of the two giggling adolescent girls heaving their bosoms at Hershey and ready to burst their plum-colored bodices. "Matilda made you up a pot of coffee," Mueller continued, "or maybe you want some hot cider—it goes better by us."

Having chosen the Old-Spice-scented stuff simmering on the back of the wood-burning stove, Hershey and I were promptly blasted by Amish-brewed lightning. "I told the other officer who was out here I'd tell you whatever it was you thought I should know somethin' about, since you're the gentlemen he said was the boss of this thing," Mueller said soberly, oblivious to his guests' uneasy shiftings in their hard chairs. "Although we don't usually have no business with English police. No need for it. We stay home; raise our families right, so's they can read the Bible; keep our *kinder* out of the English schools so's they don't learn the ways that make you people criminals and murderers; mind our own business instead of our neighbors'; take care of our own. But I'll hear you out, Officer, since we don't break our word to any man on God's earth."

Hershey had listened attentively as Mueller spun out the snarled folk-weave of his philosophy. Now he said simply, "We don't wish to disturb your routine, Mr. Mueller, or hinder your family's activities." At least six girl children—carved wooden dolls in white caps and dark dresses—had silently glided out to stand in the shadows watching us. "All we want to know is if you saw any person or noticed any activity of a suspicious nature either around Reuben Tranter Hall on the Witherspoon College campus or on the driveway adjacent to the north side of the building as you passed it at approximately 12:04 P.M. Tuesday. Anything at all that seemed out of the ordinary."

Mueller tugged at his crinkly black beard. "Most all of what I can see going on around the college when I make my rounds looks like something strange to me," he said, smiling slightly. "But this in particular I did see on Tuesday as I was passing that building. Somebody I didn't recognize dressed in those kind of clothes English college students usually wear—somebody with a hood on his head and some kind of gray shirt or jacket—was riding a bicycle right at me out of the driveway beside the building. He was coming fast, like he would run right into me. That takes care of everything, then, Officer? Something like this was what you came here to find out about?" the Amishman asked sharply, reaching for his copy book to indicate he'd spent enough time on trivia for one working day.

Hershey and I rose hastily, dipping toward each other like dance partners, touched in the head by our host's hard cider. His tree-ripened teenagers stopped suppressing their giggles as we bowed and scraped our way to the door, where Mueller's younger daughters ceremoniously clustered, swaying toward us like a nymphet seraglio. I sneaked a last look at their mother, finally realizing that even at her age she was still struggling to hatch a son.

"How about a nice Amish girl, Hershey?" I called as we charged toward the car—Don Quixote and his favorite hired buffoon questing after civilization and sobriety. "Didn't you see those come-hither-to-the-hayloft looks you were getting from Lizzie?"

"That's what the blue door is for, I believe," Hershey yelled back. "Means Mueller thinks it's time for somebody else to have a few more mouths to feed." The lieutenant lurched forward, recovering his balance and his bureaucratic dignity only after clutching at my coat, which sent me sprawling in the snow.

Laid out in my best dark suit, I screamed several colorful family curses at my friend the policeman until he exercised his option of helping me to my feet. In relatively sober silence we drove back to New Arcady, Hershey studying the dark road ahead, keeping the police calls down to a static crackle, mapping the murder in his mind. Mueller's confirmation of the hooded cyclist's existence had both closed Antonides's credibility gap and accordingly assigned us the endlessly tedious chore of door-to-door and dorm-to-dorm canvassing, unless we immediately found some bored student or trapped housewife who had looked out the right window Tuesday noon and could follow the murderer home for us. I hated to think about it; soon I'd have to start scratching the numberless days spent in New Arcady into Mrs. Vandervelde's peeling wallpaper. By now we had hit the main road; the closer we got to town, the more my throat constricted and my stomach surged with sourness; New Arcady was slowly pressing me to death under piles of church foundation stones. Suddenly I wanted to hide myself back in the hills, grow a grizzled beard, clap a broad-brimmed black hat on my shaggy head, sire stolid outdoor sons and meek domestic daughters, worry about no more of the modern world than the price of my farm-fresh eggs. Hitherto a doggedly deracinated city dweller, I likewise lost all desire to go back to Pittsburgh's tall, narrow houses and broken streets. A man could *breathe* out here, whereas I choked on the costly dry air of my dehumidified apartment.

My abused middle-aged body reminded me, however, that I had long ago leniently sentenced myself to life in the twentieth century. The cider had left a sweetish aftertaste of chain-store cologne, and my head was pounding like Adam's after polishing off the fatal apple. Hershey was offering to buy me lunch, but not before we had cornered Karen Chancellor. We stopped off at

Reuben Tranter Hall to check with Trooper Colton, back from Coal City with information about Karen's apparent decathlon at the beauty shop Tuesday that quickly returned Hershey to official life. He promptly telephoned the new mother, who said she was free to see him for only a few minutes, since she had to have Gene's lunch waiting for him when he returned from the library. So we drove down Satterthwaite Street, behind the campus proper, and went into the faculty ghetto, a semicircular cluster of small houses painted in Easter-egg pastels, like a low-budget Kiddyland. The Chancellors lived in a lavender one with a few jaundiced *arbor vitae* in the front yard.

Karen came to the door shielded by her pink-blanketed baby. Murmuring a greeting, she motioned us into the living room: a rumpled, tweedy place reeking of Gene's sweat socks.

"You had some questions to ask me, Lieutenant?" Karen said, bouncing her curls along with the baby on her knee. "I really don't know how I can be of any help to you. And I thought you had already arrested Tony Antonides for Mr. Simon's murder."

Mister Simon. How cute of her. But Karen Chancellor was the sort of cuddly little charmer people had been saying "how cute" about ever since the cradle. Baby-blue eyes, dimples, and frosted hair in a teased toadstool effect placed her as a former prom queen back at Lost Mountain High School. Possibly Gene had picked her up at a truck stop as he grabbed his large Gatorade to go.

"Mrs. Chancellor, we have a lot of loose ends to tie up," Hershey told her. "As of yet, we can't bind Mr. Antonides over for indictment, due to lack of evidence. We need to know, for example, if you were in the vicinity of Tranter Hall between 11:30 A.M. and 12:30 P.M. Tuesday, which would put you in a position to have noticed something that might be of help to us."

"But I was having my hair done," she protested, stroking her baby. "Gene must have already told you all about it. I had to get my hair fixed; I didn't look very pretty, coming out of the hospital and all that."

"Your husband told us you left the house at 11:30, in plenty of time to make your 12:00 appointment," Hershey said in a neutral tone. "But we checked with the owner of The Beauty Business, and also with the operator who does your hair, and were informed that you arrived five minutes late for the appointment that you had actually made. For 1:00. That leaves at least sixty-five minutes unaccounted for, even if it took you half an hour to get to Pine Village Shopping Center on this side of Coal City."

Karen's slightly puffy face fell like a vanilla soufflé. "Well, if you already know all about it," she said shrilly, "why worry me with it, in my state?" Sharply, she hushed her baby, who had started to cry. "And I certainly didn't kill Mr. Simon. Everybody liked him. He was a nice man."

"Your husband also told us about your previous sexual affair with the victim," Hershey said curtly. He was obviously trying to rechannel Karen's spiteful energies for his own current purposes so she'd start punching holes in her husband's alibi for murder, but I could also tell he didn't like our little mother any better than I did. "To me this says that you might have had some business that took you to Reuben Tranter Hall—even to Pete Simon's own office—Tuesday during the noon hour. Something so important that you had to lie to your husband about it, as you'd done many times before."

Karen gave the lieutenant a contemptuous glance and bent over her baby. She was taking her right to remain silent very seriously.

Hershey leaned toward her like the mad baby snatcher. "Weren't you trying to blackmail Pete Simon, Mrs. Chancellor? Wasn't the first thing you did after you left the house Tuesday morning to call him up and ask him for money? And when he sounded like he was stalling, didn't you decide to stop by his office and repeat your demands in person?"

Still, Karen said nothing. She was a stubborn little bitch. I didn't envy either Pete Simon or Dr. Gene Chancellor.

Hershey, ever resourceful, pushed the "clear" button and started all over again. "I understand your husband is very athletic, Mrs. Chancellor," he said conversationally. "Does he happen to own a bicycle?"

"Why would you ask me that?" Karen said, startled. After

hesitating for a moment, however, she apparently decided she'd be supplying sufficiently useless information to answer Hershey's question. "Yes, he does, a ten-speed French Grand Concours."

"May I see it?" Hershey asked.

"Why would you want to see it?" Karen demanded. "What does it have to do with anything? But anyway, you can't; it's being repaired right now. At a shop in Coal City."

"Do you remember how long it's been there?" Hershey asked, carefully casual.

"Well, I think for about two weeks," Karen drawled. "You'd have to ask Gene about it—or didn't you do that already?" Grudgingly, she gave Hershey the name and address of the bicycle repair place.

"I represent the American Civil Liberties Union," I said, suddenly inspired. Hershey hadn't properly introduced us, and apparently Karen hadn't kept up with current events. "I'm here to see that your interests are protected at all times," I said solemnly. "And I can assure you, Mrs. Chancellor, that the lieutenant here is not violating any of your civil rights by asking to search your cellar or your kitchen. We would urge you to cooperate with him fully."

Karen, duly impressed, swallowed my shiny new lure. With Hershey bringing up the rear, we all three trooped into the cellar. Besides an old hand mower and a few rusty gardening tools —Karen's handiness apparently failed to extend to horticulture—homemade shelves sprouting moldly paperbacks were all our quick search showed us. We noticed no choice hiding places for the missing murder weapons, nor could the ACLU allow us to pry the paperbacks loose and search every shelf.

Back upstairs in the pink-checked kitchen, Karen opened her home repair drawer, which contained both a claw hammer and a ball-peen, in addition to a few other basic tools neatly arranged on pink oilcloth. All we found out from Hershey's supervised inspection of Karen's small store of kitchen knives was that the Chancellors seldom ate steak, chops, or roasts—out of respect for either Gene's triglycerides or his salary level.

When we came out of the kitchen, Karen scooted ahead and

stood switching her skirt by the front door. Obviously, she considered civic chore time over for the day. "Mrs. Chancellor, there are a few more items on the agenda," said Hershey, planting his feet firmly on her scatter rug. "So I suggest we return to the living room."

"The baby is crying," Karen said, and bolted past him to the back bedroom. When she returned, we had seated ourselves on her sofa bed, forcing her to yield to our renewed advances.

"Mrs. Chancellor, once again, where were you Tuesday morning between 11:30 and 1:05, when you actually arrived at The Beauty Business?" Hershey demanded.

"But I don't have to answer that question," Karen protested. "Do I?" she asked, seductively wriggling toward me.

"I'm afraid so," I said in a sepulchral tone. The New Arcadian Ministerial Association really should have hired me as a part-time spiritual guide.

"But it's something very personal, and it concerns no one else except me," she argued with stubborn illogic. "It couldn't possibly help you with your case."

"That's my decision, Mrs. Chancellor," Hershey said, really angry now. "When did you make up your mind you'd try blackmailing your old lover? Were you planning on getting him fired? Maybe even thinking about getting a paternity suit going, unless he paid you out the money you wanted? How much was it, Mrs. Chancellor?"

Karen gave up with the teeth-baring snarl of a Pekingese who'd just had her turf taken over by a large Labrador. "Only five thousand," she said sullenly. "Nothing Pete couldn't have afforded if he'd really wanted to. But you aren't as smart as you probably think you are, Lieutenant! It was only a loan. And I really needed the money. For personal reasons. It was really the least Pete could do."

"And what were you planning on doing with your five thousand dollars, Mrs. Chancellor?" Hershey asked quietly.

"That really isn't your business at all, Lieutenant," Karen said with a haughty frown. "Because I wasn't anywhere near Reuben

Tranter Hall Tuesday noon! First I called up Pete from on campus. From the phone booth out behind the administration building —it's back in the pine trees, nice and private; nobody even seems to know it's there. And then I went to a legal referral service down in Coal City I'd heard about. Because I had to find out about hiring a lawyer to get me a divorce. Fast!''

"Even these days an uncontested divorce in this state still only runs about four or five hundred," Hershey observed.

"And Gene isn't going to know anything about it either!" Karen said with complacent malice. "Because I'll get my money from somewhere, and I'll be way off in New York City! With a nice apartment and a good job! I liked my job; I was a good secretary. You can ask Dr. Horton about that!" she added, daring us to doubt her.

"So you'll be leaving your husband and naturally taking your baby to New York along with you?" Hershey asked, as if idly curious about Karen's new life.

"No, I won't, Lieutenant," Karen said scornfully. "I'll bet you think the baby was Pete's! Well, it certainly wasn't," she assured us, with a sneer at Hershey's obtuseness. "Gene made me have this baby and give up my job to take care of it. So of course I had to stop seeing Pete, along with everything else. All because Gene wanted a kid just so the college would give him his tenure! You have to be a family man if you want them to keep you. But let Gene find some meek little Minnie Mouse to change the diapers for him!"

"And the five thousand dollars?" Hershey murmured, almost inaudibly.

"Pete owed it to me!" Karen insisted, her eyes aiming hate rays at Hershey and me. "Because even though we had such wonderful times together, he wanted to get rid of me! He wasn't very sad about it when I told him I couldn't see him anymore. He said that was really smart because people were starting to do some whispering, and we were right on the edge of getting ourselves into really big trouble. But that wasn't the real reason, Lieutenant. Pete had already decided he wanted to go after the little college girls! Little student twirps!" Karen spat, swelling up like a puff adder. "So what do you think of that, Lieutenant? You'd better start looking in all the frilly little suites over in the sorority houses if you want to find your murderer!"

In case she hadn't gotten across her rage and frustration, Karen snatched a heavy atlas off the coffee table and hurled it at Hershey. It landed on the floor beside his end of the couch.

"May I have the name and address of your lawyer referral service?" Hershey asked after a pause to allow Karen to remember that, at least technically, she'd attempted violence against a police officer. "What time did you get there?"

"Probably sometime after twelve o'clock, Lieutenant," Karen said in her arsenic-laced drawl. "Why don't you ask *Gene* where *he* was Tuesday noon, while he was supposed to be here at home looking after his damn baby? While I was at the lawyer referral office, I tried to call him up to ask him to take a tuna fish casserole out of the freezer for supper. And there was no answer!"

Upon this shrilled revelation, both Karen and I looked expectantly at Hershey; but, having had several premium pieces of information tendered him out of sheer spite, the lieutenant had obviously decided against pushing his luck. He held out his hand, and Karen thrust her legal referral service's smudged business card at him. Then, seeing him get up and start toward the front door, she rushed ahead of him to fling the door wide and forestall a smooth exit. She stood in the doorway clicking the latch until we'd begun inching our way down her unshoveled walk, and then she cleared her throat to get our attention. "If even the littlest bit of this gets back to Gene," she called from the door of her hostile, malodorous house, "so he can do something to stop me getting my divorce, I'll sue the two of you, as well as him, for everything you've got! For invasion of privacy!"

Grateful for the sharp vinyl smell of the car, Hershey and I drove silently back to his office in Tranter Hall. Seeing the lieutenant reach for his tape recorder as soon as he'd unlocked the door, I told him that as much as I appreciated his earlier offer of lunch, I had decided on a disciplinary fast so that I'd be too weak to want to beat up any poor defenseless females. "Thanks for finally using your head, Waltz," Hershey said as he gratefully showed me out and closed the door on me.

On my way back to the Inn, I stopped at Whitaker's Store —otherwise known as Horny Hank's, in honor of its proprietor's faithful distribution of contraband porn to class after class of Witherspoon students—for my standard four packs of cigarettes. When I walked in, Melissa Parsons, ready for the Burning Bush Bible Marathon in a stiff new sweat suit, was in the process of purchasing several packs of vomit-colored grape chewing gum to help her break the habit of living in the tense present. For all their stress on physical and spiritual conditioning, the Covenanters seemed amazingly graceless; Ms. Parsons was fumbling like Jack Campbell before her, knocking down the gum display set up on the counter and thus stirring up vile chemical odors. Then I saw that the girl was shaking all over, clearing her throat in an agonizing attempt to speak to me while sending me distress signals with those huge, soft eyes.

"What's the trouble, Ms. Parsons?" I asked, steering her out of the traffic pattern, away from the racks of thumbworn pornography.

"I kept trying to call you all morning, Mr. Waltz," she stammered. "After the funeral, I mean." She tottered backwards, right into a rack of Little Angie Cream-filled Maple Fudge Delights. "Did that mean lady at the Inn even give you my messages? She asked me what it was I wanted to talk to you about," Melissa Parsons said, her voice quavering with indignation as well as with the effort it cost her to be coherent.

Since Mrs. Vandervelde could probably have won an intimidation contest that matched her against the Ayatollah Khomeini, I had to admire this sweet, disturbed child's courage, but I was actually hoping the girl would sweep her scattered wits up from Horny Hank's filthy floor and come to the point.

"I haven't even been back to my room yet," I said, holding her up so she wouldn't crush the cookies. "What *did* you want to talk to me about, dear?"

"It really is terribly urgent!" Melissa Parsons exclaimed, snagging her sweat shirt on a pyramid of potato chips, which came crashing down to crackle under our feet. "I promise to tell you everything, Mr. Waltz—but is there anywhere else to go? To talk?" She sounded forlorn, as if we had been condemned to stand there totaling out packages of potato chips in order to hold a privileged conversation.

I couldn't take cutting through any more grease at the Golden Grill, so I boldly suggested my own room at the Inn. "Don't worry, I'll protect you," I said reassuringly, counting on the long arm of the law to yank me out of Mrs. Vandevelde's vengeful reach.

I was wishing hard for my landlady to be busy watering the cabbage soup stock over at the White Lion; however, even through the Inn's grimy east window, I could see the rusty-haired old gypsy reading room keys at the front desk. "Two girls were on the telephone for you a while ago," she said in a dilled-vinegar voice as Ms. Parsons and I humbly approached the throne. "Two other ones." She looked down at her acid-etched list. "Dr. Christensen, from down at the college. She wants you to call her back. Not too late to change your plans, she says." (For all her scandal-spreading skills, Mrs. Vandervelde made an extremely cryptic oracle.) "And a Miss Parsons. She called more than once. Sounded upset," she added accusingly, her eyes moving from me to my companion, who shrank back into her hood. "You taking this one upstairs?"

"This *is* Miss Parsons!" I said in a tone of moral outrage. "And we *are* going upstairs. On police business."

"I knew it!" Mrs. Vandervelde exclaimed. "I knew it all along! I told Dora Hammill you were really one of those plain-clothed policemen. An under-covers man."

"No, that's the Amish," I said. "They observe an old custom called bundling." Choking on my own indecent laughter, I hustled Melissa Parsons up the stairs and into my bedroom.

The girl had retained her lost orphan look and stood rigid in the middle of the room, her fists clenched fiercely. "Sit down,

Melissa," I said, sternly paternal, scrounging around for tissues, since I expected another flash flood of tears, which I actually would have chosen over her present catatonia. "What precisely is the problem?"

Slowly, Ms. Parsons turned her small housecat's head toward me. I'd thought that the girl had somehow twisted her hair up so that the gray hood would fit over it. Then I saw that she had cut it off. If *they* had made her do that, I intended to pour at least a pint of Absorbine, Jr. over Jack Campbell's scrotum and watch him writhe before I ignited it.

Melissa seemed unaware that both she and I had been wronged. "How did you know?" she said in a wan Garbo whisper. "How did you know why I came to see you?"

"I still don't," I said, a shade impatiently.

"It *is* police business. Because I have to confess," she said, impatient in her turn. "Because I murdered Pete Simon. I can't let another person be punished for it."

The girl had started shaking like a witch doctor's devil doll. After leading her to the single straight chair provided for my discomfort, I myself sat down on the bed so I wouldn't be hovering over Ms. Parsons like another pulpit puppeteer. Assuming Campbell and McKenna had rinsed her sanity away along with her sins, I still had to hear her out, without reference to secular standards of logic and reason.

"You killed Pete Simon? Why would you want to kill Pete Simon?" I asked, stupidly echoing Karen Chancellor, who had made a much more satisfying suspect than this lovely lunatic—although, according to my own earlier hunches about the Joggers for Jesus, there had had to be at least one Melissa Parsons desperately clutching at the drawstring of Jack Campbell's sweat pants.

"Because he was an evil man," Melissa said, as if she held this truth self-evident. "He deserved to die."

To me, this sounded suspiciously like a prepared press release. Someone had sent Melissa Parsons here to plague me. "Whose idea was this, Melissa?'' I asked sharply, thinking that her group must have assumed all along that John Waltz had been born in the Year of the Chump.

Melissa, however, was already answering metaphysical questions. "No one told me to kill him," she assured me. "I had to. There was no other way. I asked God to guide me." Slowly, she bowed her shorn head.

Murder made simple. Ms. Parsons, in gaining her soul, had certainly lost whatever sense of humor she'd originally been blessed with. Then I remembered Leslie Fielding's contention that whoever had shut Pete Simon off simply couldn't take a joke. "Melissa," I said, staring at her, seeing her captioned as America's Most Beautiful Cult Murderess, "that tells me *how*. Not *why*. What made you so desperate that you decided you had to kill Pete Simon? *Why* was there no other way?"

"Because of his wickedness; because God wanted it," Melissa mumbled, rocking back and forth.

"What wickedness?" I pleaded, trying to keep my tone as neutral as Lieutenant Hershey's would have been, although I was sorely tempted to slap the girl into some semblance of lucidity. Not even Christian cultists killed purely on principle. And her language had suggested something darker than a desire to speed up the divine judicial process. "What had Pete Simon done to you, Melissa?" I went on, praying for patience. "Did he proposition you? Make a pass at you?"

Silently, Ms. Parsons shook her head and set her clasped hands stiffly in front of her, as if I'd been about to truss her up for the stake.

"Or was it one of your girlfriends?" I suggested out of sheer desperation. "Did Pete Simon seduce her? Make her his mistress? Dump her because he had the hots for somebody else?" I added more crudely, hoping to shock Melissa out of her mental swaddling clothes.

The girl took one deep, shuddering breath and then started to sob as if she had literally forgotten how. "It wasn't that way at all," she gasped, waving the tissue I'd discreetly handed her like a white flag. "He said he didn't want me to make myself miserable. That he wanted what was best for me. That it had to end because I was taking it too seriously. That it was important for me to get out in the world and get a career going. Use my potential."

Although I'd heard a warped echo of the dead man in Melissa's last words, I felt much relieved since I myself was much more fluent in Recruiterese than in Neo-Calvinist Nightmarish. What interested me most was the girl's obvious need to set up someone to worship—which meant that Melissa Parsons *might* have felt a sudden maddening urge to destroy her idol after he'd so brutally stomped her with his clay feet.

"That was how it started," she was saying. "He wanted to help me. He believed in me. More than my own father, even. And I wanted it to happen. I wanted him to have my virginity," Melissa said with some small trace element of pride. "I loved him! I've never even felt anything for any *boy*."

Since I was now using any excuse not to dwell on the ugly manner of Pete Simon's murder, I found myself wondering why gorgeous young girls invariably chose to make the supreme sacrifice to some other undistinguished older man. "He thought I was something special. So *I* thought I was something special," Melissa was earnestly explaining to me. She had started shredding tissues again—handy girl to have along on a diplomatic mission. "And I never went near him after he said it was over. Except one time when I really had to see him about my résumé. And he asked me if I had any—new boyfriends! So it was all just a joke to him. *I* was just a joke to him," Melissa said in a muffled voice, choking on her own memories.

"How long ago was this? How long before—the murder?" I asked as gently as possible. At this point, Melissa Parsons needed no more betrayals by Big Daddy.

"That was just a month ago," she answered promptly. "The last time I ever saw him alone. When I found out he'd never loved me at all, and what that made me, what *he'd* made me—I wanted to die. I felt all alone. But then I talked to . . . a friend of mine, who said I should try to talk to God about it. That God would always love me. And then I found the Covenanters; God led me to them." Again the girl sounded perched on the knee of some sadistic ventriloquist squeezing hard on her voice box. "They saved me," she insisted. "And I knew I belonged to them. But I knew *he'd* never be saved. Never! So I knew that I had to kill him."

Melissa Parsons paused, lifted her head, straightened her shoulders, readied herself for battle. "But I should have realized that all of us are guilty," she told me in the strident tone of a class C sports announcer. "You heard the Convener speak to us yourself. And I talked to my friend again too. So I knew that God wanted me to give myself up because I had broken his law again. I had committed murder. So I came to you to confess."

She was back on the same scratchy tape track. The Covenanters had emptied everything out of her except self-hatred, which made me wonder if they hadn't, after all, selected her as a sacrificial stand-in, an approved substitute for the real murderer, who had made her his willing victim. Much as I hated to, I'd have to stick Melissa Parsons's head in the slime of the murder itself.

I waited until she took a time-out from tears and then asked for a factual account of the killing. She sounded convincing—or at least well-rehearsed—as she told of telephoning Pete Simon and arranging a last-minute appointment to have him assist her in making a crucial career decision. She had made her own crucial choice on Monday when she'd purchased a hammer and a hunting knife at a hardware store in Coal City, after begging a ride from a sorority sister.

"Myself, I would have gone out and bought a Saturday night special," I said to Melissa, who looked her blankest at me. "A gun," I explained, sick of my role as father confessor since the girl had just rigged up a gallery light for the dirty picture I'd been carrying around in my memory since Tuesday noon.

"But I had to *hurt* him," Melissa insisted. "And I've always been afraid of guns."

With *that* knack for incongruity, I wondered how the hell Ms. Parsons had ever passed high school geometry. Mechanically, I asked her more questions, learning that the bicycle she'd ridden belonged to another sorority sister, who'd made a long-term loan of it to her during Melissa's stint as a commuting student teacher. It was 11:46 on Tuesday morning, Melissa told me after I'd patiently rephrased several requests for the gory details; she was able to fix the time for me only because she remembered that the clock in the college tower had just struck the quarter hour (which meant she'd barely missed me and Ms. Snickelburger en route to my office.) She'd returned to Reuben Tranter Hall for her emergency meeting with Simon, parked the bike in the shrubbery, and entered the building by the front door, carrying a shopping bag containing the murder weapons and her sweat suit. After asking her former lover to pull out her own placement file, she had struck him from behind while he shuffled papers on his desk, knocking him unconscious with the first blow from her hammer.

"The next thing I remember is smearing his blood on the door," Melissa said in a forlorn voice. She had hunched herself into a fetal position. "As a sign of his guilt." Somehow she had made herself even smaller than before; her arms were locked around her knees and her nails scrabbling at them.

"Melissa," I said, harrumphing like Dr. Caldwell, the town's stodgy GP, "do you remember, by any chance, what you did with your—trophies? Pete Simon's sex organs?"

"*What?*" Melissa Parsons's head had snapped to attention. Suddenly she looked as lost as any sane person trying to speak a lunatic's private language. "I don't know anything about that at all."

I could have sworn she didn't, but I felt too backward to build any skyscrapers on top of this confessed murderess's mental blocks. Hershey would just have to drag the sludgy pond of her subconscious and dredge for additional facts, such as the disposition of the murder weapons. She sat quietly while I telephoned him.

The lieutenant arranged to meet us in the parking lot of the White Lion in a bright, new unmarked car, which would give Mrs. Vandervelde less immediate cause to conclude that I had raped and murdered a young girl in my room. Although it was too late for the lunch crowd, an afternoon bridge party was tottering its way through the slop when Hershey pulled up, his blond head shining like a beacon. The group of women stood and watched while I turned Melissa Parsons over to him. Actually, they made what these two tables of ladies would doubtless call a "lovely couple." In my own judgment, however, the three of us more strongly resembled the stricken survivors of a Polish wedding reception than the bridal party.

"I'll postpone taking your formal deposition," Hershey said to me hurriedly, "until I've had a chance to settle her down enough to get some straight answers out of her. And I'll be tied up in all the red tape I'll have to mess with to release Antonides. Today or tomorrow. Before Harrisburg decides to spend my annual salary plus Hendricks's, finding out why I had him arrested in the first place."

Hershey had put Melissa Parsons into his car as if he were rushing her to the vet's. I could tell that he, too, wanted to scrap the script and call a story conference. Personally, I felt too deranged even to drink. Besides, I still had to telephone Dr. Christensen, as the message tacked to my door—scrawled in fuchsia felt-tip by my hostess, who had inexplicably deserted her post downstairs—reminded me. In one of my previous incarnations, I realized, I had asked Anne Christensen to share an expensive evening; but at the moment I didn't much feel like expending my limited energy either binding or tenting the wounds of any more of Pete Simon's old couchmates. Nevertheless, I still wanted to see Anne, or at least find out whether either one of us intended to finish what we'd so jerkily jump-started, so I dialed her number.

"Why, Mr. Waltz, how nice to hear from you," Anne sniffed on the first ring.

"Look, I'm really sorry I didn't call you back earlier," I told her, hoping she might take *something* I said at its face value, however low she had pegged it. "Believe it or not, I had a murderess on my hand. Or somebody who thinks she's one."

"Pardon?" she said after a slight pause.

"I'll tell you about it tonight," I said wearily. "When I pick you up at—when was it, again?"

"I called to tell you that Eliot's—Dr. Blackstone's romantic restaurant—" Anne said dryly, "no longer exists. When people eat out around here, they eat greasy ethnic."

"Well, I guess we eat greasy ethnic. Unless you'd like to make yourself useful as well as decorative."

"No, I wouldn't," Anne answered. "I've got to get out of this apartment. The whole day has been a painfully legal holiday. An enforced Sunday."

"And you don't want to work on the Sabbath. Okay," I sighed, surrendering, "we'll go drown our sorrows in olive oil. Six-thirty?"

Although I'd speculated this morning on what candlelit intimacy in Anne's three-room apartment might do to us or for us, in my current state of resigned cynicism I also remembered that full-course dinners for two were inevitably followed by extortionate demands for emotional gratuities—even, or especially, if home-cooked. Nevertheless, as I drifted into a short doze full of bad dreams, I resolved to at least take advantage of Anne's remorselessly analytical mind and have her try to translate Melissa Parsons's garbled message for me, since while she might have chosen to confess to murder, I was far from ready to take her word for it.

"Melissa Parsons has a very fine, analytical mind," Anne told me that evening while she tried to dissect a few strands of Nino's special spaghetti, which he'd just given a lube job. "At least, she had one two years ago when she was my student. I can't see her suddenly getting religion. Pregnant seems a lot more likely, with her looks. Although she did seem almost pathologically fastidious. Finicky. Hardly the kind of girl to bloody up her one-hundred-percent virgin cashmere sweaters."

Nothing Anne and I ever talked about managed to remain nuance-free. "You're taking your scalpel to a girl who first joined a cult and then hacked off her own hair!" I reminded my dinner companion. "And planned out every detail of her murder at least a day in advance. And then removed all traces of herself from Tranter Hall.''

"You're contradicting yourself," Anne pointed out. "First you tell me that Melissa Parsons is so mentally disturbed she committed a kind of self-mutilation. Then you tell me she murdered Pete Simon in an extremely methodical manner."

"You're talking about trivia, and I'm talking about murder!" In my clumsy hyperactivism, I knocked over my wineglass and sullenly watched its contents make a dark red blotch on the tablecloth.

"I'm talking about someone whose personality doesn't match your description of Melissa Parsons! Still," Anne said reflectively, after offering me her napkin with a totally unnecessary flourish, "sometimes she looked . . . haunted . . . with those enormous sad eyes. Or maybe it was just sappy," she added, with a hard-edged smile.

"You sure I shouldn't drive you home so you can take to your bed with female troubles?"

"My trouble is, obviously, that I don't look tragically appealing enough for you!" Anne snapped. "Maybe I should start dying of consumption so I'd be more interesting."

"Maybe you should develop some compassion for members of persecuted minorities," I said sourly, "who not only get thrown to the Christians but stuck with the check. Look, Anne," I went on, after a long pause to prime her for a special message, "all I am is another tired middle-aged businessman who likes a little female companionship in between his monthly mid-life crises and has enough of an ego to enjoy being seen in public with a beautiful woman. So please stop thinking that during my more lucid periods, when I'm not pretending to be a detective, I sit around trying to come up with new ways to hurt your feelings."

Anne looked astonished at my apparent sincerity, then almost contrite. "It certainly isn't all your fault," she sighed. "I think I've been down at the bottom of a black hole all winter. And today it was even worse—with the funeral, and having too much time at home to think about myself, and even that pine stuff they spray in here so it smells like a dog kennel. And let's not talk about the murder for a whole hour; it's like gnawing on a ham bone with a broken tooth.'' She put her hand on mine as I paused with a forkful of salad, the first time she had ever really touched me at all. ''Speaking of what ails us, how come you were choking and wheezing in church this morning?'' she asked, making more spaghetti hieroglyphics with the hand she had hastily with drawn. ''The Sacred Cows were all afraid you were going to interrupt the service with some kind of seizure.''

I told her the story of my doomed wedding day and my sniveling excuse of a honeymoon. In turn, Anne told me of having to spend hers fetching and carrying for her widowed father-in-law, who had found her strongly appealing to his prurient interests. At night, he had stood and panted outside the young couple's flimsy door. Suddenly we were together, even close enough to snag her stockings on my shoelaces, which gave me sufficient courage to suggest we pretend we were out on a date and go dancing. And so we moved to Nino's back room, where his nephews picked out enough tunes to pay their union dues.

Despite the slight generation gap, Anne and I danced easily together. Holding her, I enjoyed as many vicarious experiences as publicly possible, thinking what a good fit we would make.

''What are you thinking?'' she asked.

''What a lovely couple we make,'' I breathed into her ear. ''How about having a drink?'' Actually, I wanted to conduct a little business under the table.

Anne let me hold her hand but otherwise seemed to be drawing demarcation lines, as if a time warp were holding us permanently back in tenth grade. I couldn't even find a demilitarized zone. ''I've really enjoyed this evening,'' she sighed. ''But it's 11:30, and I have to teach at 8:00.''

And anyway, panty hose will always protect the working girl, I thought, getting a flash of thigh as Anne settled herself into the car. My hopes blasted by freezer burn, I skulked around to my own side and, with fumbling fingers, tried to fit the right key into the goddamn ignition. My key ring rolled right into Anne's lap. She just sat there.

"Which one fits the chastity belt?" I said, sliding over and putting my hand where the keys were. Yet when we reached the moment of crisis—when a half-ounce Trojan tips the scales—Anne abruptly sat up.

"It *is* after midnight, John. We'd better drive back to New Arcady." She sounded all set to lecture me on losing our heads.

"Fine with me," I shrugged, since I'd never had much of a taste for cold canned pumpkin.

Anne sat turned away from me even after I had inched over the edge of her steep, slippery driveway. Then, with one hand on the car door, she put her face into position for a dry-lipped kiss. "I can't invite you up," she said tragically. "Because of *me*, not because of my neighbors."

"And I can't come up," I said, wanting to shake the seriousness out of her as if I were purging a vending machine of Canadian coins. "Because of your neighbors, not because of *me*. Actually, my—ah—organ has atrophied. Frostbite."

"Would you like to come up for a hot cup of coffee?" she asked in a small voice.

"Certainly," I said gravely. "But we'll hate each other in the morning."

"It *is* morning already," Anne protested.

"Okay, Professor. Be pedantic," I said, pulling her out of the car. I proceeded to surprise myself and probably my sacroiliac by picking her up and carrying her all the way up those penitential stairs.

We didn't even make it into the bedroom but began rolling around on the living-room floor like romping teenagers, strewing clothes and sofa cushions all over the bookcases, moaning loud enough to wake the living dead all along the street. Afterwards, we lay curled around each other until the cold wind rattling the windows drove us into Anne's bed, where we started all over again.

I was diving down into sleep when my ex-bedmate poked me sharply, having gotten up and made herself unglamorous in an old terrycloth bathrobe. Morning was coming, with all its creeping neuroses.

"You simply cannot stay here overnight," Anne said urgently. "My downstairs neighbor goes jogging at 5:30 sharp. And you've got to go wrinkle your own sheets."

"I love you," I mumbled, settling into the cozy hollow she had left for me. "Will you marry me?"

"I'll bet you say that to all the girls you screw," Anne laughed. Then she started to cry.

Clutching her comforter, I sat up, wretchedly tired of reducing women to tears. And I didn't even know where the hell my clothes were, so that I could go quietly.

"I'm a damn fool for letting this happen," Anne sniffed. "I tried very hard not to—which was driving us *both* crazy. My 'Unhand me, sir' routine is rather rusty. But you were being a sadistic son of a bitch about Pete Simon—and twisting your own guts out over it. And I'm not really *into* S and M, as my students would say. I'm not really into sex, even. I like being a bitter old maid."

"You'll never make it. You taste too good," I said, smiling up at her, reaching for the belt of her plain brown bathrobe—suddenly a lot limper than I was.

"Go to hell, Waltz. Go back to Pittsburgh. Get yourself a nice Jewish girl." Barefoot, Anne went into the living room and came back with my clothes, which she dumped on the floor like contaminated waste before hurrying to hide in the bathroom.

"Lady, I already did that once," I called after her. "And I'm still taking the consequences. Out of my monthly paycheck."

Hastily, I put on my stale clothes, not even waiting for my turn at the cold-water tap. "I'll call you," I shouted, wrestling the outside door open. Somehow I got my car started without human or divine intervention. New Arcady, on this first morning of spring, had been encased in ice. The Witherspoon College clock chimed out my guilty return to the inn. Five o'clock, and all was still not well in New Arcady—even though, or especially because, Melissa Parsons had confessed to the murder of Pete Simon. And certainly all was not well with John Waltz, who had briefly been born again. He *had* really better get himself back to Pittsburgh, where madness made predictable trolley-track patterns, and sex put on a happy, thank-God-it's-Friday face and scribbled phone numbers on cocktail napkins.

CHAPTER V
FRIDAY, MARCH 21

TWO HOURS LATER, I WOKE FROM A SHALLOW SLEEP TO HEAR THE clock strike seven; my subconscious, overruling all rational objections, had dictated that I stop proceeding with middle-aged caution and intercept Anne after her eight-o'clock class. My conscious mind, however, refusing to rest its case, kept clamoring for my attention all during the lusty Sousa march I sang in the shower. Not only did cold-hearted reason attempt to convince me that I could not possibly be in love with Anne Christensen, but it also brusquely informed me that I deserved to be scourged out of New Arcady with an Amish buggy whip for my neurotic compulsion to take sex seriously. Nonetheless, I scrutinized myself in the streaky mirror like a brand-new non-virgin. Reassuringly enough, I looked exactly like a tired businessman keeping his weight down through nicotine and nervous tension while somehow contriving to go neither mad nor bald. Anxiously, I searched my stubbly face for the seven warning signals of lovesickness, but I could scarcely blame my pouchy eyes or my winter pallor on too much pining and sighing.

Having noted my own normality, I put on my last clean shirt and went out into the cold, bound on a course of deviant behavior. To begin with, I was making my pilgrimage on foot. Since I suspected Anne might be tearfully sogging her toast at MacDougall Memorial Union, I cut across Garden Street to College. A fair-sized crowd had formed in front of the administration building; I could see gray hoods bobbing and cardboard banners waving above them even from here. Then, as I changed direction, I looked up at the flagpole in front of the building and saw a sweat-suited dummy dangling, hanging there by its knotted bedsheet neck. The closer I got to all the action, the more Alpha Phi Beta fraternity members—a bizarre chorus line in fluorescent turquoise warm-up jackets—I saw swinging their signs at their live opposition, huddled in a protective semicircle to the right of the building.

Preferring to observe rather than to participate in this family feud, I stationed myself under a Scotch pine to the extreme left of the gang war. Townspeople as well as students had begun to weave themselves into the fringes of the crowd; I immediately spotted the three weird sisters, glass cherries quivering with menace, moving toward the main group. Gene Chancellor, who had idiotically kept his hooded sweat shirt on, was effectively blocking the view of several UWU sisters attended by Mrs. Vandervelde, gorging herself like a lamprey on slop-buckets of gossip. I decided to refrain from making obscene gestures until I was sure she could see me. To my immediate right, Reverend Von Ruden and several junior ministers had already bowed their heads in pre-confrontation prayer.

The men of Alpha Phi Beta, along with a few members of less flashy fraternities, had begun to snake-dance around the circle of Covenanters, chanting and brandishing their placards. Wondering what kind of moral and religious convictions Alpha Phi Beta had to uphold, I read some of the signs. "Off the Joggers for Jesus!" said one; "Covenanters Are *Murderers*!" proclaimed another. A football-shouldered fellow waved a sign urging, "God Bless Fraternities."

"Covenanters, Murderers," the demonstrators chanted, and blank-faced students lounging on the sidelines began clapping their hands to the rhythm of the refrain. Three frail old men in blue uniforms—the campus security police—had started circulating helplessly through the crowd. Big Jim Smith and Fat Freddy Mays, the latter blowing dust off his bullhorn, came galloping out of their squad car to push through the crowd and stand glancing uneasily up at the cold gray sky, waiting for some visible manifestation of Witherspoon's will. The doors of the administration building finally opened, and a squat, thick-necked college spokesperson sporting a stiff black crewcut and a tiny gray mustache came forward, raising his ham-hock arms to signal silence. I was convinced this aging Japanese wrestler had to be the football coach, calling for sportsmanlike conduct but, from fragments of crowd talk, I found out it was Dr. John Knox Horton, president of Witherspoon College, still wet from the two-mile swim he started his strenuous day with. "Ladies and gentlemen," he began; but the crowd was snarling like a collection of pit bulls slavering for somebody's leg. Fat Freddy thus tossed Dr. Horton his bullhorn, which bounced off the college president's shoulder before it rolled under a burly Alpha Phi Beta's feet. The demonstrators, taking this for a tear-gas cannister thrown among them, abruptly stopped chanting and lowered their signs. Consequently, Dr. Horton ordered the marchers to disperse in the name of Witherspoon's Twelve Traditions which, in his belief, they had broken faith with, and shudderingly informed them that—as an Alpha Phi Beta alumnus—he intended to suggest national censure for their violation of fraternal principles.

Finally Horton got around to mentioning the murder, or so I inferred. "You are aggravating the circumstances surrounding this unfortunate incident," he said to his fraternity brothers, his voice husky with betrayal. "You are hindering the very processes of justice you profess to uphold. Even now, the dedicated officers of our own state police are continuing their round-the-clock efforts to return our campus to normalcy. You must go back. . . ."

The turquoise tide of Alpha Phi Beta drowned their distinguished alumnus out. "They've got the girl, so let's help them get the rest of these stupid Jesus freaks!" shouted their standard-bearer. He brought his "God Bless Fraternities" banner down on the closest Covenanter's head. A few other fraternity men started scuffling with the cowering Christian athletes, which finally set Big Jim and Fat Freddy in motion. Flapping their skinny hands while yelling, "Go get them!" the cherry-hatted old ladies had turned themselves into a cheering section, although I wasn't sure for which side. I saw no sign of Detective Lieutenant Hershey or any other dedicated state policeman; the campus security cops were timidly trying to keep all spectators stationary. Although I would have expected Holly Willie McKenna to appear with TV trays of loaves and fishes to calm the crowd, both he and Campbell were no-shows.

The edges of the crowd had completely congealed when, right under Big Jim's nose, two activist Covenanters suddenly snatched a cardboard sign and trampled on it triumphantly while Officer Smith was still threatening to bust Alpha Phi Beta heads. Additional administrators milled around their office building's double doors, frantically beseeching somebody else to do something. Then the *real* police came roaring to the rescue; Hendricks and two facelessly efficient troopers speedily collected the right culprits and sent the crowd on about other people's business. I stood silently under my pine tree, taking second glances at every passing female with shoulder-length blond hair.

"Can we catch our breaths with you for a moment, Mr. Waltz?" a voice behind me suddenly asked. It was Becky DeVore and her cropped, shrunken shadow, Lillian McKenna, who, judging from the look on her ferret's face, was figuring out how long it would take her to sear off my eyebrows. "I think we missed most of the excitement, which is probably just as well," her companion went on. "I hope no one was hurt?"

"Not seriously. But the outside world seems to have taken some notice." I nodded at the two TV cameramen filming the borough's volunteer firemen cautiously cutting down the Covenanter dummy.

"So I see," Dr. DeVore said soberly. "We all seem to be doing our best to give ourselves as much notoriety as possible. It seems to me that those of us who have to have some kind of group activity might start with offering a prayer for that poor girl who's in custody."

"I keep telling Will he should screen these people somehow," said Mrs. McKenna, rummaging through her handbag for something—a hat pin to fend me off with, perhaps. "*I* could tell this one meant some kind of trouble for us."

"Did you know Melissa Parsons at all?" I hastily inquired of Dr. DeVore so I wouldn't voice my earnest regret that the men of Alpha Phi Beta hadn't hoisted Lillian McKenna up on the flagpole instead of a bundle of rags.

"I'm sorry to say I didn't, Mr. Waltz. I keep thinking I might have been able to help her somehow," said Becky DeVore, maternal solicitude clouding her bright, rosy face.

"She looked halfway mental to me to begin with," insisted Mrs. McKenna, directing gusts of powder out of a large, heavy compact up into my nostrils. "With those big buggy eyes."

"Did you enjoy the service yesterday, Mr. Waltz?" asked Dr. DeVore, determined to make small talk for two. "If 'enjoy' is really the word, of course."

"I certainly enjoyed hearing you sing," I told her. "But the singing more than the song, I'll have to admit. A bit ghoulish for my taste."

"That's a very interesting reaction," Dr. DeVore said thoughtfully, her scholarly energies clearly engaged. "But to someone who hadn't grown up in our tradition, I expect it *would* sound that way. The Christian concept is that the blood of the Lamb of God—who gave his own life for us—cleanses us of our sins."

"Which reminds me—" I said hastily, since beside me Lillian McKenna was taking a deep breath so she could set us both straight on Christian doctrine.

"I hope to spend some time at the library later this morning," Dr. DeVore assured me with equal haste. "That is, if I don't fall asleep in there like one of my own freshmen. I won't be in any shape at all for choir practice this evening. For some reason there were lights flicking on and off and car noises on McCorkle Street last night, even after one in the morning. I hope it wasn't some of these fraternity members. I'm almost beginning to be a little afraid of them."

"It's these outside agitators; that's what it is, Rebecca," said Mrs. McKenna, bobbing her chignon around in a circle that started and ended with me.

"If you'll excuse me, I think I'd better go check in with

Lieutenant Hershey," I mumbled, waving vaguely at the ladies as I hurried off in the general direction of a couple of cars flashing their turn signals in the parking lot behind the firemen, one of whom was carrying away the Covenanter dummy like the booby prize at the county fair. I had just spotted Anne trying to cut through a mob of undergraduates to the flagstone path that led to the student union. Shoving them out of the way with far greater efficiency, I caught up with her at the edge of the walkway. When we were ten inches apart, she gave me another of those bright, impersonal smiles she'd used ever since Monday morning to set me down as a public nuisance. Like the daily Dow, our relationship was always a little off. "Dr. Horton's decided to cancel classes again today," she said after I'd silently offered my arm. "Have you had breakfast?"

"I'd really rather have you," I leered, suddenly incapable of saying anything at all that sounded as if I might want anything more out of life than a good piece of ass.

Anne had cleared her throat for a labored speech beginning, "Please, John," when Sally Richardson and Leslie Fielding, several yards away, saw us and started toward us. "How about breakfast?" they chorused, saving us from ourselves and each other.

However, having seen through us, during breakfast the two women decided that we should join them that evening for beer, conversation, and furniture-moving, in preparation for replacing their bricks and boards with some antiques they had recently purchased. "That is, if we can still find a truck to bring our things back from Mullinsville," said Fielding. "We had arranged to borrow Tony Antonides's. He said we could come get it tonight at seven. We can meet you two at your place afterwards, Anne, provided the plot unthickens a little. Are they letting him out, or what?" All three women looked at me expectantly, awaiting the latest all-county bulletin.

I had no idea whether Antonides had been released by now or not, nor did I know when Hershey wanted my own deposition concerning Melissa Parsons's confession—nor even if my friend the lieutenant was still hiring the handicapped. So I went to Reuben Tranter Hall in search of him, leaving the ladies to their scholarly activity. I intended to talk to no more women until noontime; what I really needed was a week at an Ernest Hemingway Rehabilitation Camp off in an all-male wilderness.

Having regressed into a public servant under the strain, Hershey had left me a message indicating he'd see me for a debriefing this P.M. at his earliest convenience. By now my back hurt like hell from overexertion on Anne's cold living-room floor, and my stomach whirred and buzzed with unblended emotions, so I went back to the inn for some sleep. I had made it halfway to safety when Mrs. Vandervelde materialized at the foot of the stairs. "Didn't come in at all last night, did you?" she said with malevolent satisfaction. "You'll still have to pay for the room, of course. There's no getting around *that*."

"Of course," I murmured weakly, and walked unsteadily to my room, where I collapsed on the bed. I got two hours' sweaty sleep, enough so that Dr. Blackstone would at least delay certifying me until after lunch.

The old woman's dark-towered house had been built on a hill overlooking Church Street, at the opposite end from the Presbyterians and Methodists. Carrying my complete line of urbane witticisms, I knocked on her brass-fitted door like a brash Fuller Brush man. I had expected an ancient butler to extend his mummified hand for my hat and coat, but instead Dr. Blackstone herself came flitting to the door in what appeared to be red silk lounging pajamas set off with all the family jewels. "I'm so glad you could come, Mr. Waltz," she said, extending her hand like a glittering reliquary. "Haven't had an attractive man here since I corrupted the grocery boy with a glass of beer last Christmas. Welcome to this dead old house," she went on, motioning me down a cream-paneled hallway. "Would you care to see it? As long as I'm doomed to maintaining the damn thing, I've gradually tried to make it look a little less like a funeral parlor."

She had succeeded, toning the place like an ash-tinted blonde and lighting the walls with watercolors and line drawings that seemed—surprisingly—original, along with some painfully vivid modern canvases that clashed with her monochromatic color scheme. "My husband's," Dr. Blackstone said, as I went to inspect these agonized abstractions. "Charles Carson Blackstone— you may have heard of him, since you seem to know what you're looking at. He had some small degree of success, even with the New York critics. And there are a couple of his last paintings in the Scaife Gallery down in the city."

"Yes, I recognize the style, if not the name," I said truthfully, having spent many Sundays trying to pick up hippie girls in art galleries. "But I hadn't realized New Arcady allowed any abstract artists across the moat."

"Charles had his roots here, Mr. Waltz. And besides his family, there was always my money to insure our reception here in the borough. I really think Charles chose to stay because—as he so often remarked—he painted best with his hands tied behind his back, in a straitjacket. Take this one, for example," Dr. Blackstone instructed me, pointing to a large, pale canvas pocked by spidery black splotches. In one corner of it was something I would have verbally described as an hourglass, thickly smeared on in dark red. And then I looked at this figure again and realized my hourglass was made of two roughly equilateral triangles, one inverted on top of the other so that their points touched; and I knew what Pete Simon's killer had painted in blood on his victim's office door.

"It's entitled *Arcadian Spring*," Dr. Blackstone said dryly while I stood and stared at this obscene pictograph. I saw now that the background of the painting resembled a grid, or perhaps a taut fishnet, although—given the title of the work—the black splotches burned into it could have been nightmarish needlework flowers. Actually, to my less-than-artistic eye, the middle portion of Blackstone's canvas looked more like a giant flyswatter specked with dead bugs. Yet, staring at *Arcadian Spring*, I felt the same sick horror I'd had to heave up from my guts after I'd seen Pete Simon's mutilated body.

"What do you think of it, Mr. Waltz? Why, what's the matter?'' Dr. Blackstone asked sharply. "You look as if you'd seen a cor—"

"Corpse? Yes, I did," I said, leaning against the wall. "And I think Pete Simon's killer definitely saw this painting." Then I shut up fast, wishing to hell sexual anticlimax hadn't made me start babbling like poor, mad Melissa Parsons.

Dr. Blackstone fixed her wise old cat's eyes on me and ordered me into the parlor. "You do need a drink, Mr. Waltz," she said. "So that you can talk to me—you can, you know. Quite safely. Nor do I know who the killer is," she assured me. "I'm quite cross with myself; I haven't a clue, and I do think I should be able to be a *bit* more intelligent about all this. Except that it seems to be some cult thing—isn't that the latest theory?—and I'm not at all knowledgeable about such groups. I'm even behind on my own research." She was at the sideboard now, deftly mixing double martinis, stripping lemon peel like a professional.

"Which is?" I asked, browbeaten into polite interest.

"Practical applications of neo-Freudianism, and I'd dearly love to bore you with it, but some other time." The learned old lady sat down across from me and lifted her glass. "Here's to the sun shining again on New Arcady. It's been twenty-three days, I believe."

"Now, Mr. Waltz," Dr. Blackstone said briskly, after a couple of belts had restored us both, "what bearing has that cruel painting of Charles's on this murder case?"

Rapidly, I explained my theories, and Becky DeVore's, of the possible ritualistic significance of the bloody triangles daubed on the victim's office door. "But it really looks more like a deliberate attempt to evoke that 'cruel painting,' as you called it yourself—as if the killer were literally trying to tell us something. What did *Arcadian Spring* mean to your husband?"

"Never ask an artist that, Mr. Waltz," Dr. Blackstone instructed me, "especially if he prides himself on being nonrepresentational. 'Cruel' is merely my own word for the work." Suddenly she fell silent, staring into the clouded crystal of her martini. "But, of course, what we're looking for is how the murderer felt about *Arcadian Spring*," she sighed. "So many people have stood and stared at that painting, along with all the others—my entire collection has an absolutely horrid fascination for most of my friends and neighbors, who wouldn't dream of having even one of them in their *own* houses—that I can't remember anyone in particular seeming strongly affected by it. At least, not to the point of noticeable obsession."

"What about Witherspoon students?" I asked. "Any atheistical professors ever bring their art classes here?"

Dr. Blackstone nodded. "Yes, I do see what you're driving at. Some student who simply had to run and hide from himself by joining a cult. But I haven't had a class here—I won't even allow groups larger than five; they seem to smudge up the walls—since last year."

I described Melissa Parsons to her, knowing she'd remember the face that any painter worth his camel's-hair brushes would have killed for. I also asked her about Jack Campbell. Having no clear recollection of ever meeting either one of them, my hostess shook her head impatiently.

"Speaking of the Covenanters, Dr. Blackstone," I continued, "did you ever have to hide the booze and entertain Holy Willie McKenna?"

The town's reigning eccentric laughed so hard she slopped her martini. "Forgive me, Mr. Waltz," she gasped, wiping her eyes, "but I'm an old woman who occasionally forgets everything but her memories. Yes, one year when Charles was still alive, I did have all the local ministers and their wives here for high tea. Erhard Von Ruden—whose heart seems to have gone the way of his arteries, by the by—went on and on about graven images. But Will McKenna dared to disagree, saying that Charles could even now dedicate his talent to the Lord by painting a baptismal portrait of every baby born in the borough. Will even suggested that Charles try his hand at china painting for the church bazaar. Whereupon my husband carefully poured his tea out on the carpet and shut himself up in his studio. And proceeded to excommunicate himself ever after from all Protestant churches."

"Had your husband painted *Arcadian Spring* at that point?" I asked after I had savored the old woman's story with her, since it, too, had captured the town's features for me. "Did McKenna see it, do you remember?"

"Let me think," said Dr. Blackstone. "Yes; Will did ask me politely if the title had any connection with New Arcady. I believe I mumbled something about Greek mythology and let it go at that." Having risen to refill our glasses, she paused with her high priestess's shaker in midair. "I must be far too much of a New Arcadian," she said, frowning at me, "to see these people at all clearly. What makes you consider Will McKenna capable of murder?"

Once we were both resettled with our drinks, I highlighted Pete Simon's sexual career, told her the story of Melissa Parsons, and summarized my own speculations concerning the Covenanters' role in the girl's confession. I also admitted that neither Hershey nor I had as yet actually confronted McKenna.

"Then you believe that the girl was psychologically engineered either to commit murder or to confess to it," Dr. Blackstone said gravely. "Well, it's certainly possible, although I wouldn't have thought Will McKenna knew the first thing about how to fine-tune any of his group. Now some of his colleagues—Erhard, for instance—"

The old man of the mountain, enthusiastically smashing heads with his stone tablets. Even discounting Dr. Blackstone's antipathy to clerical amateurs, I could well imagine Reverend Von Ruden orchestrating a massacre. Nevertheless, he had no discernible connection with either the Covenanters or Melissa Parsons, unless she'd neglected to tell me that before straggling after McKenna's gray cotton flock, she'd sought a rival's advice. "Tell me more about the Reverend Von Ruden," I requested my hostess. "He told Hershey and me just the other day that all you New Arcadians were strictly small-time sinners, but he doesn't seem to preach much forgiveness."

"Of course he doesn't," said Dr. Blackstone, her eyes sparkling like her own yellow diamonds. "Erhard's never forgiven himself for his own set of sins. I'm probably the only person in town who knows his tragic secret, because one dark snowy night he made a special point of confessing it to my husband—probably because he thought of Charles as a man of the world, don't you know. Well, when Erhard Von Ruden first came to this country, as a young man just ready to start seminary, he lived with an uncle out near Mullinsville and worked on his farm while he was improving his English. And one summer morning this hopelessly innocent young immigrant buggered a sheep!''

After an uneasy moment I joined in Dr. Blackstone's wicked old woman's laughter. "Sorry if I shocked you, Mr. Waltz," she finally said, wiping her eyes. "I haven't got enough life left to waste it watching my language. Charles, of course, didn't dare suggest *I* might be the proper person for Erhard to tell his sad story to. Erhard's always believed very strongly in the divinely ordained inferiority of the opposite sex. And blamed what he might call his baser instincts on it. I do believe that every time in the last forty years Erhard's ever caught himself making cow eyes at any of the women in his congregation, he's come out with a sermon damning and blasting Mother Eve for turning Paradise into something like one of those honeymoon suites over in the Poconos. And I think he's gotten even worse since his wife died; Elvira managed to make him believe some good occasionally came out of double-X chromosomes, I guess. But I've always tried to talk any woman I ever knew who was getting any pastoral counseling from him into finding somebody else who'd give her some free advice."

"You mean Von Ruden beats down all you formidable UWU types?" I said, genuinely shocked this time. "I'd think the Valkyries would ride right over the likes of Erhard Von Ruden; I've had hoofprints all over me ever since my first night in New Arcady. Even to the son of a Jewish mother, this town seems completely female-dominated."

"So you really think this is a woman's town, Mr. Waltz?" demanded Dr. Blackstone, jabbing her forefinger at me in vigorous emphasis. "It might appear that way to outsiders, but I know better than anyone else that we 'formidable UWU types,' as you called us, are psychologically battered women. Men like Von Ruden and Will McKenna and Horton at the college—and even Peter Simon, I'd say, given his public persona—make all the rules in New Arcady. We women merely enforce them. The town fathers want dutiful daughters to do the donkey work for them.''

The shrewd old psychiatrist gave me a look that told me she'd personally long ago given up any attempts to muster an army of liberation. ''But I shouldn't wonder, Mr. Waltz,'' she said so vehemently that I suspected the town's presiding tyrants had more than once made her fall flat on her well-padded pride, ''if one of us doesn't someday decide on revenge, in some form or another. Provided we don't all o.d. on Christian love first,'' my hostess added, rising abruptly and ushering me into the dining room, where she'd set up an A-list buffet.

''I think Melissa Parsons beat you to it,'' I said, having gotten up just in time to give Dr. Blackstone my arm. ''She's the most psychologically battered woman I've ever met. And I'd love to have a few comments on her situation along with my meal, if I may,'' I prompted the old psychiatrist, seating her ceremoniously.

''You're quite right, Mr. Waltz,'' Dr. Blackstone reflected, sipping white wine. ''As you describe her, the girl has been brutalized: terrorized into her hysterical confession both by her own strong sense of guilt and by some form of external pressure, perhaps exerted by somebody who's filled the psychological void left by Pete Simon when he ended the affair. Maybe even by the killer himself, making an awfully clumsy attempt—which *does* sound something like Will McKenna—to make her take the rap, as they say in those wretched TV things I watch at 2:00 A.M. to take away the taste of the neo-Freudians.'' The old woman poured herself more wine from her Waterford decanter. ''However,'' she said meditatively, ''it's still psychologically plausible that the girl could have savagely murdered her former lover out of a sense that he had raped her, abused her, mutilated *her*, physically and emotionally.''

''And so, adding parricide to incest, she decided on revenge,'' I said mockingly, to ease my own psychic tensions.

"Or someone else did," Dr. Blackstone said quietly. "And, although we may both wish you were joking, your analysis is actually quite sound."

"And we still have to worry about *Arcadian Spring* as well," I said glumly, moving my half-empty plate away.

"Well, you can certainly mention it to Lieutenant Hershey, but do stop being obsessive-compulsive about it," Dr. Blackstone commanded. "I think I shall ply you with brandy while we have our coffee so you'll talk to me about Anne Christensen. What do you intend to do about her?" she asked, pouring out a libation of Four-Star Hennessey to whatever gods were forming a jeering section.

"What does she intend to do about *me*?" I asked plaintively. "Besides send me away."

"Well, if she does, it's absolutely your own fault," Dr. Blackstone said severely. "You could at least be audacious enough to offer her a job. A little economic security might make a new woman of her. Or, be even bolder and ask her to marry you!"

"You mean if she wants the world and the flesh, tell her the devil comes with the deal? Frankly, I think we'd both rather brood over what might have been. It's a hell of a lot less scary that way."

"And I think you're a damn fool!" Dr. Blackstone snapped. "And that the least you can do is to put temptation into Anne's path. Provide her with a few contacts in Pittsburgh."

"Yes, ma'am," I said meekly, thinking that in another century the church hierarchy would have heaved a sigh of relief as it burned Vanessa Blackstone. Besides, I needed to get myself out of reach of the heavy hand she had laid on both my psyche and her own liquor cabinet. Surely the sober folk of New Arcady, WCTU capital of the world, were conspiring to turn me into a hard-core alcoholic.

"Well, it's been delightful, Mr. Waltz," my bad angel said, draining her glass and dismissing me. "I *do* generally lie down after lunch. Please tell Lieutenant Hershey I'm available for consultation. And please forgive me for being a meddlesome old woman. But don't let her go, Mr. Waltz. Don't do that to yourself."

"I'll think twice about it," I promised her half-seriously.

"And that's *precisely* your whole problem, Mr. Waltz," Dr. Blackstone said, nudging me toward the front door. "Even in terms of this murder."

Needing a second opinion, I went to Tranter Hall to talk to Hershey, who by now had probably done enough second-guessing to have pole-vaulted himself at least fifty feet over the truth. He sure looked like a sufferer from cogitational burnout when I walked into his office.

"Waltz, you'll have to wait about half an hour until I can run you through all the formalities," he said, as if he were officiating at my wedding. "Not that there's any point to them; Melissa Parsons is still swearing she killed Simon, but her story stinks like a cheap cigar. She did ride to Coal City with her girlfriend Monday. But we ran a check on every hardware, discount, and department store down there; none of them sold any customer either of the items in question on that particular day. When I called her on it, she said she'd been lying because she'd taken the weapons from friends of her family when she went home two weekends ago, and she was ashamed to admit being a thief! Jesus Christ!" Hershey groaned. I had already noticed that, as well as warping the lieutenant's incomprehensibly positive mental attitude, our mutual frustrations had been gradually corrupting his language.

"Miss Parsons also says she borrowed this same friend's car Wednesday night—which, believe it or not, she really did do —and threw the murder weapons into the Passatawkey River, across the Ohio line. This all has to be taken down, transcribed, typed in triplicate. And it's all totally meaningless," Hershey said in disgust, "because the incisions in the body—and the amputations—were pretty clearly made with a double-edged dagger blade, say maybe even a German Army Kommando Korps issue, circa 1943—like Antonides's. Anyway, Pete Simon wasn't cut up with a crescent-style sheath knife, which is what Melissa Parsons had in mind. Not that *she* knows the difference. And I wasn't about to break the bad news to her." His brown eyes filmed with fatigue, the lieutenant slumped down in his chair.

"Speaking of Antonides, has he been released?" I asked quickly.

Hershey nodded. "At eleven this morning. He said he hated to leave; New Arcady was a worse jail than the county's, and even the food was better there. Which I can believe after eating at the Golden Grill," Hershey said, trying to smile.

"You haven't mentioned New Arcady's all-time fun couple, Dr. and Mrs. Gene Chancellor," I reminded him while his attention was still more or less focused on me.

"I guess Karen's in the clear," the lieutenant said, almost disappointedly. "Colton talked to the legal referral service she gave us, and they do remember her coming in sometime between 12:00 and 12:30 Tuesday. Unless these people's memories are all screwed up, she wouldn't have had quite enough time to rush over to Tranter Hall and slice up her old boyfriend before she drove down to Coal City."

"And Gene?"

"Gene," Hershey said, rummaging through his pockets for something—contact lens cleaner, I saw— "came storming in here this morning trying to accuse us of confiscating a couple of his office reference guides. And it took me at least twenty minutes to get him to admit he left his kid alone Tuesday morning for maybe about forty-five minutes while he was supposed to be minding the store. As a matter of fact, Gene left the house about fifteen minutes after Karen did. And you know where he says he went, Waltz?"

"Out to buy a pistol so he could blow Karen's curly little head off when she got back from the beauty shop?" I suggested. "Or maybe his own?"

"He says he went to the goddamn library, Waltz!" Hershey said, slamming his fist down into his desk as Tony the Greek might have done. "And guess what Professor Chancellor says he was researching this time? In the stacks, of course—he's not sure anybody even saw him go in or out. Do-it-yourself divorce!''

"Cheap bastard," I growled, emulating Antonides in my own turn. "But I guess that means Karen can look forward to being a free woman any day now. So all her worries are over."

"Well, her husband's sure as hell aren't, and neither are mine," Hershey said plaintively, and began squinting at some kind of messages he'd left for himself.

Determined to postpone my dismissal until I'd been filled in on *all* my least favorite people, I asked about McKenna and Campbell. The lieutenant gave me a sour-lemon look that suggested he'd been seeing too much of Mrs. Vandervelde. "Well, if you must know, Waltz," he sighed, "Campbell swore up and down he's never had any direct contact with our current detainee, Miss Parsons. You know how *he* is; the guy always sounds like he's just been groped by the Holy Ghost. Even offered to take a polygraph test to take the heat off his followers and polish up his halo. Shrewd sonovabitch," Hershey said grudgingly. "Anyway, it looks like the demonstration this morning scared the shit out of Campbell. If Dr. Horton orders any student organizations off campus, he's not going to start with Alpha Phi Beta Fraternity."

"Unless Holy Willie gets him key privileges at his favorite foolish virgins' club," I said. "I have a few things to say to our man McKenna himself—although, having met the missus, I suppose I ought to feel sorry for him."

Hershey was busy breaking the points off all his red pencils. "She told me he won't even be back from Coal City until eight o'clock tonight," he said, disgruntled. "He's putting in a twelve-hour day addressing the annual BASH conference: Businessmen Against Secular Humanism. Kicked it off with a prayer breakfast bright and early. And we don't even have enough on McKenna to make him knock off early and get his ass back here."

Since the lieutenant was now giving a few preliminary shuffles to his piles of papers, I told him about Charles Carson Blackstone's grim painting before he could bury himself in the rubble. "Then, in addition to coming down hard on McKenna, we'd better look fast for some artsy-craftsy Covenanters," Hershey said, his eyes brightening. "Hendricks has all their half-assed membership records. I'll get him going checking out their old course schedules in the registrar's office. Tell him to take a break from bicycle-tracking. And Waltz, you go get some coffee—sounds like you could use it—and be back here at 2:45."

Having been officially terminated for the time being, I murmured my thanks for the information and opened the door of Hershey's office—almost into the startled face of Mary Sue Simon.

"Lieutenant, there's something I have to see you about right away," she said before I could even offer her one of my all-purpose apologies. Realizing I had no intention of tactfully withdrawing while he dealt with Pete Simon's widow, Hershey resignedly motioned me to shut the door.

"Oh, hello, Mr.—Waltz, I believe?" Mrs. Simon murmured, distractedly poking at her glazed coiffure. "I didn't know about this at all when you interviewed me Wednesday, or I certainly would have brought it up then," she said to Hershey.

The lieutenant, his face bland, motioned her to sit down, and Mary Sue did, on the edge of her hard chair. "I know you've got that girl who made some kind of confession in jail and've let Tony Antonides back out," she said breathlessly. "But that's all wrong, Lieutenant Hershey; you really shouldn't have. Because somebody called me up just this morning and told me that while he was having coffee over at the Grill one day last week, he heard Tony Antonides tell one of the other maintenance workers he wanted to—*kill*—my husband! For all the things he claimed Pete had done to him."

"Do you mean you received an anonymous telephone call to that effect, Mrs. Simon?" Hershey asked briskly, wholly revived by this fresh complication.

"Oh no, Lieutenant Hershey," Mary Sue assured him in the same breathless tone. "The caller was a faculty member here at the college—Dr. Chancellor from the English Department. What I'd call a nodding acquaintance of ours. I mean, of mine. He said that when he heard you'd released Tony Antonides, he felt it was his duty to tell me about the threats Tony had made against my husband.''

"Funny Dr. Chancellor didn't think it was his duty to tell *me*," Hershey remarked, mainly to himself. "Thank you very much for your information, Mrs. Simon. Believe me, we do appreciate your coming over here to bring this to our attention.''

"And how soon will you be rearresting Tony Antonides, Lieutenant Hershey?" Mary Sue asked hopefully, as she rose to clasp his offered hand.

"I'll certainly see that you're kept informed, Mrs. Simon," Hershey said, graciously showing her to the door. I could hear Mary Sue murmuring at him out in the corridor for several seconds before the lieutenant came back in, sat back down, and said, "Okay, Waltz, I *will* take your testimony now. And that's absolutely all. No theorizing, no questions, no comments!"

After I'd duly complied, I went back to my room at the Inn to theorize in solitude. Tacked to my door was a note admonishing me to call Dr. Christensen "right away," with the latter boldly underlined in peacock blue and further emphasized by a puce exclamation point. Mrs. Vandervelde was working very hard at injecting color into her drab little life.

When I reached Anne, after several suspicious busy signals—Dr. Blackstone was no doubt hammering away at her psychological dents—she explained she'd called merely to confirm our arrangements for seven o'clock. After a blanket apology on my part for any thoughtless remarks this morning or, under the same, last night, she also offered me a quick supper at six—which, of course, would allow us no time to drink ourselves into a stupor or out of our clothes. Already I was anticipating peanut-butter-and-jelly glasses, which turned out to be not far enough from the truth; Anne's supper consisted of cheese-stuffed hot dogs and a dismal marshmallow salad tasting of Sacred Cow recipe-swapping parties. Since I had briefly enslaved several Scarsdale Diet dropouts with my French omelets—only to have them all convert back to anorexia nervosa—I told Anne that she'd have to come to Pittsburgh to eat my cooking and gave her an epic catalog of my culinary triumphs. "My mother always told me I'd make a good husband," I carefully explained. "Especially for a *shiksa* who can't even circumcise her own wieners," I added, heaping my paper plate with frozen onions.

Anne, however, heard my overdone joke as a further indictment against her. "Maybe it's another sign I should stay out of the real world," she said darkly. "Go jump off my ivory tower, even. Or maybe I'm putting all my creative talents into driving you away. '

"For my own good," I said, with a saintly simper stolen from Willie McKenna.

She laughed, and we were friends again. We forsook her condemned man's meal for beer and popcorn on the couch; and when I draped my arm around her like a drive-in make-out artist, she settled against me. I was helping her out of her unyielding stretch jeans when the telephone rang. The clock, we saw, said ten after seven: time to zip up for the outside world, unless Richardson and Fielding had had the foresight to be unavoidably detained for another hour. "Hello," I said eagerly into the receiver. All I heard was a muffled gasp, as if an emphysema sufferer were breathing into my ear. I was about to tell the gang at the Alpha Phi Beta house to go string a few of their pledges up on the flagpole when a faint voice pleaded, "Please don't hang up, John. Please don't. It's us, I mean it's me—"

"Les? Leslie?" I was scared out of my few remaining wits. "What is it? Where are you?"

Leslie Fielding, as far as I could tell, was trying hard to say something intelligible, but all I could comprehend was the word "please" again. There also seemed to be a lot of background interference, people moving around, somebody murmuring to Leslie in a low, hoarse voice.

"Please come," Leslie got out at last. "Tell Anne. When we came down here—" She made a harsh, scraping sound in her throat. Then her voice was gone again.

"When you came down here, what?" I said sharply. "Where?

Leslie, where the hell are you?" Anne, who had gone to comb her hair, was back beside me, asking no questions but pacing the length of the couch, having picked up both my fear and my numb bewilderment.

"John," a second voice said tonelessly. "It's Sally Richardson. Les and I found Tony. With his throat slashed. Ripped, sort of. Like some dog had done it. We're here at Becky DeVore's. Upstairs," she added needlessly.

So human error—Hershey's and mine—had cost us another murder. While the state police filled out forms in triplicate and their court jester played art critic, the murderer—in pursuit of omnipotence—had had to kill Tony Antonides. Tear his throat out. So we'd know it wasn't an outsider, some drunk from down at the Eagles' Club swiping at Tony with a kitchen knife.

"We'll be right down," I told Sally. "You've already called the police?"

"Yes. The borough cops, too," she said wearily. "Could you bring us some whiskey? Les is about out of her head."

Praying we'd arrive before the borough police, Anne and I hurried down her hazardous steps, cut through her neighbor's snowcrusted yard, and ran into the dank green house where Antonides had been arrested only two nights ago. At what sounded like an alarmingly slow shuffle, Becky DeVore, wrapped in a blue velvet bathrobe reminiscent of her funeral costume, came down the steps to let us in. "I'm so sorry, Anne," she said in a pathetically thick voice, when she'd at last reached the storm door, her eyes so vague I wasn't quite sure she knew who I was. "I suppose—somebody ought to walk me around. In the snow. And all I wanted was just one good night's sleep. . . ."

Embarrassed for all three of us, I followed Anne and her guide, now leaning into the bannister, up the stairs. Sally Richardson—very much in charge and in control, belying my own previous type-casting of her as the soft, dependent femme of the pair—came out on the landing to conduct us into the living room, where Leslie, her dark, handsome face streaked with dirt and tears, sat slumped on the couch like a disjointed doll. Just as Anne splashed some whiskey into a teacup for her and handed it to Sally, Becky DeVore sank down on the couch and closed her eyes. With some difficulty, Sally squeezed her over to the end of the sofa and began forcing whiskey down her lover's throat. "Tuinal—I looked," Sally explained. "We had to knock and knock to wake Becky up at all. She must have taken more than one pill. That was what about finished Les," she added with a shiver. "We thought that after that—thing—had finished—in the cellar—he'd come upstairs after Becky *too*."

"Why don't you go make some tea for her, Anne?" Sally suggested in a firmer voice after a moment of anxiously stroking Leslie's throat to make sure she kept down her bourbon. "Les could use some, too."

Wishing I could help myself to enough Tuinal for a three-day blackout, I sat down in Becky DeVore's armchair, facing the three women crowded uncomfortably together on the couch. "What happened?" I asked, of no one in particular, since I wasn't even sure what we were talking about at this point. Dr. DeVore, who'd briefly opened her eyes, seemed to be going into another nod. It occurred to me that I'd soon have to assume my proper masculine role and go look at the body. Frankly, I much preferred making *any* kind of conversation and would have welcomed the company of Big Jim and Fat Freddy, who had inexplicably failed us. And what the hell was keeping Hershey?

Sally helped herself to some whiskey. I noticed that she was sweating slightly. "Tony said we could still have it. His truck," she said in a monotone. "As long as we left him Les's car. So we got here a few minutes before seven. The lights were all on. The truck was in the driveway. But we couldn't find him. We went around to the side of the house. The cellar door was half-open. Then we *found* him," she finished, forcing the words out.

"He was on his back. I think they turned him around. Over," said Leslie, slowly and painfully coming to life. "So they could cut him like that." She made a metallic sound in her throat. In the same moment we heard, for the third time in four days, sirens breaching the peace of New Arcady as police cars skidded down dark, silent McCorkle Street, where Anne's neighbors had already shut themselves in for the night.

"Mr. Waltz? Have you been here long?" Becky DeVore said in the sudden jarring silence after the law had braked out front. "I'm ashamed for you to see me like this. Although I think I must be beginning to wake up a little—" She broke off to stare out the window behind me, as if hypnotized by the winking red lights.

I looked out the window also, to reassure myself that I was seeing a state car instead of the borough boys' tubercular Chevy. By the time I made it downstairs, Hershey and his men had thumped across the porch and were pounding loudly on the front door, waking up the entire neighborhood and thus guaranteeing the formation of a crowd—especially as there was nothing else to do in New Arcady on a Friday night except slash buggy tires.

"Waltz," said Hershey, pausing at the foot of the stairs, "did we really have to let this happen?" He too held us jointly responsible. "Don't tell me *you* found the body," the lieutenant went on, peering at me closely—not that I could say that I blamed him; even to myself I seemed an extraordinarily logical suspect.

"No, I didn't," I said grimly. "I just can't seem to shake this black cloud that's been hovering over my head like a homing pigeon ever since I left Pittsburgh. Around here I think they call it predestination."

"Well, whatever they call it, I've got to go take a look at Antonides, so I can get the coroner going on all the fun parts," Hershey said, impatiently checking his own reflex glance about a foot above the top of my head. "Anybody call in what's-his-name —that fussy old maid of a doctor—and have him go through the motions yet?"

"Hershey," I said, falling in behind him, "there's a maiden lady upstairs who's had a few too many downers, and two girls having hysterics. How the hell were we supposed to remember the doctor?"

"Colton, get the town GP here until we can be sure the coroner hasn't lost his brakes on 125," Hershey yelled at the trooper ahead of him. "Ask one of the women to faint over the telephone, if you have to."

"We'll use the outside door to the basement—just the way the killer did—but I'll have your ass if you move it as much as a millimeter," Hershey said on our way back downstairs. "I don't want a single goddamn thing down there disturbed. We'll have to check DeVore's entrance to the cellar too. Naturally, we weren't bright enough to stick to our original plan and search this house today," he mumbled, like an old wino who'd reached the end of his last pint of Rainbow. "Anybody see anything? No, of course not," he answered himself before I'd had time to tell him that upstairs we hadn't even arrived at the stage of sensible questions.

We walked through the snow to the cellar, trying to prevent ourselves from increasing the confusion of footprints. We stopped short at the basement door; somebody had left the overhead light on, so we could see that there was no blood on its peeling surface. Even in the cold, we smelled mildew, urine, the tainted-meat odor of death. The body was in the near corner, along with the washer and dryer. Dirty socks dangled down from the top of the dryer; the washer was mounded with a dark, sodden mass of work clothes. From the doorway, the feet that stretched out toward us seemed much larger than the head, as in a gag photograph. This time, however, the joke was on us.

And this time the murderer had been even tidier than before; except for a few garish splashes on the white enamel of the washer, which had been moved slightly away from the wall, most of the blood was in a thick, dark puddle around the body itself. But the red mush where Antonides' neck was supposed to be made me have to edge myself out the door and stand in the snow, forcing air through my lungs while Hershey scrawled his notes. Up and down the street, I could see lights blinking on, New Arcadians coming out onto their porches, calling to each other in high, anxious voices. A car crawled by, turned around in a driveway, and inched its way back up the street. One of Hershey's men promptly came out of the house to keep concerned citizens technically off the premises. Another car pulled up: Dr. Caldwell.

"Good evening," he said, nodding cordially at me. "And how are you tonight?"

I was about to give him an anatomical answer when Hershey came back out to stand silently a few feet away from me and wait while the doctor rapidly went through his routine.

"Well, I guess Antonides didn't do it," Dr. Caldwell said, briskly shutting his bag as he hurried back to his wife's warmed-over creamed chicken. "Must make your job all the harder. But people are expecting you fellows to bring things back under control; I hear they got a little out of hand over at the college this morning, while the state police just stood around and watched."

Caldwell smiled when he said this, since he'd meant only to expose us to the facts of life in New Arcady; but Hershey and I were looking out at the street, increasingly clogged by students and townspeople, some of them supplied with sandwiches and coffee, standing and watching the lieutenant's men like a sneak preview.

After the doctor had walked around to the front of the house—waving cheerily to a woman in the crowd—Hershey informed me that, as far as he could tell without moving the body, the murderer had again used a claw hammer to stun his victim, before turning this one onto his back to slash his throat. "These two women who found the body—how much do you know about them, Waltz?" the lieutenant asked me grimly. I could tell he'd mentally begun two new files.

"Any college could use a few more like those two on the faculty," I said. "They're both so smart they scare the hell out of me. Told me the murderer has to be somebody with no sense of humor because who could take Pete Simon, or his sex life, all that seriously?"

"I see," said Hershey. "Any chance either or both of them could have been involved with Pete Simon?"

"Not unless they're faking it. They look like a devoted lesbian couple to me. But—" I shut up fast, alarmed at the creative possibilities presented by suspecting my friends of murder.

"Yes, Waltz?" Hershey said, folding his arms like an Indian pondering Paleface asininities. "Or shall we stand here all night and make funny faces at the crowd?"

Much to my own chagrin, I had just remembered the late Peter Simon's definitely unchivalrous remarks about "dykes" Tuesday morning, after Leslie Fielding had stopped by his office. Dutifully, I repeated his comments to Hershey. "Simon told me he didn't think either Leslie or Sally was going to last long at Witherspoon College, so I suppose he could have been planning to make that a self-fulfilling prophecy and/or already quietly trying to get rid of them," I conceded grudgingly. "And both of them are strong women—physically and mentally. And certainly handy with tools. But why in holy hell would either one of them want to kill Tony?" I demanded, in a voice as shrill as Lillian McKenna's. "Not that either one of *us* even has any kind of logical explanation for the killer's encore in there tonight."

"Your friends just might be taking their sweet revenge on men who still think you can't argue with anatomy," Hershey said after a long, cold pause. "So I'm just going to have to break up the act and question them separately. And let's hope old Caldwell's brought Miss DeVore back to life. I have a few questions for her while I'm at it."

We had hoped to slink around to the front with our flashlights off, hugging the pine trees along the side of the house; but the coroner pulled up just as Caldwell came down the stairs, signaling applause for the medical men and scattered boos for Hershey and me from the crowd, as if we'd been a visiting basketball team.

"Anybody still alive in there, Doc?" somebody hollered, snorting like a horse.

"If there is, it's no thanks to the police," a woman in front answered, hefting her picnic jug. "What are we paying our taxes for, anyway?"

Trooper Colton, who was six-feet-four, went to edge the crowd back with a measurable amount of silent menace, his right hand casually resting on his revolver. Then, presumably to stop the whole show, Big Jim and Fat Freddy came coasting down Mc-

Corkle Street at fifty miles an hour, escaping multiple charges of vehicular homicide by only a few inches. Nonetheless, the crowd cheered the arrival of two of their own.

Shielded by Fat Freddy's bulk, Hershey and I slipped upstairs, where Dr. DeVore—fully dressed now, and apparently fully conscious—was offering tea to Hershey's two remaining subordinates.

"You girls entertaining the troops?" I murmured to Anne. Hershey promptly told Richardson and Fielding to count on spending the rest of their evening at Reuben Tranter Hall, where he would be holding his own all-night vigil after the body had been removed from the basement and every dirty sock duly itemized. Hendricks was already tackling Tony's apartment, and with reluctant politeness Hershey told Becky DeVore he'd have to keep her up for a while examining the indoor entrance to the basement.

"Lieutenant, there's something I probably should have told you the minute you got here—if I'd been able to make any sense," Becky said slowly, in a tone that clearly indicated none of the rest of us could possibly judge her as harshly as she had herself. "Except that I'm not really sure how much I should trust myself. For all I know, I might have been—how do the students put it? —freaking out? Hallucinating," she articulated fiercely, her eyes on a throw rug the lieutenant's men had ground cinders into, rather than on her interrogator's face.

Hershey, who was too overwrought for his usual display of forbearance, impatiently signaled our hostess to tell him the rest of it.

"Well," she began with a troubled sigh, "between the funeral yesterday and life in general, I felt I just couldn't keep going unless I took a day off and did nothing but sleep. For sixteen hours or so instead of my usual four and a half, which is about all I usually manage—" Becky DeVore was talking to Hershey, but she looked straight at me, so I nodded my sympathy; for tonight I could quite honestly state I knew just how she felt—"so at two o'clock this afternoon I took one of the pills Dr. Caldwell had prescribed for me and went to bed. When I woke up, it was dark, and I'm ashamed to say I had no idea how long I'd slept. But by the clock it was only just before six; so I got up for a drink of water and, I must admit, another pill—Dr. Caldwell's already given me the scolding I deserve for that, but one just doesn't seem to work anymore. . . .''

This time Hershey gave Becky DeVore an all-forgiving nod, since the poor woman was sitting there literally wringing her hands, which I'd never been quite sure it was even possible for a human being to do.

"Well, I thought I heard a noise, so I wandered into the living room," Dr. DeVore went on, inhaling and exhaling with her entire rib cage. "I've always been afraid I'll find rats in this old house, coming up from the cellar—" This time she stopped to look for confirmation from Anne, who made an appropriate face.

"Then I looked out this front window here; for some reason, I felt *afraid*, not that I've ever believed in what some people call premonitions," Becky hesitantly assured the lieutenant. "Actually, the street light out front—the one right across from the house—was shining in; it can make an awful glare in here. And—" she quavered, after another pause for an audibly deep breath, "right under the light I saw somebody walking down the street. Somebody dressed like a Covenanter. In a gray sweat shirt with the hood up."

With a look on her flushed face that belonged to a St. Francis caught tearing the wings off his private collection of horseflies, Becky DeVore broke off again to glance anxiously around the room at each one of us, all of whom must have looked just as glassy-eyed as she had thirty minutes ago. "Do you think it might have been something like the power of suggestion?" she asked us anxiously. "Certainly the Covenanters have been a lot on our minds lately; and most of us seem to be carrying tales every time we open our mouths, even when we don't mean to. And now here I am adding more fuel to the fire, since I really can't be sure I saw what I thought I did."

"This individual dressed like a Covenanter you think you saw this evening at about 5:55 P.M.," said Hershey, clearly remaining neutral, "was walking under the street light across from the house? Continuing on down the street? Not crossing the street or standing still?''

"Oh dear," Becky sighed, pressing her hands to her feverish cheeks, "I don't *think* the person was standing still, or crossing the street. But then I can't be sure about that either."

"Did you happen to notice how tall this person was, Dr. DeVore?" I put in. "Did he seem unusually tall or short to you?" I hoped she'd immediately tell me she thought she'd seen a gray giant so Hershey and I could cross everybody off our maddeningly long list except Gene Chancellor, who had seemed to want to make sure the dead man down in the cellar was indicted for Pete Simon's murder—or, of course, the Covener of the Covenanters, Jack Campbell.

"Let me see," Becky said, after staring out at the street light for a moment. "I don't remember the—figure—seeming especially tall. Maybe more on the short side—even shorter than average. I *think*, Mr. Waltz," she broke off doubtfully.

"And what did you do after you looked out the window and noticed this individual under the street light?" Hershey asked her.

"I went back to bed and back to sleep," Dr. DeVore said with another long sigh. "And, oh, how I wish I hadn't!"

"And you didn't see or hear anything else? Say, between six and six-thirty? Any noises downstairs? Voices? Doors banging?" Hershey said, likewise resorting to the power of suggestion.

"If I had," Becky said, gripping the coffee table in front of her to prevent herself from wringing her hands again, "it might have saved Mr. Antonides's life. *That* ought to keep me awake at night! No, I didn't hear anything, Lieutenant," she assured him, blinking back tears, "until Leslie and Sally—Dr. Fielding and Dr. Richardson—started pounding on my downstairs door at—what time was it again? Just after seven? I'm not being much help to you at all, Lieutenant, am I?"

Without waiting for an answer to her obviously rhetorical question, Becky DeVore lifted her eyes to the ceiling as if she could actually see my black cloud up there. Automatically, I followed her gaze, easing my own tensions by picturing a fat white dove dropping down with the secret word we so badly needed, with the needle stuck as it was on "Convenanter."

"When you two drove down McCorkle Street and pulled in the drive here," Hershey was saying to Richardson and Fielding, "did you pass any other cars? See anybody biking down the street? Anybody out jogging after dark? Taking out the garbage? Did anything on this street specifically attract your attention?"

"Nothing besides John's car which, just as Anne's neighbors do, we expect to see here," Leslie said with a small smile.

Hershey was listening to her explain that she and her housemate had conscripted Anne and me for the evening. "And what did you say you were doing between 5:00 and 7:00 P.M., before you came over here to pick up Antonides's truck?" he quickly asked Sally. She hadn't said a damn thing, but I could tell the lieutenant was trying hard to divide and conquer.

"We went to Coal City. To pick up some supplies. The last place we stopped was the liquor store. That was probably around 6:30. Since it's Friday night, it was fairly crowded, but any New Arcadian hiding behind the Carlo Rossi would probably remember us," Sally said dryly.

"If you promised them a fresh start somewhere else, they might even come through with an alibi for us," Leslie put in, having recovered her scorched-earth sense of humor.

The coroner came up the stairs and, staying well out of it, motioned to Hershey from the doorway. Secure in my unofficial capacity, I followed him downstairs to Antonides's apartment, where the police had found nothing of interest except—unavoidably—a forgotten sack of potatoes fermenting under the kitchen sink.

The coroner told us he thought that the Greek had been killed sometime during the hours between five and seven; the cold of the cellar had probably hastened the onset of rigor mortis, making it difficult to fix the exact time of death. Again the murderer had chosen to mutilate a dying man; struck at the base of the skull by his assailant's hammer, Antonides, halfway in a kneeling position, had toppled over face down onto the cement floor. In the coroner's judgment, the killer had continued to batter the back of his victim's head for several minutes before he turned Tony over to hack out his throat.

So far, the coroner's findings were giving me nothing besides a bad case of combat fatigue. Then Hershey and I heard something to restore us to the path of foolish optimism and bring our blood sugar levels back up. In moving the body out of the basement, Hershey's men had discovered that the killer had hauled his victim around in an imaginary semicircle, making the body lie parallel to the front of the washing machine. Initially, however, the corpse had been at an oblique angle to the left side of the washer.

Ignoring the crowd out front, who seemed ready to throw rock-centered snowballs at us, Hershey and I headed back to the basement. "Why would the killer want to change the position of the body?" I asked. "You wouldn't think he'd be all that worried about how things looked down here." Unaccountably, I was wondering how Charles Blackstone would have painted this scene in the cellar, on this first day of another Arcadian spring.

Hershey was carefully measuring the space between the washer and the wall. "I was positive Antonides had shut this thing off in the middle of a load to perform an autopsy on it, which he was involved in when the killer came up behind him, but the Greek sure didn't leave himself much room for that," he said, puzzled. "And why would the killer take a sudden interest in do-it-yourself projects? Assuming he moved the body to take a look at the washer."

"Or behind the washer," I said excitedly. "Hershey, I'm going to have you suspended for stupidity. Your men found no tools on the body, or anywhere around the body. Or anywhere near the washer. So Tony was doing something else besides screwing around with the washing machine."

"Okay, Waltz, what?" asked Hershey, pantomiming polite resignation.

But I had struck gold instead of rusty water pipes for a change.

"He'd found something down there, damn it! Something stuck behind there. While he was trying to figure out why his washing machine had started doing a St. Vitus's dance."

"What are you telling me, Waltz?" Hershey demanded, having absolutely no faith in any revealed truths from me. "What was supposedly down there behind the goddamn washer? In your exalted opinion, of course?"

"Something connected with Simon's murder that the killer had hidden there: one, to implicate Antonides or, two, just because it looked like a good hiding place. If we buy alternative two, it must have been something even Antonides wouldn't have been dumb enough to ignore. So that the killer had to commit another murder to get it out of here. Especially if the killer was Gene Chancellor! We certainly don't know that this shorter-than-average person in a sweat suit Becky DeVore says she saw across the street just before six o'clock was—if not the result of too much stress and Tuinal—actually the person who killed Tony. And the reason Gene Chancellor may have wanted Tony safely back in jail was so he could sneak over here and get the evidence out from behind Tony's washer."

"Well, Waltz," Hershey said with a skeptical grin, "you still have to tell me: one, what Gene Chancellor stuck down behind the washing machine and, two, where Gene Chancellor has it now. *If*, of course, the killer *is* Gene Chancellor!"

"Since you give me so goddamn little credit, Hershey," I said, "I think I'll pass the buck. And get out of this frigging cellar before I have to figure out whether to hold you or Witherspoon College financially responsible for my hospital costs."

Although the crowd outside seemed to be shouting its acclamation, Sergeant Hendricks was now standing at the basement door impatiently waiting for a chance to deflect his superior's energies. "Lieutenant," he said in a harrassed tone, "you'd better come tell the TV people cruising around to move their ass out of here. Colton's keeping them back, but those two local yokels playing cops and robbers are trying for their own series."

By the time we made it out front, however, Big Jim and Fat

Freddy, posturing for the Mobile Mini-cam unit struggling to film from the top of their van, were already has-beens. Holy Willie McKenna, whom I wanted to hang by the roots of his bright Barbie-doll hair, was standing under the street light across from us, preparing to preach to the multitude, who had turned their backs on us to hear him. The driver of the WACK-TV van was trying to turn his vehicle around (if not his sinful life) to capture this charismatic freak on film. Hershey went up to intimidate McKenna just as the old loony put himself into public prayer position, his arms raised in a sweeping Cecil B. De Mille gesture. Determined to make a nuisance of myself, I followed the lieutenant across the street.

"McKenna, I'll have your head for obstructing the police in the performance of their duties and inciting to riot!" Hershey barked at the titular head of New Arcady's cosa nostra. I could tell my friend was in no mood to make allowances for the frailties of old age.

"Lieutenant," McKenna protested in his high-frequency voice, "I merely wanted to ask these good people to open their troubled hearts to the Lord. Surely it can never be interference to offer a prayer." His tone hinted that Hershey would have made it big in the KGB.

"McKenna," Hershey said ominously, "at this point, you'd better offer an alibi. And tell these good people to go home—quietly—before my men start making arrests. And I'll see you at Tranter Hall at nine tomorrow morning. Unless you want a personal police escort to take you there in a squad car."

"Good," McKenna beamed at him. "In the matter of keeping the peace, we do have certain things to discuss of mutual interest. My own Christian young people—the Covenanters—have been persecuted by all this adverse publicity. And what do you intend to do about that poor child, Melissa Parsons, still in custody?"

Since Melissa Parsons had obviously never harmed anyone except herself, I considered this an excellent question, which I had tactfully refrained from asking Hershey myself. Considering McKenna's own probable contributions to his protegee's delinquency, however—I was almost positive he was the "friend" and adviser who had exhorted Ms. Parsons into her nervous breakdown—I regarded his inquiry as not only a tactical error but also a virtually non-negotiable demand for a broken nose.

"I may take some more of you in to keep her company," Hershey said, pointedly stepping aside so that McKenna could move along.

"Actually, Lieutenant, I had planned to formally request her release into the care of myself and Mrs. McKenna," the old man persisted.

It was high time, I thought, to interfere, especially with Hershey there to prevent Big Jim from hauling me in for verbally assaulting a minister. "God damn it, McKenna," I yelled, "you sure as hell *should* hold yourself responsible! You damaged that girl a hell of a lot worse than Pete Simon ever could have! She as good as told me you talked her into joining the Covenanters—and then when she asked you to help her out with her problems, you told her she ought to confess to a murder she didn't commit! For the good of her soul! You really screwed Melissa Parsons up good! The killer should have chopped *yours* off while he was at it!"

I had nudged myself close enough to McKenna to stick my five-o'clock shadow right in his blank white face; but even before Hershey could yank me out of trouble, I abruptly retreated. Even to myself I had sounded too goddamn much like some aberrently foul-mouthed New Arcadian skirmishing with satanic forces every time the carillon in the clock tower changed its program. But Dr. McKenna, apparently too stunned to consider hinting around to the crowd to tear me to pieces, immediately stepped forward for a man-to-man talk. "I have heard you out, Mr. Waltz," he assured me, "but I can't understand a single word you've been saying." His lips trembling, the old man tried in vain to position them in his usual long-suffering smile. "I wish I could take credit for the good you have laid at my door, but Melissa Parsons was inspired to seek out the Covenanters without my own personal help or guidance. As for the evil you accuse me of—" He shook his head in despair at all the false witnessing I had done. "Mr. Waltz, I have never been consulted by Melissa Parsons on any subject whatsoever, personal or otherwise. I've never even spoken to the girl privately!"

Silent at last, Holy Willie began rolling his eyes and tugging on his own wrists as if he'd just developed grand mal. Even without any prompting from him, some members of the crowd had already started stamping around in place and muttering carefully unintelligible threats at Hershey and me. I halfway expected them to start scraping Amish horseshit off the snow to pelt the forces of justice.

"That's what your boy Campbell told us too," Hershey said in a tired voice. "Go on home, folks," he called to the crowd. "There's nothing else here for you tonight. Except some more bad publicity. McKenna, I'll see *you* in the morning."

"Lieutenant," said McKenna, with some dignity, "people have called me many things in my time, but never a liar." He started walking away toward his car, parked back up the hill, then made a deliberate detour straight through the crowd, which rustled after him like a whole village of rats.

"Well," I said in grudging admiration, trailing Hershey back to the house. "Talk about a power play. McKenna took everything right out of our hands. And I'm beginning to think I'm as cuckoo as Melissa Parsons."

"Waltz, what you and your brilliant ideas are beginning to do is get in the way, so why don't you collect your girlfriend and worry about having a meaningful relationship for a while?" Hershey instructed me, looking at the checklist he had scrawled an hour ago. "Or you can stay up there and babysit Miss DeVore if you want. I'd watch it with that lady, though. She seems to think you're a hell of a nice guy for a Jewish atheist."

"You're not planning on making any arrests tonight, are you?" I asked, only half-jokingly.

"I'm planning on crawling over this whole house inch by inch, in case the killer might have left a few droppings this time around.

Instead of jumping to any more screwball conclusions, Waltz. And don't start agitating over gay rights at this late date. Go on and walk your girl home like they used to do in the movies."

Shaking his head, the lieutenant walked briskly away to the basement. I went dutifully upstairs after Anne, praying that in the last hour she'd been blasted by a cosmic headache so I wouldn't have to treat her as a sex object. At this point in my own warped time frame, I could barely manage the stairs, let alone a vigorous romp on the living-room floor. But if I had expected Anne to greet me with passionate restlessness, she looked up from the Scrabble game now therapeutically absorbing all four women at Becky DeVore's with some slight annoyance at this rude male thrusting himself in.

"Let me know how it turns out, will you?" she said to the rest of them, handing me her purse while she hunted her coat.

Oh well, I reflected, walking up the street with this slave to the dictionary and her own spinsterish impulses, *there's more than one form of coitus interruptus*. "You didn't give me a progress report," Anne said as we paused, nervously, at her outer door. "You men must have gotten something done—justice, maybe? —while we women all waited up there for the executioner. Even though we're both exhausted, would you like to come in for a little while?" she asked hesitantly.

"I'll tell you all about it some other time," I said. "No, I would not like to come in. I do hate to disappoint your neighbors, but I am far too tired to make any fresh assaults on your virtue." I bent down to give her a chaste good-night kiss under the porch light, realizing too late that this public display of commitment was even more dangerous here in New Arcady than tom-catting around at five in the morning. Moreover, my behavior was also demonstrably hazardous to my failing mental health.

"I love you," I said, holding Anne for a moment against me. Then I stumbled down the stairs to sit cowering in my car, expecting Big Jim along any minute to arrest me for indecent emotional exposure. Had I said it? Yes, I had said it. Obviously I needed a good long rest. Oblivious to the doomsday preparations in progress all over New Arcady, judging from the lights and the noise, I went back to the inn and stumbled into bed with all my clothes on. For a few hours I slept like one of the Methodist dead in the cemetery behind the Borough Building.

CHAPTER VI
Saturday, March 22

AT 5:30 I JERKED MYSELF OUT OF A DREAM THAT COULD HAVE WON the Rome Prize for some hallucinogenically abstract expressionist and produced several neo-Freudian footnotes for Charles Blackstone's widow. For all I knew, the old lush herself had haunted my nightmares, urging on the fire-eyed nymphs who'd dragged me in triumph around the Astrodome, towing me behind their rusty tricycles. Yet, I reflected, raining ash on my graying sheets, surely I ought to love my enemies for having broken me of a vicious male habit: hormonal dependence on logic. Although Lieutenant Hershey would probably have brained me with his tape recorder for placing any trust in intuitive flashes, my subconscious had just corkscrewed around to the absolute certainty that Pete Simon's and Tony Antonides's killer was definitely not Gene Chancellor; nor Jack Campbell or any of his group; nor one of New Arcady's ruling elders like Dr. William McKenna or the Reverend Erhard Von Ruden, whom it had briefly occurred to me to start building a case against in the absence of sufficient evidence to convict either Chancellor or the Covenanters. Instead, I knew in my aching bones that our fiendishly clever murderer was a woman: a UWU-er, a Sacred Cow, a she-wolf in a fleecy spring coat.

Until now, the lady with the knife had managed to keep Hershey and me all lathered up, running after every bit of fluff shrugged off a sweat shirt while she silently kept score, exulting in our impotence, our willful misunderstanding of her labyrinthian female mind. She'd led me personally astray far enough that I still didn't know which active member of the Christian Women's Club she was. I did know I was forever in her debt, since I owed every quilting scrap of my own half knowledge to the women of the borough of New Arcady—to Anne Christensen and Leslie Fielding and Sally Richardson and Becky DeVore and Vanessa Blackstone, M.D.

Anne, who still thought of herself as "one of them," had initially diagnosed for me the chief cause of this town's hypertension: its codified intolerance of human error, its methodical attempts to monitor all of its inhabitants' vital signs on a mammoth Putrid-Apple computer. Anne had also instinctively known that the killer was female; "someone in a mad rage finally striking back," as Leslie Fielding had informed me; a holy warrioress riding out to perform her bloody ritual. Becky DeVore's cryptic gloss on the Valkyries, the "choosers of the slain," now made perfect sense to me, since yesterday Dr. Blackstone had supplied me with the murderess's initial motive: redress of grievances; revenge against the arbiters of her female destiny, the local lords of creation who'd gang-raped her, kept her eternally putting out—in missionary position—serving up their endless covered-dish suppers and polishing the gilt right off the collection plates, and made her hustle her way to heaven.

Now I had to yank at a stuck door and choose the tigress, crouched to spring. At this late date, I adamantly refused to entertain any ingenious suspicions of Anne. However, as the skeptical Hershey had done, I briefly considered the possible case against Leslie Fielding and Sally Richardson, both—at least on the surface—as eminently sane and rational as they were self-sufficient. Nevertheless, I reflected, if Pete Simon had actually planned to force them out of Witherspoon College—or even if Leslie and Sally had merely believed he was contemplating a covert campaign against them—then the two women might have been impelled to act out their galling resentments against a man who so hypocritically maintained the community standards that damned them. Under these particular circumstances, I had little trouble imagining the two of them (all kinked up from the false positions New Arcady kept forcing them into) deciding to strike at the root of all evil by coolly and efficiently cutting it off. I'd been halfway listening for a fault to open up under their wisecracks. When I'd sounded the two women out on Pete Simon's murder the day after, over coffee at the student union, Leslie had scoffed perhaps a little too loudly at the notion that anyone could have taken Simon or his sexual behavior with the deadly seriousness his—female, she'd insisted—killer obviously had. Both Richardson and Fielding, moreover, were quite capable of offering me elaborate psychological insights in order to lead me straight past the plain truth, if only to satisfy their cravings for irony. And while I was also sure that both women were armor-plated with alibis that pretty well removed them from the right places at the right times, on the basis of what they'd told Hershey last night, they'd had just enough time to drive straight to Tony's from the liquor store in Pine Village Shopping Center, batter him into permanent silence concerning whatever he'd found in his basement, and deposit themselves on Becky DeVore's doorstep so they could feign hysteria at having walked in on a corpse. And if some hideously twisted desire for revenge had driven Leslie and Sally to murder, in my own judgment that automatically made the two women capable of doing a psychological hatchet job on Melissa Parsons that included intimidating *her* into permanent silence on the subject of any recent conversations she'd had with Witherspoon faculty members other than Dr. William McKenna.

Since my own thought processes were about to drive me into a phobic despair that might have kept me cowering behind the door of my room until Mrs. Vandervelde came around for her daily no-knock search and opened it into my face, I tried to assure myself that there had to be other women here in the borough besides my good friends who had unimpeachable motives for murder. Then it struck me that in mentally absolving McKenna and the Covenanters of direct participation in murder, I had tried much too hard to be fair. I remembered wondering for a moment last night why Lillian McKenna had neglected to join the crowd so she could see to it the starch stayed in Will's backbone throughout his confrontation with secular authority. But if little Mrs. McKenna had been the undersized Covenanter Dr. DeVore thought she had seen across the street from her house last night, naturally the woman would have found it more prudent to remove herself from the scene and hear the details of the evening secondhand from her long-suffering husband. And the evening after Pete Simon's murder, Lillian had bitterly condemned the dead man for having introduced the poison of "sex education" into her church's Sunday school and had thus even posthumously grudged him his apparently unassailable position among the movers and shakers at the First Presbyterian. If Mrs. McKenna had also found out about one or more of Simon's after-hours entertainments on his office sofa, I could see the woman immediately losing such sanity as she possessed and—inflamed with rage, armed with the strength of her own monomania—ending Pete Simon's career through murder and mutilation. Moreover, given Lillian McKenna's implacable fanaticism and her shrill glorification of organized violence in the name of her own priorities, I was also sure she would have taken an equally savage pleasure in reducing Melissa Parsons to a raving heap of gray cotton rags.

Needing some more reliably damaging information on Mrs. McKenna's general demeanor and any particularly blatant aberrations that might make her an even more promising candidate for the violent ward at Dixmont State Hospital, I decided to disturb Dr. Blackstone with a telephone call, rationalizing that she'd be delighted to return to active duty. The old woman answered, in fact, on the first ring, her ear still attuned to medical emergencies. "I'm truly sorry to bother you at this hour, Dr. Blackstone," I began, "but—"

"No, you're not, Mr. Waltz, so do get on with it, without building up any suspense," she croaked expectantly.

So I told her what I'd been thinking for the last forty-five minutes, insofar as it concerned bolstering my case against Sally Richardson and Leslie Fielding or, as I fervently hoped, Lillian McKenna. "Have any of these three women been over at your house lately?" I concluded. "Have you gotten stuck holding any long, dry luncheons for the girls in the last month or so? This might be a lot more important than it sounds," I explained into the skeptical silence at the other end of the line.

"Especially if Lillian or Leslie or Sally had a fainting fit over *Arcadian Spring*," Dr. Blackstone finally said. "Or am I reading your mind right, Mr. Waltz? I've had to hold so many enforced social affairs here that I sometimes think this house should be declared in the public domain; I really can't keep track of all the women's groups who come and coo over my decor. But I do believe all three of them were at my indoor picnic for UWU at the end of February. The only reason I remember that particular occasion is that somebody dribbled pickle juice down the gray squirrel collar Lillian was so proud of having found at the after-Christmas sales."

"And what did Mrs. McKenna do about it?" I asked eagerly. "Choke the poor soul with it?"

"Oh no, Mr. Waltz. Poor Lillian was almost in tears over it, mainly because Leslie, as I recall, suggested she might want to give her fur piece a decent burial. Becky DeVore finally had to play peacemaker, and—"

"Has Lillian McKenna ever made any nasty cracks of her own about your husband's paintings?" I broke in. "Can you remember her telling you she doesn't quite trust modern art? Or asking you what she was supposed to be seeing on that big, ugly canvas called *Arcadian Spring*?"

"Every woman in New Arcady who gets invited to any of my functions here *of course* asks to look at Charles's paintings, no matter how many times she's been here before, and loads them with adjectives. 'Powerful,' is, I believe, the current favorite. If Lillian has a minority opinion, she's managed to keep it to herself. No, Mr. Waltz," my reluctant informer protested, "I don't think you have much of a case against Lillian McKenna, although I can certainly see why she strikes you as almost a textbook murderess. Nor do I think *Arcadian Spring* is going to solve anything for you. And how do you know, by the way," she asked abruptly, "that *I* couldn't have killed those two men? I'm rather hurt that you automatically ruled me out. Anger can actually generate tremendous physical power. And I might have more reasons than you'd ever care to hear to want to take my revenge on this town," she added in such a somber tone that for a moment I thought my imagination hadn't run nearly wild enough. "Or I could have bought myself some student and furnished him with one of those sweat suits so he could do my dirty work for me," the old lady suggested brightly.

"And I could be keeping Mrs. Vandervelde chained up naked in the closet, a sight to make strong men piss in their pants!" I retorted. "I wish you'd tend to your television set, Dr. Blackstone. Or conjure up my murderess for me. Why can't you find me the right one of you?"

"Perhaps I haven't unearthed your murderess for you yet, but I certainly found you the right woman, Mr. Waltz. Have you done anything more about Anne Christensen yet, by the way?" the old woman demanded.

"No, I haven't," I said irritably. "You might call it a matter of priorities. I'll get back to you," I told my self-styled therapist, annoyed at her attempts to force an emotional quadriplegic like me out of my wheelchair. "*After* I've done my daily chores for Lieutenant Hershey. In the meantime, since you seem to know who *did* kill Simon and Antonides—and I get the distinct feeling you do, even though you probably won't even admit it to yourself—try to bring yourself to blow her cover."

Suddenly I believed every word I'd been saying. After a long pause, in which I could hear the old woman doing what sounded like yoga breathing exercises, she finally answered me, with audible reluctance. "Well, Mr. Waltz, I don't think I had the slightest idea until about ten seconds ago," she admitted. "But since I haven't a scrap of evidence on which to base anything I might be thinking, it might be better for both of us if we just assumed I'm getting senile at last. All I can point to is a feeling I have about—this woman—that the only way she could let it all out was by murdering somebody. And as someone who's supposed to be least a semi-scientist, I don't really think I ought to start drawing conclusions from what some people call psychic intuitions. Or let you and Lieutenant Hershey draw them. And I have every confidence the two of you can hang onto the ball without my running interference for you.''

"We're supposed to wait until she creeps up behind us with her handy hammer?'' I shouted into the receiver. "All you seem to be concerned about is protecting one of your own, like all the rest of these goddamn soul-suckers!''

"Mr. Waltz, if I thought she meant you any harm at all, I'd tell you this instant,'' Dr. Blackstone said soberly. "I can't imagine she ever meant to kill Tony Antonides. *If* she's guilty of anything at all. I'm not terribly convinced myself. But if you and the lieutenant haven't come up with anything by Monday morning—and if she hasn't broken down by then, as I suspect she might—I'll go to work on her myself. Hand you her head on a platter, as it were. But you have no idea how much I hope I'm wrong.''

"I hope you are too, because it would sure make things a hell of a lot simpler for all of us, especially me and Lieutenant Hershey. Thanks so much for your cooperation with state and local law enforcement agencies, Dr. Blackstone.''

"You're most welcome, Mr. Waltz,'' she replied, sublimely indifferent to my sense of powerlessness. "And you'd better get busy. Tomorrow's Sunday, you know—our day of rest. Here in New Arcady we don't even cut our grass on the Sabbath. Goodbye, Mr. Waltz,'' my tormentor said airily, and hung up.

Trying—contrary to habit—to accentuate the positive, I realized that I'd run out of cigarettes only fifteen minutes before Horny Hank's opened for business, which would also allow me to escape from my room and my own dark thoughts of revenge on Vanessa Blackstone and every apprentice witch in her coven.

While shaving, however, I had the great bad luck to remember, on the basis of enforced exposure to TV evangelism, which Biblical malefactor had actually had his head served up like the Businessman's Special: John the Baptist. The prophet's lips had been sealed, moreover, by a wrathful woman. If I was going to be prone to prophetic nightmares, at the moment I would have greatly preferred to have been named Ezekiel or Jeremiah.

I went out into what passed in Western Pennsylvania for a spring thaw with a great sense of relief, although the Edwardian fog that had come in with the cold drizzle would have had Jack the Ripper convinced he ought to relocate here in New Arcady. This morning I seemed strangely alone on the misty moors; no Covenanters huffing and puffing their way to the pearly gates came crashing blindly into me; no faculty wives desperate for Froot Loops mowed me down on my way into Whitaker's. Instead, I sent the heavy door swinging into Becky DeVore's soft mid-section just as she struck me with the point of her furled umbrella, which wedged itself between my ribs, while wet folds of flowered taffeta clung tenaciously to my coat. To release myself and the door, I made a quarter turn and fell into Dr. DeVore's arms. By executing a kind of amateurish minstrel-show shuffle, we at last got free of each other. Unable to come up with any more gracious form of apology, I stood out on the pavement while Becky entered the store, and went in myself only after I had seen her disappear into the maze Horny Hank had laid out for his customers.

Since I had to duck down the sundries aisle for some shaving cream, I caught up with Becky again at the checkout counter. "This time of the morning, I guess I'm even more clumsy than usual," I said to her, trying to smile a second apology. Old-maid snoopy myself, I glanced down at Dr. DeVore's few purchases: a frozen dinner, a tiny jar of instant coffee, a can of butterscotch pudding, and some cough syrup which worked by pickling the sufferer's sore throat. I was positive the poor woman didn't know this particular remedy was sixty proof.

"I don't normally do my grocery shopping at this hour either, Mr. Waltz," she said, after she'd checked my unseemly stare by adding some wintergreen Lifesavers to her small hoard of necessities, "but, as you can imagine, I couldn't sleep at all after the police left last night, and I guess they'll be back today to go over the house again. And I must say I had to get out of it for a while."

"Can I buy you some breakfast? A cup of coffee?" I suggested, out of craftiness as well as conciliation, since I wanted to hear

Becky DeVore's unrevised version of what Hershey had accomplished last night after getting me off the premises, and also try for a second opinion on whether Simon's and Antonides's murderer might not have been imitating Charles Carson Blackstone instead of the Book of Exodus.

But the moment I'd made my gentlemanly overtures and stepped closer to Dr. DeVore so I could pay for my own purchases at the cash register, I found myself staring again, this time at an elaborately old-fashioned brooch on the stiff collar of her blouse, twisted out over her coat collar. What had caught my eye was the gold-clasped center of her heavy piece of jewelry: a glass oval enclosing a lock of reddish hair.

"My mother's. It's called a mourning brooch, Mr. Waltz," she murmured. "And I'd be delighted to share breakfast with you." She immediately nodded at Horny Hank, noisily digging detritus from underneath his fingernails while he slouched at us from behind the counter, to hand me her bag of groceries.

I pointedly stayed put until my companion had started out the door, which I closed after us with a perfectly executed follow-through. "Do you often walk in the rain?" I asked, casting about for introductory remarks. Since Dr. DeVore had set me a brisk pace down Main Street, I assumed any woman with a sensitivity to match her cup size would feel honor-bound to say, yes, she just loved to stroll in a steady downpour.

"I've always been a great walker, even in the rain," Becky told me, slowing down enough for me to struggle up beside her and no doubt splatter mud on her nylons all the way past Frank Fitzmeier's Friendly Hardware. "Sometimes it will even send me to sleep. But even though they say humid air's so good for the throat, all the rain we have here in this part of the country seems to ruin my voice every spring."

I murmured something suitably empathetic about spring colds and added that on rainy days in downtown Pittsburgh, one seldom ventured forth on foot unless one had already been nudged toward suicide by the endless weeks of perfect funeral weather.

"I know just what you mean, Mr. Waltz," Becky agreed. "Up

here, when we go on so long in the spring without seeing the sun, we seem to start feeling the dampness all through us. Even in our souls, if you don't mind my saying so. Right around Easter, even those of us who really ought to set an example can get so terribly—discouraged. Dispirited. What word am I looking for, Mr. Waltz? As my students sometimes tell me, I don't seem to be saying exactly what I mean."

"Claustrophobic?" I suggested, since for the duration of my house arrest in New Arcady I'd been frantically searching for an oxygen tent.

"I guess that's more or less what I meant, Mr. Waltz," Becky DeVore said judiciously. "I was just about to describe this feeling I'm talking about—in my own roundabout way—as something like being caught underneath a net that somebody up above keeps stretching tighter and tighter. Or, have you ever seen insects of some kind on your screen door, crawling and crawling all over it—almost frantically—trying to find just one little break in the mesh? I think that must have been exactly how that poor Melissa Parsons must have felt, Mr. Waltz. What made her go to you. And the police.

"But I'm being much too morbid!" my companion cried with a sudden hectic gaiety, while I tightened my grip on her limp paper bag. "This time next week we may even have some spring sunshine for Palm Sunday."

"Not to change the subject," I said hastily, "but is New Arcady planning to hold any kind of funeral services for Antonides over at the First Presbyterian?"

Actually, I had to call myself either an imbecile or a coward for changing the subject while I'd had Becky painting me word-pictures of a large blotchy canvas called *Arcadian Spring*, something like a grid with ragged-edged holes burned into it or, in my own words, a giant flyswatter festooned with dead bugs. Or a screen door crawling with frantic insects, as Dr. DeVore, with her more delicate sensibilities, had so revealingly put it. If I'd been brave enough to bring up Charles Carson Blackstone's contributions to New Arcady's cultural heritage, I might even have been offered her unique interpretation of the hourglass-shaped emblem in the lower left-hand corner of the artist's masterwork: the figure she'd found striking enough to reproduce on Peter Simon's office door as part of her own bloody handiwork.

I should also, of course, have found some ingenious method of asking the woman marching through the rain three strides ahead of me if—like her living victim, Melissa Parsons—she had any intention of using me as an intermediary, one who might smooth her way to the sterner and shrewder Lieutenant Hershey. I had the distinct feeling, however, that Becky considered herself, and whatever she had to communicate, consciously or otherwise, much too subtle for either one of us. The brooch she wore to display her trophy, the lock of hair so suspiciously like Melissa's that she'd carefully sealed inside, visibly testified to her—entirely justifiable—contempt for our powers of observation. Certainly Hershey and I, both of us solicitously inquiring after Becky's insomnia, had been holy idiots to swallow her sleeping-pill story the same way she'd supposedly tossed down her Tuinals. And neither one of us had even bothered to question the identity of Melissa Parsons's friend and counselor, the confessor who'd sent the girl straight to a hell of guilt and self-loathing. In this entire matter Dr. McKenna had been guilty of nothing but his sublime stupidity—fully equal to our own.

Charles Carson Blackstone, on the other hand, who'd summed up his own situation here in New Arcady by saying he did his best work with his arms in a straitjacket, probably could have solved Pete Simon's murder five days ago. No doubt New Arcady's least-honored prophet would have immediately understood that Becky DeVore had tried to hack her way through the net she'd felt tightening around her by killing one man who'd managed to find a break in the mesh and another she might have succeeded in having tried for and convicted of murder—if in a moment of panic she hadn't chosen the wrong hiding place for her self-incriminating piece of evidence. And I finally understood the grudge Antonides had borne his upstairs neighbor for what he thought was her tacit encouragement of the Covenanters; he must have seen Melissa Parsons at some time or another in her gray hood and recognized her as the beautiful girl he'd seen more than once on her way upstairs to Dr. DeVore's.

If I'd been some kind of innocent bystander, I suppose I would have already ruptured myself shrieking with laughter at this dumb jerk sloshing down Main Street behind the murderess of two men, carrying her groceries for her. Instead, I found myself shivering violently; I had just remembered Reverend Von Ruden's firm conviction that God had somehow marked Pete Simon's murderer. If only Becky DeVore had felt conspicuous by virtue of her considerable talent, I reflected miserably, rather than the physical endowments she so despised, she might not have had to turn Pete Simon's office into a bloody stage for acting out all the horror inside her.

"I hope *you're* not catching a spring cold, Mr. Waltz," she was saying, having seen the shiver I hadn't really been able to hide behind my soggy brown paper bag. "But you were asking about Mr. Antonides. Probably he had relatives somewhere who'll want to bury him in his own religion; but if not, we'd certainly hold services for him here, where he lived and died. After all, he was one of us."

"And of course you'd sing at Antonides's funeral?" I asked in a hypoallergenic voice. I had no idea how I was going to dynamite this woman's warehouse of guilelessness.

"I always sing at funerals," said Dr. DeVore, her eyes empty. "And at weddings too, of course."

"Of course," I echoed solemnly, concentrating on the choreography of getting us through the door of the Golden Grill and seated conference-style in a back booth. The yawning student waitress breathed last night's beer into our faces as she flicked on the overhead lights; we were her only customers.

The murderess left her coffee conspicuously untouched until she had my attention, then softly asked permission to say grace. "I guess I really should have asked for some sunshine to cheer us all up," she said when she had finished, with an almost flirtatious smile, her tone completely uncorrupted by irony.

Somehow I was going to have to win a psychological advantage over Becky so I could seize the initiative Hershey had sought to deny me—on the grounds of my general ineptitude—and triumphantly lead my prisoner to Tranter Hall. Since, like the woman across from me, I vastly preferred to believe things were just what they seemed, I was taking this all very personally—including the gloating she'd done over my own imperception. Thus I was determined I was going to break her down somehow, make her tell me exactly why she'd had to kill Pete Simon as well as how she'd engineered his murder, even if it meant rubbing her smiling face in the obscene messes she'd left last night and Tuesday noon. Resenting the strain her party manners were putting me under, I decided on shock tactics. "Here's to a real old-fashioned Arcadian spring," I agreed, raising my tomato juice. "And another Charles Blackstone to paint it."

"Then you know that particular work of his, Mr. Waltz?" my breakfast guest asked me. Her voice was steady, but she had begun to compulsively crumble her toast.

"Know it and understand it," I nodded. "Just the way Pete Simon's murderess did. We both saw something there we weren't supposed to," I added, deliberately ambiguous.

"You saw something, Mr. Waltz? Connected with these horrible murders?" Becky asked, studying the jigsaw puzzle she'd made from her pieces of toast. But she'd finally said the wrong thing, having neglected to show either alarm or curiosity at my assigning specific sex characteristics to Simon's killer.

"And so did you," I insisted. "Two triangles, one inverted so that their points touch—making a figure roughly in the shape of an hourglass, and about the color of dried blood—in the lower left-hand corner of Charles Blackstone's most notable work. Faithfully reproduced on Pete Simon's office door in his own blood. So that it looked like somebody's crude idea of a cult murder. I imagine you would have eventually found us a ritual popular with pre-Christian teenyboppers that any Covenanter literate enough to use the library might conceivably have tried to copy. After you'd made me waste another week or so worrying about whether or not the killer was a little mixed up on the Passover story—although I get the impression you actually had that in the back of your mind as well as the painting. Putting your mark on your chosen victim.''

Her cheeks burning bright pink, Rebecca DeVore gave me a little-girl look that had probably grossed crates of Easter eggs for her thirty-five years ago. ''I think my mind must still be in a muddle this morning, Mr. Waltz,'' she told me with one of her tinkling laughs. Then she turned expectantly toward the front door of the Grill, which had just come rattling open to let in wind, rain, and a large individual in a pungent black rubber raincoat, shaking water off himself like a St. Bernard. It was Gene Chancellor, who nodded sheepishly at us with the air of a man who'd never admit even in the middle of a marital break-up that his wife had stopped cooking him breakfast, and went to sit at the counter, well out of earshot.

''I hope Karen hasn't been taken ill. Or the baby,'' said Becky, a frown of concern on her face. ''Or maybe their basement has flooded again, the poor things.''

Somehow I had to return the conversation to matters of life and death. ''If it does, I'm sure Karen can take care of it,'' I said, carefully scanning my companion's large, calm face ''She swings a pretty mean hammer herself.''

''What?'' said Becky, giving me the same glassy stare that had so unnerved my subconscious last night. ''Does somebody think poor Karen could be mixed up in these murders somehow? With a brand-new baby?'' She had dropped her voice in sentimental homage to madonna and child. ''But I guess things aren't always what they seem, are they, Mr. Waltz?'' she sighed, rolling her eyes at me.

''Wednesday night you tried to tell me you usually thought otherwise, Dr. DeVore,'' I reminded her. ''But you're right. Things generally aren't. Not to police detectives—although they can be made to see only what they'll believe. And certainly not to painters—who were probably the first private investigators —they've trained themselves to look for hidden truths; pretty or

171

not, here they come. If they're real artists, that is. If they aren't, they're only another kind of murderer.''

Dr. DeVore, hand on aching head, had begun to beg for a change of subject, but I made a papal motion with my arm and silenced her. ''Both artists and murderers are apt to develop God complexes,'' I went on, stiffening my spine against the back of the booth so I was up a little higher than the woman across from me. ''But the difference is this: murderers can't stand to see things as they are. So they try to rub out reality. As if it were a bad likeness. Or rewrite it, like a hymn tune nobody could possibly fit any nice words to.''

Here I paused, fresh out of parables, but the woman opposite, immobile, seemed to be waiting for more. And to get her to make some irreparably damaging admission, I had to enmesh her in a tight net of words. ''All murderers think they're larger than life, Dr. DeVore,'' I said gravely. ''Epic heroes. Valkyries.''

Becky DeVore stubbornly refused to admit she had run out of time and evasions. ''And so you have another riddle for me to solve, Mr. Waltz?'' she said, casting her eyes upwards, asking heaven to please be patient with us both. ''You're certainly speaking in riddles—too many all at once. And I've never been any good at all at guessing them. Have you finished your breakfast?'' she asked, positioning herself to slide out of the booth. ''Please let me leave the tip.''

I laid my hand heavily on my reluctant prisoner's wrist. ''Was your method more direct with Melissa Parsons? Did you tell her she ought to confess to the murder you so carefully described to her to save herself from a life of sin? Or to punish herself for being young and pretty? How long did you think you were going to keep me convinced you never knew her? That little off-the-cuff lie wasn't nearly up to your usual level.''

Becky DeVore winced like a drunk waking up in somebody else's bedroom. I had broken through. ''I didn't want Melissa to be hurt anymore—I had no idea she'd come to you with her confession. Because she'd already come to *me*,'' the murderess said sadly.

For a moment she sat silently fingering the brooch on her collar. Then she said in an angry murmur, "I looked on her almost as a daughter, Mr. Waltz. Before *he* took her away from me. But I still tried to help her—after the murder. To comfort her. We women have to comfort each other, and forgive each other. So many of us seem so weak, Mr. Waltz. So easily led. And I told poor Melissa that if I could forgive her, then God could forgive her too. And love her. Like a bride. Cherish her forever. I never thought Melissa would turn to the Covenanters," Becky sighed. "But she came back to me after all, Mr. Waltz. The poor weak thing was nearly out of her head. She seemed to feel she was responsible for the death of the man who had made her suffer so much. And I told her to talk to God about what she ought to do. To take her guilt to God just as she'd brought it to me. Not to go running to the police!"

"Who might come around and keep you up past your bedtime asking embarrassing questions," I said angrily. "Did you chop off Melissa's hair for her too?"

"Of course not, Mr. Waltz," Becky said in a shocked tune. "How could you even think such a thing? The poor child kept saying, over and over, that she had to cut off her wicked hair. Her wicked hair. And when I saw there was nothing at all I could do to change her mind, I asked if I could snip off just one lock with my kitchen scissors. As a keepsake."

Whatever the irregularities of my imagination, picturing Rebecca DeVore rooting around for the kitchen scissors to shear off her memento made me realize that at this stage of my—winning—game, I certainly ought to anticipate Hershey's quest for tangible evidence and find out where my prisoner had hidden her actual weapons: the hammer she'd used on Antonides and the commando dagger she'd kept to slash him up as well as Pete Simon. "And where did you decide to hide your knife and your hammer, Dr. DeVore?" I asked, rejecting all further experiments in indirection. "Have you got them tucked away in the kitchen drawer too?"

"Putting the rags of those ruined clothes down behind Mr. Antonides's washer just wasn't a good idea at all, though," Becky sighed, obviously lost in her own second thoughts. "I really didn't think he'd be let go quite so soon." The murderess shook her head at me as if I'd thoughtlessly pulled a silly prank on her. "It's too bad all those things were stained so," she said absently. "I was always so fond of that skirt. Everything really should have been burned, but there's an ordinance against burning inside the borough limits, and it would have made such an awful smell for all the neighbors."

I'm sure they'd all be pleased to know you were thinking of them," I muttered into my ashtray, trying to think up some trick method of staying on top of the situation—or at least maintaining my own precarious mental balance without permitting Becky to send me sprawling into the nets. "So you only meant to kill Pete Simon to begin with?" I asked bluntly. "Mainly because of Melissa?" Out of the corner of my eye, I saw the waitress start toward us with her coffeepot and hastily pointed at Gene Chancellor, who seemed to be scouring the counter with a whole ream of paper napkins.

Across from me, the murderess lifted her chin and squared her shoulders, her eyes fiercely triumphant, her face suddenly hardening into beauty. "God is not mocked, Mr. Waltz," she said sternly. "God is not mocked. 'Whatsoever a man soweth, that shall he also reap.' As we are told in Galatians, chapter six, verse seven."

"In other words?" I asked, picking up my cue so that the woman opposite couldn't willfully withdraw from this hellish conversation again.

"If you live by the flesh, Mr. Waltz," she said, pausing for one full beat, "you die wallowing in its filth. And only blood can make things clean again." The murderess leaned forward until she seemed to fill up all the space in the booth.

"So you told me yesterday," I said, looking fixedly at her glass brooch in an effort to dissolve my extraordinarily clear mental image of the bloody carcass that had been Peter Simon.

"But there are worse sins than even fornication, Mr. Waltz," Becky assured me after another long pause to stare at me for several seconds with those avid, round eyes, the palms of her large, white hands unyieldingly pressed together. "The sin of pride, which is the source of all others. Self-love, which makes weaklings think they're strong enough to live outside the law. Bend the rules, break the rules, and make everybody look the other way. And have their way with people even weaker than themselves. Mr. Simon had a way with people. Why, his daughters worshipped him—or so I'm told. And his boys in Sunday school. And *she* worshipped him too. They all worshipped him. And so he got away with it."

"*You* almost didn't," I told her, jumping in while there was still a chance of making some kind of sense. "*I* almost caught you. You must have walked in the front door of Tranter Hall just about ninety seconds after I showed a student down the hall for her job interview. And I had a lunch date with Simon at 12:15."

"Oh, but there was an allowance for that, of course. That was when Mr. Simon generally left for lunch; he was quite regular in his habits. But that still left ample time for it. And if you'd been there in the hallway with your student, there was always another day for it. Another Tuesday noon. As you said, Mr. Waltz, Peter Simon was a marked man."

Rebecca DeVore's eyes were now burning with a dangerously low blue flame. "Under the circumstances, I don't know what prevented him from taking his own life," she said in a soft, hissing voice. "He was at his desk looking for Melissa's folder when he was first hit. From behind—anyone might walk around behind his desk to look at all the things he had up on the wall, or just to look out the window. But he had started to straighten up a little because he had started to laugh. When he was asked how many others there were. How many whores he had besides Melissa. And he started to laugh. And so, Mr. Waltz, as for his prideful and sinful manhood, it's been put away in my freezer."

My hands seemed quick-frozen to the table, too heavy to lift.

My lips were numb. *This must be what rigor mortis feels like*, I thought, experimentally moving my jaw muscles. "That explains Pete Simon," I said, with the calm detachment of a drowning man. "But what about Antonides? He did his rule-breaking right out in the open, and he was hardly in a position of power. And he gave you good women a lot of free labor. Did you actually decide you had to kill him before he took it into his head to look down behind his washer?"

"That did make his death necessary right away," the killer said, keeping her burning blue eyes on my face. "But of course it would have had to happen before too long. Mr. Antonides was a terrible liar; he lied to me every day of his life here. Oh, he always seemed polite and deferential—'Yes, Dr. DeVore,' and 'No, Dr. DeVore,' and 'You tell me if the noise down here ever bothers you any, Dr. DeVore.' And he'd do little jobs for me; he was replacing a light fixture for me last Saturday when he had his key to the padlock he'd put on his basement door taken from the table in the hall. But I knew he sat down there every night, and he drank with his sluts—and he laughed at me. He got on my nerves so, I couldn't sleep, just knowing he was down there underneath me, snoring away. Even with all my medication, Mr. Waltz, I do have such terrible trouble sleeping."

Becky DeVore had raised her voice enough on those last blankly terrifying words that Reverend Von Ruden, carefully draping an enormous gray Inverness cape over the coat tree beside the cash register up front, smoothed out one last wrinkle and made for our booth, calling, "You're finding this good sleeping weather, then, Becky? I am also. But, as you must know, I never sleep through the constitutional I have set myself to take every Saturday morning. And how are you, sir?—Mr. Waltz, I believe? How do you find this wet spring we are having?" inquired Von Ruden, pausing beside the booth to peer at me, and waiting to be asked, with all due respect, to sit down.

Becky DeVore had already begun smiling and nodding as if she and I had actually just been talking about the weather. "Hello,

Reverend Von Ruden," she said brightly while the old minister patiently hovered over us. "Mr. Waltz and I were out walking in the rain, too; and when we met, he insisted on taking me out to breakfast."

"We were just leaving," I cut in, really angry that this woman had tried to make our encounter sound like a romantic adventure. "Dr. DeVore had a lot of excitement last night, so she really has to go home and get some rest." Throwing down a five and signaling Becky to gather up her belongings, I purposefully stood up, holding her bag of groceries like a shield.

"Then you're still not sleeping well, dear?" Von Ruden asked, quirking his bushy eyebrows at us. "These are dark times for us all. But as I have tried to tell you so many times, Rebecca," he said, playfully waggling his finger at my companion, "when we know we have a clean heart, we should all sleep like little children."

"We'll go get my car, and I'll drive you home so you won't catch cold, Dr. DeVore," I said, unctuously solicitous in my own turn.

Murmuring pleasantries, Becky meekly followed me out of the Golden Grill, leaving Reverend Von Ruden to tinker with the soul of Gene Chancellor, still scowling over his empty coffee cup at the counter.

"We're walking to Tranter Hall," I said coldly, once we were safely outside. "Because, as old Von Ruden just said, when you know you've done the right thing, maybe you can finally get some sleep."

"Of course, Mr. Waltz," Becky said quietly. She seemed her usual self again, whoever that was. "I'll gladly go with you and make a statement—is that what it's called?—to Lieutenant Hershey. But I have a favor to ask of you first, Mr. Waltz," she added almost shyly, her cheeks girlishly pink again. "The Music Building is on our way, and I have a key. The first time you and I ever talked, we talked about music. Now I would like to sing for you—something more to your taste than our Christian hymns.

Some Wagner, perhaps, if you would like to hear it. A farewell performance, Mr. Waltz.'' She gave me a hesitant half-smile and inclined her head, plainly indicating surrender.

I agreed at once, since I not only admired Becky DeVore's sense of timing but also felt sure that in the afterglow of her command performance she'd willingly tell me where she'd hidden the murder weapon. And, in her own chosen words, the precise nature of the revenge she'd sought to exact through the murder and mutilation of Peter Simon, so that we could ring the curtain down. I also had to hear Dr. DeVore sing Wagner, out of my ineradicable awe at her wonderful voice, as well as the burdensome pity I felt for her. I strongly suspected that narrowing her range in the name of religion had caused much of this lost woman's mental anguish.

Equally convinced that Erhard Von Ruden had probably offered her forty-five years' worth of accumulated platitudes for her pain, I asked my companion, clinging to my arm while we strolled casually in the direction of the Music Building—and Reuben Tranter Hall—if she had ever had any counseling from the old minister. ''Yes, I spent hours and hours with him a few years ago,'' she answered readily. ''After my father passed on. I was so close to my father, Mr. Waltz. It seemed too much to bear. But talking it out with Reverend Von Ruden was a great comfort. He became a second father to me.''

I shivered, and not from the cold drizzle. Melissa Parsons had also been Daddy's girl, using almost the same words to eulogize Pete Simon. Dr. Blackstone had described the women of New Arcady to me as ''dutiful daughters.'' And now Rebecca DeVore was seeing herself as her old German pastor's handmaiden.

''My problems all seemed to disappear like magic after I'd spent a few months learning from Reverend Von Ruden how I could cope with them,'' Becky DeVore was saying in an almost worshipful voice, which forced me to remind myself one more time that this women was totally incapable of committing the sin of irony. At the corner of College and Garden, a passing bicyclist making a muddy left turn—one of several New Arcadians now groping their way through the fog—missed taking off my leg by inches, which reassured me that the world of daily routine, with its full quota of minor triumphs and major annoyances, lay just down the block, within shouting distance. This near-mishap also reminded me that I had neglected to ask the woman beside me to explain how she had contrived to ride her bicycle away from the scene of her first murder.

When I did, she changed key on me once more. "All this snow was a lucky thing, Mr. Waltz," she said in a tone of self-commendation. "Because the bicycle could be put in the shrubbery under the proper window last Sunday without anyone at all knowing it was there. And if it had had to wait another week, all anyone would have found was a stolen bicycle, right where the fraternity boys had left it after they'd had their fun. It was easy enough to park the car on McKendree Street, just a few doors away from them, and to walk to Tranter Hall with the shopping bag. And afterwards, it was easy enough to change clothes in the rest room and climb out the window and ride the bicycle back near the car, to the shed where Sergeant Hendricks found it. Of course, there was an extra coat in the bicycle basket to put on over that ugly sweat suit. And time to drive home for a catnap before my two o'clock class."

"Not to change the subject," I said quickly, since we had reached the Music Building, "what's the program for this morning?" The star performer was rhythmically jingling her keys as she led me through the front door of the building and down a linoleum corridor to the theater.

"I never announce the program in advance," Becky said solemnly. "And, as a music lover, you should surely recognize my selection, Mr. Waltz." After guiding me to the sixth row for the sake of the acoustics, she ran breathlessly back up the aisle to the balcony in order to extinguish the house lights and focus a single spot on center stage.

I had been coughing and fidgeting far more anxiously than the average concert-goer; but once Rebecca DeVore, her face impassive as a goddess's, stepped into the spotlight and began to sing, I forgot everything but the music. Then I indeed recognized the selection the singer had so carefully chosen for me: the exultant hymn to death at the end of *Tristan and Isolde*, the "*Liebestod*," or Love Death. As the soaring voice achieved its climax, I began sliding my way from seat to seat toward the center aisle. But after her song was finished the singer merely stood there in the spotlight, head bowed, hands clasped.

Compulsively I cried, "Bravo!" my voice trailing off absurdly in the empty auditorium.

Standing in her spotlight, Rebecca DeVore made a graceful bow. "I could have had such a thrilling career, Mr. Waltz," she said, softly but quite clearly, her trained voice carrying in the empty theater. "But my father wanted me to be a scholar. And to stay here at home with him; my mother died quite young, you see. And my father always told me that when God gave a talent, he meant for it to be used for his greater glory. That's in the New Testament, Mr. Waltz. In the Gospel according to St. Matthew. And so I gave all the talents I had back to God, Mr. Waltz. To his church. And I taught his worship."

Becky had spoken these last words in an almost inaudible whisper. She seemed to be staring at her own clasped hands. "But they worshipped that man Peter Simon!" she suddenly cried, flinging her arms wide. "They worshipped him! They gave him awards, and they gave him applause. And they gave him their love. But nobody gave *me* love, Mr. Waltz. Nobody—ever —gave—me—love."

Head bowed, fists clenched, Becky DeVore stood for a long moment in the spotlight before she straightened up and walked off the stage to retrieve her coat and purse from the center aisle seat in the first row.

"Would you tell me where Tony's knife is? And the hammer?" I asked, as softly as the singer herself had initially spoken, while she slowly buttoned her coat and twisted her brooch out over the collar.

"They're in my own bed, Mr. Waltz," she answered, looking straight at me. "Underneath me. Between the mattress and the springs. The police would never have thought to look there."

Then she bent her head again to hunt through her purse for the right key to lock up the building, while I stood silently behind her.

"I'm all ready for you now, Mr. Waltz," Becky said. Then, with amazing quickness, she turned and arched herself toward me. In the darkness something long and shining flicked at me like a snake's tongue. Instinctively, I jumped aside and twisted myself toward the section of seats on our left, wedging myself in between the third and fourth rows before realizing that I'd have to back my way to the fire exit before the killer reached me with her razor. For a moment my enemy paused to smile at me, raising the ivory-handled weapon like a bandmaster's baton.

"Isn't it beautiful?" she said. "It belonged to my father. I've kept it sharp ever since his death. But it's never been necessary to use it before." Then she lunged at me, slashing at the seats in the row in front of me while I scuttled sideways like a crab.

"You're crazy!" I yelled, although this was certainly neither the time nor the place to state the obvious. "You'll never get away with this!" But help, I had to remember, arrived on the heels of bad dialogue only on the late show. I was trying to clamber over the seats behind me when the blade arched toward me again, neatly slicing my wrist. She was going to kill me unless I could snatch the razor away from her, hurt this woman, beat her bloody—kill her if I had to—smash that staring doll's head against the metal seats. Without her weapon Becky DeVore was no match for me, but I had trapped myself by taking refuge between the rows of seats.

"Help!" I screamed. "Help! Help, somebody! My God, my God—"

"Did you mean to say a prayer, Mr. Waltz?" my murderess asked softly, holding her razor still, offering me my moment of silence. Then she swiveled toward the main doors at the rear of the auditorium.

In that heart-jerking second I had heard it too: voices in the hallway, heels clattering on the linoleum. "Help!" I shrieked. "Please! Help!" and whipped around to run toward the center aisle, leaving Becky to bump her way after me through the row of seats that had been between us. Then Richardson and Fielding burst through the center doors, hesitated for only a blade's flash, and went straight for Becky, who reversed her course and started running back toward the stage. But Leslie did a *grande jeté* over the seats to tackle the larger woman from behind, while Sally ran to intercept Becky at the side aisle. Wrapping powerful arms around her opponent, Leslie knocked the breath out of her and had her spread-eagled ignominiously over the seats by the time Sally came around to pry her colleague Dr. DeVore's fingers loose from her father's ivory-handled straight razor.

"You all right?" asked Leslie, seeing me slumped down in the aisle seat I'd chosen to watch the rest of the show from. She spoke in the same brisk tone in which she'd inquired after my health Monday night, after she and Sally had picked me up off the ice in the parking lot of the White Lion.

"Ladies," I said, my voice cracking like a thirteen-year-old's, "I owe my life to you. And I mean that."

"What happened?" asked Sally, staring dazedly at the razor she held in her hand.

"And please don't ask me what happened," I mumbled. "You can always catch the rerun."

"Maybe he's in shock," Leslie suggested, holding onto Becky DeVore like a large carp she had netted.

"No more than I am," said Sally. "After all, all I came over here for was a book I'd left in my office."

"You'd better go get Lieutenant Hershey, Sally," Leslie instructed her lover. "Unless John here wants some fresh air. Was *I* that bad last night when—"

"When we went upstairs with her, and she kept staggering around the room into the furniture—right after she had killed Tony," Richardson finished for Fielding. "You want me to run over there for the police, John?" Sally asked, turning to consider my welfare only after she'd carefully deposited the murderess's razor on the seat in front of her.

"No!" I protested, shaking my head with exaggerated vigor

and struggling to rise to the occasion as well as from the seat I had somehow glued myself to. "No more crowds. No more freak shows. We'll all four of us take a short walk up the street to Tranter Hall."

The two women heaved Becky, inert as a corpse, to her feet while I managed to make it to mine. Four abreast, we hiked to Tranter Hall, Leslie propelling Becky while Sally held *me* up. When we came staggering up to the door of Hershey's office like a punk rock group looking for the right party, Holy Willie McKenna, who had kept his 9:00 A.M. appointment, was requesting the lieutenant to kneel with him in prayer. "And won't you others make a little circle with us?" he cried enthusiastically, seizing Leslie's free hand.

"For God's sake, McKenna," I said, sagging against the door frame, "you bastards prayed this woman here all the way to Murder One. She did it for you. So what more do you want?"

Mercifully terrified into total silence, McKenna edged his way out of the room, leaving Hershey to break up the act and arrest Esther Rebecca DeVore for the murder of Peter Simon, the murder of Stavros Antonides, and the attempted murder of John Waltz. At that particular moment, I couldn't recall ever having met the latter and wondered idly if he were a stranger in town. Seeing the state I was in, Lieutenant Hershey, red-eyed and rumpled from his all-nighter at Tranter Hall, worn out by a workaholism even worse than the late Peter Simon's, kept his questions as anticlimactic as possible. The murderess, silent except for the slight hiss of her breathing, had made herself into a manacled statue.

"When are you leaving here? I'll buy you a beer before you go," Hershey said in an uneager voice as I left the room.

"Yeah," I agreed, with an equal lack of enthusiasm.

Leslie and Sally, excused earlier, were waiting for me at the front door of the building. "Sorry we forgot the whiskey," said Sally. "But our car's still parked at the Music Building, and it's a five-minute drive to our house."

Although Richardson and Fielding deserved a Chinese banquet's worth of toasts for saving me from the nearly fatal consequences of my own stupidity, there was another woman on McCorkle Street still waiting to find out just how dumb John Waltz intended to get. I knew I had to see Anne right now, even if it meant setting a trap for myself twice on the same stormy morning. "Ladies," I said, "I'm going into temporary exile. But I promise to stop by for several drinks before I permanently leave this delightful town, which has·given me memories to carry to my grave and almost shoved me right into it."

Leslie and Sally merely nodded, well aware of my destination. "If you're not leaving town till tomorrow, why don't you come watch the six-o'clock news with us?" they called as I cut across the College Green to McCorkle. "We've all been too busy lately to bother keeping up with small-town scandals."

When I reached Anne's front walk, I tried hard not to look at the dingy house set back among dark, dripping pines two doors down the street, but I had a shell-shocked veteran's vision of a large woman leaping out of darkness at me with a razor. And thus, when Anne answered the door, I toppled into her living room like a corpse falling out of a Hitchcockian closet.

"My God, John, what's the matter?" Anne gasped, exactly as she had done on our unforgettable second encounter in Reuben Tranter Hall. Then, seeing the state I was in, she brought her arms around me for a moment—sodden raincoat and all—before leading me to the couch. As I sat down I felt something sticky leaking through my coat onto my trouser leg. Then I realized that I still held Becky DeVore's bag of groceries, containing a TV dinner now defrosted by my own body heat. To my own horror, I tossed the bag to Anne and started laughing like a long-term lunatic. Anne quickly took the remains into the kitchen and came back with a Ronald McDonald tumbler full of brandy.

"I'll even say, 'Here, drink this,' if I really have to," she said, trying to remove us both from the reality of whatever losing battle I had fought that morning. "Looks like Jack Campbell jumped you out behind MacGregor's IGA," she added, handing me the glass.

I had forgotten the crescent moon cut on my wrist, which had bled less than the Halloween carving the head Covenanter had done on himself a few days ago. But, looking at it under a hundred-watt bulb, I concluded that I'd bear a slight scar; Esther Rebecca DeVore had literally left her mark on me. "No," I answered Anne, "it was your nice neighbor lady down the street —you know, the one who sings at her victims' funerals."

Struggling to maintain my coherence, I recited the events of the morning, beginning with my phone call to Dr. Blackstone, touching on that ghastly last breakfast shared with Becky DeVore before she sang me her swan song, and ending with my rescue and her arrest. To my amazement, I came out sounding as disengaged as the murderess herself, who had angered me by refusing to refer to her crimes in the first person—as if some higher power with the mind of a rabid rat terrier had been working out its ugly purposes through her.

"That's Calvinism again," Anne reflected after I had finally brought myself to mention Becky DeVore's frightening air of detachment toward her own handiwork. "Carried to an extreme. The notion that we're all God's puppets and he sits there deliberately snarling up the strings. And probably a lot of people in New Arcady would prefer to blame fate, or even their own God, for these killings; it makes more sense to them than holding Becky DeVore responsible for murdering two men with malice aforethought. Or even than considering her criminally insane. I still can't believe it myself," Anne shivered. "How did Dr. Blackstone figure out who it was? Or was she just performing some kind of weird psychological experiment on you?"

"I'll let you know," I said, "after I've been up there to burn a cross on her lawn."

"Think positive!" Anne said with scholarly enthusiasm. "Actually, Dr. Blackstone turned you into a hero."

"Yeah," I said. "David and Goliath. Only she forgot to put my slingshot in along with my sandwich and cookies."

There was a long pause while I sipped Anne's roach-killer brandy and stared at the brown, spidery blotch staining her ceiling, the result of a congenitally leaky roof. Then Anne inquired casually if I planned on going back to Pittsburgh in the morning. I was about to ask if she planned on giving me a suitably tearful send-off when the telephone conveniently rang.

"That was my departmental chairman," Anne said after a brief and monosyllabic conversation. "Dr. Horton has decided to move spring vacation up two weeks. So school is officially out." She picked up the fresh ashtray she had just given me and started toward the kitchen.

"Then come to Pittsburgh with me," I said, on my feet fast, cutting off her retreat. "Come live with me and be my love."

"You forget that being an English teacher, I know the companion poem to that one," Anne said, her lips trembling. "The girl tells the would-be Don Juan—he's a shepherd—she's saving herself for the local robber baron. Because she doesn't want a leaky roof over her head."

"Sure the shepherd didn't work for Witherspoon College?" I asked, pointing upwards. "And for a Don Juan, my score seems to be pretty low."

Anne took another step backwards, holding the ashtray protectively in front of her.

"Come work for me then. We can take each other on a trial basis. Or I'll recruit you for somebody else. Somebody who can only get it off with papaya-shaped Polynesian brunettes," I hastened to add, having had several second thoughts of my own.

"Last night—" Anne began earnestly.

"Last night I was neither drunk nor *non compos mentis*. Nor trying to get into those baggy old-maid underdrawers you wear."

"John," Anne said somberly, her eyes slowly leaking large, messy tears, "I'm afraid I won't lose you."

"Well, you can sleep on it. One step at a time. If you feel you want to risk your present happiness, then come to Pittsburgh with me. We can save the big words like 'commitment' for whenever they don't scare the hell out of both of us. Anyway, I'll plan on picking you up at ten o'clock tomorrow morning. At the First Presbyterian Church," I added in a sputter of inspiration, thinking that grim, sooty building an appropriate symbol of all I earnestly hoped we were both leaving behind us forever.

Anne was now using her ashtray as a tear-catcher. I got my coat and made for the door. "One thing you'll have to learn if you want to go into business," I said, willing her to lift her head and look at me, "is how to make a quick decision." Then I turned and went down the stairs, theatrically slamming the storm door behind me.

I had forgotten I had to walk all the way back to the inn. Saturday shoppers, English and Amish, shoved each other off the broken sidewalks. In the fog I kept lurching into well-camouflaged Covenanters; I began looking forward to getting back into Pittsburgh's truck ruts. Suddenly I was thrust up against Mary Sue Simon, carrying her groceries back to the parking lot behind the IGA. "Sorry, Mr. Waltz," she murmured. "How are you this morning?"

"Oh, just fine, Mrs. Simon," I assured her with asinine heartiness. "And how are things with you?"

"I didn't have a chance to ask you yesterday, Mr. Waltz, but do tell me what you thought of the funeral," she said sternly.

"Well," I said, wondering if they had authorized any coed dorms at the nut house, "it was good to see your husband had so many friends."

"Do you know what I think, Mr. Waltz?" Mary Sue demanded, looking straight at me. "Pete had his faults, but he was my *husband*! All at once I've been left a widow—and *they* did it. This town killed my husband. It does that to people, you know."

And I had assumed Mary Sue Simon was a stupid woman, except when it came to picking out paint samples. "Yes," I nodded, "I know."

When I got back to the Inn, I decided to have both my bill and my hash settled at once, rather than making tomorrow my day of reckoning. "Well, Mr. Waltz," said the old gypsy, scratching away at endless columns of figures in a whole rainbow of inks. She had donned a diarrhea-colored dress for the occasion. "You owe me ten dollars more than this total here," she said ominously, pointing at an illegible sum. "You burned a hole in my best linens with one of your cigarettes. Bottom sheet, upper right-hand corner, about an eighth of an inch from where the pillow is supposed to be."

"Fine," I said. "Then you'll have to change the bed for your next victim." But at least I was able to write my landlady off, along with all my emergency travelers' checks, since Mrs. Vandervelde refused to take my credit card.

I used it instead to toast myself into oblivion at Nino's. After glutting myself on basketball and championship bowling, I had little appetite for the six-o'clock news, willfully wandering in and out of focus. The boys at the bar, who had all switched from draught beer to Johnny Walker Black on the tab of the out-of-towner, jeered and hooted as their neighbors up the road in New Arcady charged each other with cardboard signs and menaced the camera with styrofoam cups.

"Look at them dumbasses," snorted the large Muppet reject on my left. "The problem with them churchy people is they don't even know what life is all about. Think them murders up there ever happened?" he demanded, poking me in the ribs in order to punctuate. "Maybe them TV people just wanted to create a little stir up our way—depressed area and all; you bet your everloving life we could use the business!—and made every goddamn effing thing up."

"Maybe so," I told him. "These days you can't trust anybody. And it used to be you didn't even have to lock your doors."

I then parted enough of the crowd to make it to the public telephone, get Richardson and Fielding's number from Information, and receive patiently reiterated directions to Tulip Tree Lane, in the town I had tried so hard to get out of, from my two best friends in the world. They even put a blanket over me after I passed out on their living room couch.

CHAPTER VII
Sunday, March 23

"YOU'LL BE LATE FOR CHURCH," SAID SALLY, NUDGING ME URgently at nine o'clock. It was Sunday morning in New Arcady and the sun was beating at my shriveled eyelids. Like a nonagenarian on the lam from his sheltered care facility, I shambled into the kitchen in search of some vitamin B. While making me an emetic protein milkshake, Leslie informed me that Lieutenant Hershey had been asked to publicly receive the surplus thanks of the Presbyterian population that morning. Whatever debt New Arcady owed John Waltz, who had delivered it from evil, the town had already torn up its promissory note. Smoggy-eyed and unshaven, I drove back to my lodgings for the last time, crouching low over the wheel so as not to frighten all the blonde, blue-eyed children being quick-stepped to Sunday school. Judging from their starched and ironed smiles, the adult residents of the community, in their best Sunday-go-to-meeting sackcloth, were highly dismayed that yesterday's downpour hadn't signaled the start of another Flood, a sure indication that their God was going to do it over again and create a new order out of their current chaos.

Back in my room at the inn, my stomach rolling like Noah's lifeboat, I tried to caulk myself up enough to tow along a weaker vessel, even though this meant struggling into the clammy shirt I had washed and hung in the shower. Before carrying my suitcase downstairs, I thoughtfully emptied my ashtray in the middle of the unmade bed.

On this unreasonably sunny morning, with church bells chiming out their competition for previously unowned souls, hard-sell Presbyterians lined the sidewalk outside their church as if they were waiting for another procession of pallbearers. Several do-and-die Calvinists frowned at me as if slightly disturbed by their inability to place my vaguely non-Aryan face. Big Jim Smith, his hair apparently coated with crankcase oil, offered me a nod as stiff as his Sunday suit, and Lillian McKenna came bustling up beside him to give me the evil eye. Her husband and Reverend Von Ruden, waggling their white heads in three-quarter time and mumbling like co-conspirators, paused long enough to offer me prepared smiles of remote pity. The three old women with the fruit-flavored hats, however, waved at me enthusiastically—or so I thought, until I realized that they were affording Hershey a hero's welcome over my shoulder. And suddenly the two of us were clapping each other on the shoulder like teammates after the big game.

"Waltz," said Hershey, "we couldn't have done it without you making an ass of yourself trying to be Highway Patrol. Which also means you'll have to come back up here to testify at the trial. But thanks anyway. Hendricks said to tell you you're a hell of a guy. And I still owe you a beer."

"Also some more information," I told him. "What's going to happen to Melissa Parsons?"

"She's going home to her parents, and I guess they're planning on getting her to a shrink. She'll be finishing school in the summer. Already she's snapped out of it enough to tell me to say thank you until she can write to you herself—and could she send you a new résumé? And here's something I forgot to give you the other day, Waltz," Hershey went on, flashing his straight-arrow smile and handing me the pocket handkerchief—freshly washed and neatly folded—appropriated last Tuesday by Ms. Snickelburger. "One way or another, Waltz, you leave your mark on the ladies."

"Yeah," I said absently. I was going to have to worry about how Hershey might hit it off with my daughter some other time; I had spotted Anne, disconcertingly bridal in a pale suit, standing beside Dr. Blackstone at the extreme end of the walk, both of them frozen on the first flagstone step leading up to the church door. "Since I won't be here for your finest hour, Hershey, break a leg. McKenna can always pray you back on your feet." Hurriedly, I wormed my way through the churchgoers to where the two women, the young one and the old, smiled mysteriously down at me. Dr. Blackstone, blinking her lioness's eyes, might have been muttering either a blessing or a curse. But when I reached her, she stepped forward and took my hand in her two aristocratically skeletal ones.

"I am truly sorry, Mr. Waltz," she said, her voice shaking with sincerity. "I had no idea your own life would be in danger. I completely misread the situation."

"So did I, Dr. Blackstone," I said, seeing the tears of frustration behind her tinted glasses.

"I've turned into a coward, Mr. Waltz," she said bitterly. "Too old and too scared to look down into the snake pit. Best retire from the God business altogether. Chuck the neo-Freudians and take up tatting."

"Never," I said, kissing her Chanel-scented cheek. As I let go of her, both of us were knocked back against Anne by the sudden full-court press of the crowd. A large body of Covenanters, led by Jack Campbell, who had elevated himself to a scarlet jogging suit, came tramping through, stomping their sneakers like jackboots. Incorrigibly flirtatious, Darla, the girl who had sought my soul and tried my patience last Monday, peeked out from underneath her hood at every passing fraternity man. Anonymous voices assured me that, under the pressure of adverse publicity and the resultant hysteria of parents and teachers over the threat posed to their respective authority by religious cults, Dr. Horton had revoked the Joggers' right to exist under the protection of Witherspoon College; however, he'd hardly been able to bar the church door to these vigilant foes of armchair Christianity.

Seeing me turn aside and attempt to shield myself behind the two women, Campbell halted his troops to confront me. "For I have seen violence and strife in the city," he intoned. "Wickedness is in the midst thereof: deceit and guile depart not from her streets."

"Actually, I was just on my way out of town," I told the Convener of the Covenanters.

"And so was I," Anne said in a firm, clear voice, taking my hand so I could guide us both to the parking lot. "But I am taking my own car, John. In case I have to make a quick getaway."

"So you can drive away to bury yourself in another peaceful small town stuck back in the hills somewhere? If it's sex and violence you want, I really think the two of us can manage to keep each other pretty well supplied with it for a while."

"I did rush out and buy some more suitably sinful underwear," Anne admitted.

"Well, I hope you burned your bathrobe along with your bridges," I said solemnly, just as Leslie and Sally came up for a communal embrace.

When in our separate cars we reached the crossroads where Route 34 would wind us back to the Interstate, I exultantly accelerated, after winking at Anne—following closely—in my rear-view mirror. Then I had to brake so abruptly that we almost wrecked each other before we even got to Pittsburgh. Gnashing my teeth in time to the church music triumphantly crackling over the car radio, I settled back for the long, slow descent to the secular city behind an Amish horse and buggy.